CLOISONNÉ

It was never about the jewels

by

Patricia Steele

Other books by PATRICIA STEELE

Memoirs
A Roundabout Passage to Venice
Mind the Gap in Zip It Socks
Fairydust to Daffodils

Spain Trilogy - Travel Memoirs:
Touching Spanish Soil
Spain Calling
A Spanish Haven

Novels
Tangled like Music
Cloisonné
Slutty Memories

Callinda Beauvais Series:
Shoot the Moon
Wine, Vines and Picasso
Thorny Secrets & Pinot Noir
Flamenco Strings Uncorked

By PATRICIA RUIZ STEELE
Genealogy and Historical Fiction
Spanish Pearls Series:
The Girl Immigrant – Based on a true story
Seeking Duende in America
*Silván Leaves – Out on a Limb-
*Ruiz Legacies - A Malagueño Odyssey

*Family History Books

Cloisonné

All characters are created for this fictional story.

Printed in the United States of America
Plumeria Press
ISBN: 9780996606356
www.patriciabbsteele.com
www.facebook.com/patriciabbsteele.com

Cover design by SelfPubBookCovers.com/RLSather

ACKNOWLEDGEMENTS

The second paragraph in this story originated from a dream. I was preparing to embark on my first ocean cruise to Mexico, and the scene played through my mind, prompting me to write it down. I believed I might use it in a book someday. Two days before my departure on that cruise, I had written forty-two pages, and the words jostled against one another, eager to make it onto paper.

Once I was on the cruise ship, I explored every corner for my research, jotting down notes and taking photos. I found Rina and her hairstyle, and the girl with the tattoo on the Lido Deck, Ash, were in the Atrium, while Magda sat at our dining table each night in the Botticelli Dining Room. I had a marvelous time visiting every inch of the Ruby Princess ship, enjoying the fabulous food, and sharing my virgin cruise trip with my friend, Jeannette Rhodes, who invited me to join her on this cruise in the first place.

During the writing process, I realized there were scenes where my expertise in the police arena was about zero. To make my story credible, I turned to my friend, Bob "Roberto" Wilcox, a retired police detective. He asked me thought-provoking questions after reading several of my questionable police scenes. Without his excellent help, I would have had too many cops barging through a door on a "maybe" and interrogators making too many mistakes. So, thank you to my police expert.

Also, thanks to Tina Heller, a retired nurse and childhood friend, for sharing her expertise on the types of car accidents that can cause specific health conditions.

Contents

CLOISONNÉ

It was never about the jewels.

Patricia Steele

One

Goosebumps rose on her arms like a plucked chicken. He sat too close, but she had no intention of acknowledging him. She ignored the world, particularly men, to savor the bliss of her first cruise and to slow down her life enough to breathe again. And she liked it that way.

"You aren't going to waste this beautiful cruise reading, are you?" His deep voice was nearly drowned out by the wind that whistled between the chaise lounge chairs. The deck of the Princess Cruise ship buzzed with activity, with some passengers hollering from the swimming pool and others sipping drinks from chilled glasses nearby. The air was warm as the ship sailed south along the Pacific Ocean coast, moving deeper into Mexico. The laughter of children as they raced around the pool added a vibrant touch to the relaxation she had envisioned.

Rina Silvan snapped her book closed and lowered her sunglasses to glare at the man. Her right eyebrow shot upward, a clear sign of annoyance. Squinting against the sun, she asked, "And YOU are…?" Her fingers tapped a staccato rhythm over the edges of the book she had saved specially for the cruise.

She watched the man scrape his lounge chair a few inches closer to her. His sunglasses glinted in the sunlight as the massive ship sped toward Mazatlán. His long fingers gripped a small, round metal box. "You remember me. I sat near your dinner table last night when you wore that glitzy red blouse and…" His whispered words held a torrent of urgency.

Rina raised both of her winged eyebrows this time before dropping the sunglasses back onto her freckled nose. "Go away. It may look like wasting time to you, but I plan to read this book and maybe another." She lifted her book again, but a loud shout nearby made her drop it back into her lap.

"Damn, not now," the uninvited stranger hissed before hooking his fingers in the side of her lounge chair and yanking it to touch his own. "Please take care of this for me." He moved away and disappeared.

Rina placed a hand on her thumping chest and took a deep breath. Yet her heart continued to beat like a mariachi band.

Two men rushed past her chair, and the other loungers arranged like dominoes near the swimming pool. They were dressed like golfers, sprinting in unison across the sun terrace. Everyone stopped to stare. Swimmers bobbing in the pool looked visibly surprised and curious. Rina bit her lip. They didn't appear to be police or ship employees. Whoever they were, she sensed the stranger wasn't going to stop for a chat. She gazed after them for a few seconds and then reached for her book once more. As she scrunched down in the chaise to get comfortable, she winced at something digging into her leg. When her fingers reached beneath her lacy swimsuit cover, she felt metal.

Oh, God, now what? Her mind raced, recalling the man's parting words as her fingers wrapped around a bright blue cloisonné container. She scanned the deck for the stranger and the men who clearly wanted to talk to him. Then she shoved the box into her swim bag, along with her book, and grabbed her water bottle.

Watching for the men, she scampered across the terrace. As she wove between rows of deck chairs and white tables in the windowed areas, where people ate their breakfast from the buffet, her mind was focused on one thing: what to do? She didn't want to get caught up in something that could knock her socks off. She had plenty of adventures over the past year, thank you very much. She just wanted peace. Muttering to herself and holding her bag close to her chest, she climbed the stairs and flew down three flights to the Aloha deck on twelve.

Minutes later, she emptied the bag onto her bed and stared at the box; it was a beautiful, bright blue. Strips of flattened wire placed edgewise on the metal backing separated the enamel, glass, and gemstones. She had seen a similar box in her uncle's antique shop, but this one was different, much heavier, and more elegant. Her fingers shook. Her thumb gently smoothed over the lid's etching that reminded her of the maze on the grounds of Leeds Castle in England. Intricately painted birds circled the box, their wings sliding downward in a spiral tapering toward the middle to touch the gold fringe that marked the box's clasp.

Her book now forgotten, she sank onto her bed and cradled the small box in both hands. Should she search for the guy? Return it to him and revert to her mantra of 'relax, read, and forget'? She had finally walked away from her problems. She had won her lawsuit, and her bank account was fuller than ever before. Her sister didn't know where she was. She wanted to keep it that way.

The massive cruise ship amazed her with its opulence; the brightly painted decks, captivating shops, numerous restaurants, and visually appealing sea motifs kept her eyes wandering in all directions. She always sat alone, just far enough from other passengers to avoid conversation. She smiled at the servers but carefully maintained her distance from others. Now, this man was invading her personal space. She pretended he wasn't there.

Just breathe. That is what she wanted to do. She had dreamed of days like this—hours to spend as she pleased. Massages followed by music in the Piazza, featuring live entertainment from around the world. She wanted to immerse herself in the local culture and watch movies under the stars. That is what she had promised herself by taking this short cruise. She wanted to reinvent herself. Nobody knew her on the ship. She had kept to herself, waltzed away from conversations with strangers, and she had begun to feel peace again. Now this.

Rina glanced toward the ocean, which whipped against the ship and wandered erratically beneath her. Her cabin's sliding glass doors reflected the beauty she had enjoyed each day, a beauty that brought peace from a tiny balcony on the twelfth level of the ship. She felt as if she were standing at the top of the world, even though she was one of hundreds doing the same thing. She stood at the railing and experienced the freedom she had hoped for as the wind blew through her tousled hair and ruffled the shaved underside.

She returned to the cabin and brought her eyes back to the box that suddenly felt cold in her hands. She licked her lips and lay her head down on the fluffy pillow on her bed. Lifting the blue beauty above her head with outstretched hands, she couldn't take her eyes off its shiny surfaces. Tracing the lines draped across and around the birds and the maze on top with all of her fingers, she shuddered. Balancing it in her hands again, she sat up and leaned against the headboard. The anticipation and mystery left her a little breathless. She had fallen right in the middle of something, and she was unsure what she was going to do about it.

Then she flipped open the box.

Two

Ashton Mahone hugged the corner behind the stairwell and closed his eyes to catch his breath. He had watched the woman since she walked up the gangplank, knew she was alone on the cruise, and hoped he could trust her. She had avoided everyone, both in the restaurant and in the sleepy Piazza on the Atrium's open deck. All alone. She seemed perfect. At first, he wandered around, squeezing the blue box as if it held the answers to his questions. He hurried down the corridor and moved along the carpeted hallway, slipping into his own room.

The leather satchel was wedged between the mattress and the wall where he had left it. Breathing a sigh of relief, he ran his hand through its opening. After assuring himself that the packet of papers was still inside the bag, he sat back on the bed. His mind drifted back to boarding the ship and reflected on the intricate steps he had taken to stay out of the men's orbit.

But somehow, they knew he was here. How could they have followed him? Where was the connection? Who was watching him? Damn. Damn. Damn. He thought he would have more time. He recognized that getting to know the woman before asking for her help was no longer possible.

And she now had the cloisonné box. He took a breath, closed his eyes, and pressed his lips together. What had he been thinking, giving it away to a stranger? If he hadn't promised to return the box to its owner, he wouldn't be in this position. His mother's eyes had pleaded with him, filled with tears, begging him to promise. So, of course, he did. That was two weeks ago. San Francisco felt far away now, as did his mother.

He had seen the blue box as he grew up and knew there was a story behind it, but his mother would only smile when he asked her. Now that she was dying, it was a different story. Once she began telling him about the small box, her words flowed out in a chaotic waterfall of memories. With each piece of the story, her porcelain face became more animated, and his heart tightened as she revealed its glittering history. It wasn't just an elegant blue box; it was her connection to another world, a world he hadn't known she ever inhabited. And now he was tasked with bringing it home again.

Initially, he wasn't sure where to begin. His life had taken a downward turn after his mother was diagnosed with cancer. He had been an embedded journalist attached to military units in war-torn areas, but that lifestyle had lost its allure months, maybe even years, earlier. He hoped that the silver lining of her illness would bring him back to San Francisco. He missed the tall buildings and narrow streets lined with thriving shops, as well as the winding cobblestone roads. He missed his mother, too. Now, she was nearing the end, and returning this box was the last thing he wanted to do. But he had promised. And he couldn't shake the image of serenity on her face when she placed it into his hands. He had agreed.

"Ashton, you will recognize Jacob when you find him. I know you will. Look at the top of my bedroom closet. There's a loose board on the wall. There are papers and photographs for you. There is a young woman and a man with dark eyebrows…That's me and my Jacob." Her lips had quivered, and her fingers had dug into his arm.

"Your Jacob?" He looked confused. The hairs on his arms stood up as his mother's face changed; all her wrinkles smoothed into a wan smile.

"Yes, son. Your father." Her voice took on a softness Ash had never heard before. She gazed into his face, encouraging him to ask questions, yet clearly afraid of what they might be.

"My father?" Curiosity battled shock, and Ash recalled how the blood had rushed to his head. "Who was Dan Mahone, then? The man I've always believed was my father?" The words poured out of him, laced with resentment. She recoiled from him, her kind eyes darting around the room before settling on him once more. He recognized the pain.

"My darling son. Dan adopted you when you were two years old. He was your dad, always remember that. He was special to me…always. But he could never take the place of my Jacob. Dan didn't want you to know he was your stepfather. And he loved us enough to…" Her clear brown eyes pleaded for understanding as her words fell silent.

Ash felt heavy now, reflecting on the conversation that followed. He'd lived for fifty years believing he was Italian. Now, he realized that his father was a Jew and his mother was a Gentile. She'd been a good daughter, aware she could never marry a Jewish boy. However, the week before she and her family fled Europe to emigrate to America, she and Jacob had been alone together. As it turned out, her parents disowned her anyway when they discovered her pregnancy. She'd been cast out like dirty dishwater. She should have married Jacob.

Now, his mother lay dying, sending her only son on a mysterious mission to find a father he didn't know. Dan Mahone, his dad, was already dead. Jacob Safra, his biological father, was still very much alive. And Magda Mahone knew where the man had lived all this time, leaving Ash's legacy in a blue box to mark him as Jacob's son.

He had never felt anything other than Dan's son. He had given him the love and support of a father that some of his friends envied. He'd always wished for a brother or a sister. Being an only child left him lonely. His friends used to tease him because he had more of everything. After all, there were no siblings to share his parents' love or the toys at Christmas. But he disagreed with them; he would have loved sharing his parents and his toys, knowing there would also be laughter, camaraderie, and sibling memories.

Ash shoved the small leather satchel back into its hiding place. The shock he had experienced regarding his parentage was only the first of many. Now, he understood that the blue box was more than just a beautifully decorated, glazed metal piece that a young girl kept to remember her long-lost love. It was a work of art worth thousands, and its contents were a labor of love...

Its value was one piece of the story his mother had neglected to tell him before he showed the little box to his friend, Harry Dalton. Harry told his art gallery friends, who shared the information with others. When he realized its value and later knew he was being followed, he guessed what they wanted. He wracked his brain to figure out who it was and how they knew about it. But Harry had a lot of friends in and out of the gallery all the time. Who knew?

The strangest part of this scenario was that his mother had no idea it was valuable beyond the contents. She cherished the metal box for its memories, never considering what it might be worth.

"The only time things are worth money," she said, "is if you plan to sell them. And that has never entered my mind." Her eyes had teared up, and her face turned inward when she talked about it.

Ash couldn't shake his bittersweet memories of her. He was unprepared for the fallout that followed. That night, after leaving Lola's Bar with one too many beers, he struggled to make sense of his mother's story, and his reactions felt sluggish. A block away from the bar, he was sucker-punched while waiting for his Uber. He wasn't naive; Ash didn't drive after drinking. He had an agreement with Sam, the bartender, who called for an Uber when necessary. Since many drinkers thought they could still drive after having too much, they often tried. But Ash had seen guys who never lived to tell the tale. So, Sam kept an eye on his patrons, especially his friend Ash.

They came at him quickly and knocked him onto his butt, his back hitting the sidewalk like a two-ton truck. When he tried to get up, he saw two men who thought he was down for the count. Sluggish thoughts scampered around in his head until they made sense, and then he was ready for them.

"You have something we want, mister." One of the men growled at him. His voice sounded like gravel, familiar yet unsettling.

The man's cohort had snickered and raised a foot in the air to kick Ash in the ribs. When the shoe was close enough to cause some damage, Ash feinted and grabbed his leg, sending the man crashing to the ground. He was pleased to see his head slam into a parked car at the curb. One guy was out.

The other one, however, wasn't ready to give it up and came toward Ash, who was now standing near the car with his fists at the ready. His jacket hung askew, but his feet were spread apart; the man was prepared for action.

And Ash gave it to him. His fists found the man's jaw, and then his knee came up to swing into his crotch. When the big man groaned and bent over in agony, Ash slammed his fist into the back of his neck.

The Uber driver arrived. Ash jumped into the car and said, "Step on it." He grinned at the expression on the driver's face as he lifted the flap of his jacket to wipe his forehead. "They're the bad guys, not me."

"You sure about that?" The driver edged away from the curb but swung his eyes between the road and the rear-view mirror. He stared at Ash as he drove away, his shoulders rigid and his face unsure. The driver glanced back at Ash several times.

"Yes, keep driving." Ash turned to look out of the Jeep Cherokee's rear-view window. He knew the men couldn't possibly be up and running after him since he'd put them out of commission, but he'd learned not to take anything for granted. These guys meant business and didn't care if he was collateral damage. His back hurt like hell, and he'd snapped his neck when he went down.

Now, these same men were on this ship, a place Ash Mahone had never imagined being after his heart had been ripped out and put back together again. With growing worries after the encounter, he had altered his travel plans. But here they were again.

Ash laughed miserably. Who would have ever thought he would be headed toward Paris by way of Mexico to take a tiny box to a Polish Jew he'd never met whose blood ran through his veins? And that box was now somewhere on this cruise ship in a strange woman's hands. He pushed weary fingers through his prematurely graying hair and looked in the mirror. Sky blue eyes below dark eyebrows stared back at him, and a small scar by his bottom lip seemed to stand out more than usual.

Blowing out a frustrated breath, he approached the door of his cabin. He never imagined he'd feel like a captive on a massive ship, uncertain about the next few minutes of his life. But he couldn't wait any longer. Slowly opening the door, he peeked into the long hallway. He looked both ways but could only see cleaning carts and two women whispering three doors down from his cabin. Music filtered down the hall, making one believe it was a paradise without chaos waiting to pounce. Ending up on a cruise ship had never been his intention, but he was here now, and his stomach felt as tight as a rubber band. He glanced back down the hallway just to ensure nobody lurked in a shadowed doorway.

All clear.

Now he had to find her.

Three

She had promised herself that she would enjoy this cruise incognito. No electronic devices. She brought real books—no phone, Kindle, or iPad. Now, she stared into a tiny box filled with so many small jewels that her eyes nearly crossed. And she had no internet to research the box unless she paid by the minute.

It wasn't as if she couldn't afford that, but she didn't want to break her promise. Were these jewels stolen? Was the man who confronted her a thief? Why would he toss this magical box to her and run away? Do I have 'trust me, I'll help you?' written on my forehead? Her head ached. She snapped the box closed and moved around the room searching for a hiding place. She couldn't very well carry it around with her while men chased the thief... if he was a thief. Oh hell. Out of one mess and then dropped into another.

The room didn't have any hidey-holes. She whistled through her teeth. She knew the safest place was probably in her bag, so she dug through its depths to explore inside. Then she grinned when she remembered the small zippered compartment at the bottom of the purse. She'd laughed when she bought it, wondering what in the world she'd ever use it for. Now she knew; oh...a little blue box.

Rina brought her hands to her face and felt the heat throbbing there. Yes, she realized she was scared. Those jewels must be worth a fortune. She didn't need to be a mathematician to figure out the money. Math had never been her strong suit, but she knew that sparkles meant value. On the other hand, she wasn't sure whether she should be more afraid of the man who asked her to hold it or of the contents inside the box.

She wanted a glass of wine and some food. After she zipped the little hidden pocket closed on her purse, she pressed her fingers into the bulge to make sure it was securely wedged inside. Opening her door, she imagined him lurking outside or waiting to pounce on her when she entered the dining room. He'd mentioned that he had seen her the night before in her red slinky blouse. She glanced around inside her mind and shook her head; she didn't remember him at all. She would have since he was a good-looking man, maybe four or five years older than she was. She begrudgingly accepted that he had a very nice voice; yes, she would have definitely remembered the voice.

The carpeted hallway bustled with other passengers preparing for dinner, filling the area with laughter. Music filtered through the sound system, and she smiled for just a moment when she heard Neil Diamond's voice singing September Morn. Jeff's favorite song. Her heart stumbled for an instant. However, she walked steadily toward the steps leading to the dining areas and the bars located several floors below her room.

Jeff was one of the reasons she was on this ship. She had wanted to sail away from the memory of him with Jenna. Jeff and Jenna. Her sister was the flamboyant one, while Rina was the quiet one. Her sister skipped college to play and have fun, whereas Rina was the sister who wanted to learn about the world and travel. She had been sure that Jeff was her kindred spirit. But she was wrong. She felt relieved when Neil Diamond's voice faded away as she stepped onto the landing. Jeff was dead to her, and so was Jenna.

Now, she kept her eyes open. Rina felt both excited and frightened that the man would find her. She needed to make better choices. She grimaced, thinking about the poor decisions she had already made. She wanted to turn a new page in the chapter of her life, but the challenge now felt as overwhelming as the jewels that screamed and jittered from her bag.

The Wheelhouse Bar was crowded with people in fancy clothes. The sounds of clinking glassware filled her ears, momentarily distracting her from thoughts of the man. As she sat at a corner table to keep an eye on the door, she began to consider what she'd say to him. She twisted in her chair and pressed a hand to her tight throat to soothe it. When she turned back around, a glass of Cabernet rested on a linen napkin. She smiled at the waiter, who winked and glided toward the table, balancing his tray of drinks like a pillow.

Rina surveyed the room, squeezing her feet together to hold the purse firmly beneath her chair. There were men and women of all sizes and shapes on the ship; many were overweight. Did they cruise because there was so much food available? Or was it because the entire holiday could be enjoyed aboard the ship without any exercise? At a loss, she wondered if they were simply lonely and consumed an abundance of food to relieve their sadness.

She watched three large women laughing next to her, thoroughly enjoying themselves. Being overweight did not diminish their happiness, and she was glad to see it. Rina reflected on all the weight she'd gained and lost over the years, always convinced that being thin would make her happier and prettier. A different hairdo, new shoes, a different dress. She suddenly realized that happiness comes from within, not from the outside. Her fingers tapped on the tabletop when the music started, and the three women tapped their own feet on the floor with each beat. When the ladies got up to dance, she smiled again.

She sipped her red wine and began to relax. When she closed her blue eyes for a moment to reflect on her epiphany, she opened them again to take another sip. Almost choking on it, she recognized the two men who had rushed past her that afternoon toward the stranger. Should she leave now or pretend she was calm and unaware? Unlike her sister, Jenna, she wasn't used to subterfuge. No, she had always been a straight shooter and walked the walk, so people knew where they stood in her life.

She lifted her glass of wine and pretended to watch the ladies on the dance floor. Their laughter surrounded her, and she nearly believed she had vanished into the crowd, as she had been doing since boarding the ship. But her hopes withered when the men glanced toward the dance floor that surrounded her table.

Her heart dipped, and she nearly dropped her glass. "Stay cool," she whispered. Don't meet their faces. She contemplated her wine. Posing an uninterested bearing, she acted oblivious to them. She lowered her eyes as if she didn't have a care in the world and lifted a bacon-wrapped, stuffed olive to her lips with a toothpick. Surely the men don't suspect me? When one of the men headed in her direction, she felt the olive spin and stick in her throat.

When he approached her table, her stomach lurched with fear. As he turned toward the long bar to stand beside his friend, she felt her insides smile with gratitude. They had been talking, and she wondered if they had noticed her at all. Maybe she had just imagined their interest? Maybe she was paranoid just because her purse was filled with jewels worth a fortune. She nonchalantly swiveled a few inches in her chair toward the dancers again.

Someone tapped her on the shoulder, and she almost swallowed the olive whole.

"Would you care to dance?" The man looked interested, but she did not.

She shook her head with a smile to soften the blow. "Sorry, I'm nursing a broken ankle and it's not up to dancing yet."

The man smiled in disappointment and approached another woman who was sitting alone with her glass of wine not far away. He had better luck this time, and soon, they were dancing alongside the ladies.

When she finally glanced at the bar moments later, only one of the men remained. His companion was nowhere to be seen.

Another sip of wine.

Another olive.

Ok, I can do this.

Four

Ash navigated through each of the elegant dining rooms before slipping into the Wheelhouse Bar. He remembered she had wandered in before dinner the night before. The bar was always lively at night, boasting perhaps the most active dance floor on the ship. Blues bands typically performed there, embracing vintage and nautical themes from the early 1900s. In contrast to Club Fusion and Skywalker's Nightclub, this space wasn't cluttered with multiple televisions. Instead, it offered a booming sound system, ceiling-mounted dance floor lights, and comfortable seating in various arrangements. This bar nearly spanned the width of the ship with a throughway aisle on one side.

Happy hour offered two-for-one drinks from 4:00 to 6:00. When he'd seen the woman lounging in one of the beautiful wing-backed chairs the night before, he'd sat in a wine-leather chair angled for a better view of her. She'd looked like a two-fisted drinker with a glass of red wine in one hand and another glass on the small table before her. She was definitely getting her money's worth. He hoped she'd follow the same path tonight. Perhaps he could pull her out onto the deck for a nice chat?

For some reason, she had seemed safe last night and again this afternoon, but now... not so much. Maybe because he had no idea where she was or what she was thinking. Ash was sure she had looked into the small box by now. God only knew what she thought about it or about him. He needed more time.

He pulled his 49ers baseball cap down low over his eyes. He didn't care if he stood out among all these men dressed in elegant casual attire. His khakis and pullover sweater worked fine for him. He wasn't fussy. He liked the term, simplify. He hoped to live his life that way. Lately, however, that was a laugh. Between his mother's illness, his disenchantment with his job, and now being unemployed, he wondered, would his life ever be simple again? Yet, he admitted he thrived on action, not simplicity. What a conundrum, he thought.

Musicians began strumming guitars, and a drummer tapped out a beat in sync with his thumping heart. Several Asian dancers filled the dance floor, thoroughly enjoying the music and each other's company. The beautiful wood floors gleamed like glass. Ash swallowed hard, ordered a Jack Daniels neat, and waited. Surely, she would make another entrance, and they would have the chance to discuss his dilemma. He hoped he hadn't made a terrible mistake by trusting her at face value.

Sipping his Tennessee Sour Mash whiskey, he leaned back against the wall; he didn't want to be blindsided by the men. His knuckles were still raw from his encounter with them in San Francisco, and he wasn't looking forward to seeing them again. How they managed to find him after he'd made such convoluted travel plans to reach old Jacob, he had no idea.

As he thought about the jewels in that little box and the love they represented, the whiskey wouldn't go down. Thirty-two years. Thirty-two jewels. It had taken the old man eighteen years to…

His head jerked slightly when he saw the woman sitting at a table near the musicians. A wooden railing separated her from the dancers. He noticed a man tap her on the shoulder, and she rose with a smile, hardly the same woman who had avoided others after all. As they started swaying to the music, he observed the man pull her a little too close, prompting her to step back with a frown on her face.

He saw the man laugh and bow his head. The music sped up, and they began doing the swing. After the music stopped, the man walked her back to her table, where she sat down, thanked him, and lifted her glass of wine. Now what? Do I wave at her? Stand up? Walk over to sit with her? Stare her down? Just as his mind was flooded with indecision, he noticed her staring at him.

Rina tilted her head slightly toward the bar, where a man stood casually with his foot resting on the foot rail, a cold beer raised to his lips. She subtly moved her head and gestured with her hand from the chair to her palazzo pants toward the door.

The dancer approached her again, but she shook her head, lifted her wine for the last drop, and stood up to leave.

Ash's forehead creased for a moment as he grasped the message, finished the last of the Jack, and pushed his baseball cap down over his brow. Without turning his head, he shifted his gaze toward the man at the bar. He then eased out of his chair and sauntered unhurriedly toward the opposing entrance before stepping outside. A group of laughing patrons entered the bar, concealing his escape.

He grimaced as he walked into the hallway. The woman was nowhere in sight. He exhaled a disgusted breath and then felt a hand on his arm. When he looked down into her angry blue eyes, he smiled.

"You think this is funny?" Rina's expression wasn't exactly a scowl; it was more one of curiosity, but it definitely wasn't a smile. She glared at him for a few seconds before pursing her lips.

"No, I don't, but I'm happy to see you."

"Really?" She glanced back into the bar. Rina pulled him away from the doorway as if he didn't have a smart thought in his head. Hustling him away from the bar, she seemed like a woman on a mission.

Ash grinned again and followed her.

"Come on. There's nothing to it but to go to my room. They both came into the bar, but only one guy stayed. So, they're looking for you everywhere…" The rest of her words were lost in transit.

He had to pick up the pace to keep up with her. She was several inches shorter than his 5' 10" frame, but the woman could move. He heard her mumbling as she rounded the corner at nearly a trot and pressed the elevator button.

"Are you out of your mind? And my next question is, are you a thief? I know what's inside that box, and I don't want any part of it." Her chest heaved rapidly as she murmured the words. When the elevator door opened, she yanked him inside after her as if she were the teacher and he was the kid. She pressed twelve, and her eyes swung back toward him as the door snapped shut.

He grinned again. He admired her spirit and hoped he could talk her down, explain everything, sort of. The next thing Ash knew, they were on Deck Twelve and she slid her room key into the slot. She pulled him into the small room with her, and he gazed out the glass doors toward the balcony and the ocean beyond. Her room was more spacious than his, and he didn't have a balcony. Huh. He had only a moment for further thought when she moved behind him to lock the door. When he turned around, she pushed him toward the only chair in the corner.

The woman stood with her arms crossed over her chest. "Now talk, mister." Her chest heaved, and her dark eyebrows arched. Her small stature didn't diminish the anger directed at him as he looked down at her.

Two sets of blue eyes met.

"First, let me apologize for putting you in this situation, Ms...?"

"What? You need to know my name to tell me why you pushed that little box of gems into my chair and then ran like hell?" Her eyes narrowed as a wisp of medium brown hair slipped over her left eye. With a huff, she pushed it back from her forehead and sat down on her bed to stare at him.

He stared back at her, waiting.

"Okay... It's Rina. What's yours?"

"Ash."

"Good, now we're introduced. What in the world is going on with you?" She grabbed her purse, unzipped the bottom, and handed him the beautiful box. Her fingers hesitated to let go of the metal, and she was confused by the connection it held for her.

He didn't immediately raise his hand to accept it. He slipped his hands into his pants pockets, urging her to listen to him.

She lifted her hand toward him once more. "Take it!" Her eyes flashed, and she was breathing heavily. When she reached for him again, her hands curled protectively around the box.

"I need your help, Rina." His blue eyes smoldered as he began to talk, briefly recounting what his mother had shared with him. The anxiety he had felt when his mother told her story surged up to slap him in the head again as he recounted nearly everything he'd been told.

Rina's eyes sparkled with curiosity as she settled the little box onto her lap, where it nestled into the folds of her black palazzo pants. Her dark, arched eyebrows furrowed together as she listened to his story. He felt relieved to see her relax, as if her belly had unclenched.

"What can I do? You know these men want it. They saw you talking to me. When one of them came toward me during dinner, I nearly spit out my wine. When he walked past me, I nearly kissed the floor with thanks. And I'm a little afraid." Her light, luminous eyes began to fill. She quickly closed them again before gripping the box in her lap once more.

"I'd planned to get off the ship in Cabo on Thursday, but that plan has evaporated since they found me. Instead, my last chance may be in Mazatlán tomorrow. Maybe I can lose them in the city. I need to get on a plane to Paris. I thought I'd be invisible cruising on the ship instead of flying out of San Francisco, but the men followed me." He ran his hands up and down his thighs as he tried to get his brain working.

She sighed deeply. "Why on earth did you get on a ship to Mexico when you need to go to Paris? The port in Los Angeles is a long drive from San Francisco..." Her curiosity was piqued.

"The story is very complicated." He leaned over and lifted both his hands to cover hers, still tightly linked around the small oval box. His blue eyes pleaded with hers, and a few strands of hair fell over his forehead.

She didn't move.

"Hold this awhile longer. Please trust me. I'll leave from Mazatlán. If I can avoid them until Thursday, when we're at the pier, don't get off with me. Instead, let's meet at the end of the pier past the rental car kiosks. I'll be waiting for you. I'll have a plan by then. What do you think? Can you do this for my mother? She's a sweet woman, and I ache to think of letting her down. This is more than just a cloisonné jewel box. Her heart resides inside it. I can't lose it." He knew he was rambling, but he couldn't help it.

Rina blinked and rolled her eyes. "You're full of it, aren't you, Ash? You don't have to lay it on so thick. I can see how important it is to you, but I'm not on this ship for an adventure, I'm here to unwind."

His eyes didn't leave hers.

"Oh, Okay! We can try to lose them in Mazatlán or wait for Cabo or…? Different boat. End of the pier. First group out. Now, go somewhere so I can read my book." She showed him the door.

His eyes sparkled as he stepped into the brightly colored, carpeted corridor. When the door clicked shut behind him, he felt a burden lift. He appreciated her spunk and her eagerness to help him. Now, he needed to stay out of their grasp long enough to leave the cruise ship with Rina in tow.

During his long walk back to his room, another plan began to form.

Five

The men sat in leather easy chairs inside the Crooner's Bar; both sets of eyes glued to the Atrium's elevator lobby. Music floated through the room, but they didn't notice. Brad Latham and Gabe Pizelli gripped metal Bud Lite bottles while their eyes swung like a pendulum between the decorated, swooping staircases and the elevators.

"This ship can't hide the man forever, Gabe." His cohort lifted his beer to his lips, his eyes still scanning inch by inch across the expanse of the Atrium and beyond. Christmas decorations clung to every corner, winding between each tiny column on the balustrade.

Gabe didn't answer.

"You should have grabbed him when he first got on the ship. All this wait-and-see crap is getting on my nerves. One man, one little box, and we are still sitting around like idiots waiting for it to drop in our laps. Dalton said the box was worth a mint, but the jewels inside were amazing. Why don't we….?"

"Shut up, Brad. Let me think, yeah?" Gabe swallowed the last drops of his beer and set the bottle on the table beside him with a hollow thump. He saw a crowd entering the elevator area, and his eyes narrowed.

"Well, think of something solid. I'm getting tired of this…"

"When he was talking to the dark-haired woman on the Lido Deck, she didn't look happy about it. Now that I think back, I wonder if she's helping him. They didn't come on the ship together; I'm sure of that. Maybe we should start looking for her instead. I saw her at one of the bars on Deck Seven a while ago." His thick eyebrows scrunched down over his eyes as he thought about it. Gabe pinched his nose.

Brad turned to Gabe. "What? We can't even find one guy, and now we need to find two people?" He dropped his beer bottle on the table. "You're taking your vengeance a little too far on this guy, aren't you?"

"Shut up. They may be together. Let's split up." Gabe opened the small accordion map of the ship and spread it out on the table in front of them. One fat finger pointed to the Explorer's Lounge. "We'll take one level at a time. I'll go here, you go back to the Wheelhouse Bar, and then we should go to Gatsby's. The guy may be hiding in plain sight at the casino. I wanted to take a look in there anyway. We need to get that box before we get to Mazatlán, dammit." He fisted his right hand into his lap and grabbed the map with his left.

Brad Latham grunted. They both left, heading in opposite directions. The bars were beginning to fill up as the sun set over the western horizon. Music and beer flowed along with wine, cocktails, and sweet drinks. The Wheelhouse Bar was packed. Brad glanced at his watch and surveyed the room; his gaze lingered on each table as if he were taking a census. When he came up empty, he sidled up to the bar to wait, turned toward the door, and slapped his cruise card on the bar. Moments later, he guzzled down his first beer.

Gabe slipped into the Explorer's Lounge and noticed the tiered seating arranged in a huge semi-circle. He raised a finger to order a scotch and soda as his eyes scanned the room. The noise escalated in tandem with the crowd's alcohol intake. Sipping his drink, he wondered where the man was hiding. Ashton Mahone owed him, and he wasn't letting this one go. He'd pay for his malicious news article.

As he remembered his anger during the last few days he spent in the military, he admitted it still simmered. He tightened his fingers around his glass. There had to be a perfect plan to hurt the guy, and stealing that box of jewels was the answer. He was sure of it. His mind considered other options. The Passenger Services desk? Maybe he could trick one of the older ladies. His eyes darkened. After placing the empty glass on the bar, he scanned the room once more and headed to the stairwell.

One level down in the three-level Atrium was a sparkling sight. The Christmas tree in the corner glittered and dripped with tinsel. Elaborate fronds of greenery slipped in and out of the post railings on the curved stairwells. Gabe made the trip slowly, his eyes on everyone below, until he came to the long desk. He grimaced. Only one young woman, the rest were all men who might not give him the time of day.

He waited in line like everyone else. Finally, it was his turn. Damn, he got the man instead of the woman. Taking a deep breath, he smiled at the dark-skinned man in front of him. "Hey, I have a strange request."

The Filipino man smiled at him and waited patiently. "How can I help you, sir?" His thick head of dark hair was cut close, and his shirt was starched to perfection. The other people behind the desk chattered as the line grew behind him. It seemed he wasn't the only person with a problem.

"I'm sure I saw one of my old friends on the ship yesterday, and I've given up trying to find him again. His name is Ashton Mahone. Can you check your database for his name and cabin number?" Gabe smiled innocently. He knew there were about 3,000 passengers on the ship and fourteen bars. He could never watch all of them to find one man in that massive crowd.

The man pursed his lips for just a moment before answering. "No, sir. It is against policy to give out that information. Perhaps you could go back to where you saw him last, and he might be there again? I am sorry."

Gabe's fingers curled into his palms. "Yeah, I understand. Thanks." As he walked away, his thoughts turned dark once more. Time was running out. Standing at the ornate railing, he glanced down to the lower level. A woman with red hair played a lively tune on a shiny white piano, while a couple danced across the floor in perfect rhythm. Laughter filtered upward, and he almost wished he were on the cruise ship to enjoy the scene, the camaraderie, and the people. But he wasn't there for a holiday, and he knew it.

As those whimsical thoughts slipped through his mind, he noticed the dark-haired woman enter the Atrium. She moved toward the back of the room, walking beneath the balcony where he stood, and soon she was lost from view. Gabe hurried toward the curving stairwell, but it was clogged with other passengers and children moving too slowly for him to get past. When he finally stepped onto the level below, she was no longer in the Atrium. He slapped the newel post. Of course, she wasn't.

Brad continued to wait in the Wheelhouse Bar, scanning the room while downing his second beer. As the room swayed slightly and the ship moved toward the next Mexican port, he lifted the glass to catch the last drop on his tongue before placing it back on the bar. When the bartender raised an eyebrow at him, Brad shook his head, indicating no.

He thought the casino was one level down on the other side of the Atrium. The ship was large, and he kept getting turned around. The beer wasn't aiding his navigation skills, but he exited through the port door in search of Gatsby's, where he knew the gambling buzzed.

~

Ash entered through the aft door of the Wheelhouse Bar just as Brad turned the corner toward the hallway. If Brad had done his homework, he would have realized there were two doors to the bar. Ash had counted on the man's dysfunction. He had watched him order both beers and hoped the liquor would slow down the man's thinking and movements.

He hurried out the other door to follow him, losing himself in the crowd of passengers until he spotted the big man heading toward the casino. It buzzed with sounds and laughter as he eased his way into the doorway. It felt good to be the hunter instead of the hunted. What can they do to me in a crowd?

Ash saw Gabe pacing a hole in the carpet across the large room behind the blackjack table, while Brad walked toward him with his hands jammed in his pockets. He figured the man probably wished he had taken that third beer.

Every corner of the casino buzzed with noise and was brightly lit. The walls were lined with slot machines, while gambling tables were centered in the room. Ash idly wondered how many passengers spent their entire cruise in this room, overlooking the beautiful ocean and all the wonders the ship offered.

One man sat at the blackjack table. He looked like he had been there for a while. He moved his hand to cup his chin and lightly tapped his forefinger against the side of his jaw as if he thought the cards in his hand would change any second.

Ash shrugged and turned his head toward the men he'd followed. His gut ached, and uncertainty overwhelmed him. He hadn't intended to become a hybrid of Mission: Impossible and Double O Seven. And he didn't like it much. Maybe he'd read too many adventure books or written too many war chronicles. The thought of stepping into any one of them made his breath catch. His heartbeat raced against his ribs as if it had taken on a life of its own.

His eyes never strayed from the men as he moved closer. The other guy looked familiar. He hadn't gotten a good look at him the night they'd ganged up on him. Now, a tickle of memory brushed against his mind. Where had he seen the man before? He pondered if he'd met him while he'd been embedded with the media. Did he work on the newspaper with him? Newspaper? The magazine? He didn't seem like the type to sit in front of a computer for long. Damn, he hated not being able to put a name to a face. He knew the guy. But from where?

As Ash watched the men converse with their heads bent toward each other beside the billiard and blackjack tables, a crowd of gamblers began to gather next to them. Ash knew it was now or never and shook his head. He'd try to put a name to the face later. When he slipped around the craps table and approached them, he visualized the man in a uniform in his mind's eye. Military? Then it had to be while he was in Iraq or Afghanistan covering the war. He bit his lip in frustration as the memory nagged at the back of his mind.

The carpet felt thick beneath his feet. Huge, round spirals of colorful circles covered every inch, enough to make his eyes spin. The sounds of raucous laughter filled the spacious room as he weaved his way past another small crowd of gamblers. Once he stepped beyond the gaming tables and slot machines, Ash confidently approached them, one hand tucked into his pants pocket.

"Hey, you guys. Long time, no see." Ash stood firmly before them. He didn't like confrontations like this, but it was better than glancing over his shoulder every time he left his room. He raised an eyebrow and tucked his other hand into his waistband. Ash refused to let the men see how on edge he felt.

Gabe and Brad's heads swiveled around so quickly that Ash nearly laughed. They were clearly thrown off balance, each taking a step toward him. But when the men realized they were caught in the middle of a gambling party, Ash couldn't hold back his laughter anymore.

"I know you guys think you're pretty smart following me onto the ship. I also know you want something that doesn't belong to you. If you get in my way again, you'll be spitting out some of your teeth," Ash said with a smile on his face for the benefit of those around him.

The men sensed the air around them becoming hostile. One of them still stumbled forward, but a gambler raised an arm to celebrate a winning number and stopped him.

When Ash turned on his heel to leave the room, Gabe leaned forward again, but Brad pulled him back. "Don't do something stupid. Do you want to end up in the brig? The ship probably has one, you know." Brad yanked Gabe's elbow and squeezed hard.

Gabe huffed out an angry breath and punched the air. "Holy shit. Let's go!" The room was bustling with gamblers who paid no attention to the men until they pushed into them. Several men jumped out of their way as they were shoved aside without a hint of civility.

"Hey!" One man shouted as he shoved Gabe backward. Gabe's jaw tightened, and he turned toward the man with a sneer on his face. Several others looked up from their cards to stare. A security guard noticed the disturbance and started to move across the room. He nodded to his partner, and both men entered the fray.

"No problem, mister." Gabe answered absentmindedly as he focused on Ash's retreat and headed toward the doorway. The lights were bright, and Gabe didn't want to lose him. He paid no attention to the whiner he'd nearly knocked down in his haste to get out of the room. However, the man wasn't going to let Gabe leave without a confrontation.

"That's what you say. We're here to enjoy ourselves, not mow everyone down in the process." The big man tucked his green shirt into his trousers and glared at the men as they shifted around the gaming table.

His cohorts began to surround Gabe and Brad, appearing as though the evening adventure had just begun for them. When they moved closer to Gabe, he seemed oblivious to their interest until he heard their voices grow louder behind him.

Soon, the room felt much smaller than before, and the card table grew quiet. The casino was so crowded that a party could be happening unnoticed by others. This time was different, and the men weren't going to let Gabe off easily.

The security guards were almost right on top of the group before they realized it. Time seemed to move in slow motion as each man stepped back upon seeing the guards' faces.

Gabe gave the man a cod-liver oil stare and lifted his eyes toward the others. "I'm not here to make a ruckus, guys. I'm just minding my own business. Sorry if I was..."

The guards turned toward Gabe. Their organized approach didn't escape his notice. They had done this before. Their body language indicated they meant business, and no one was going to disrupt the camaraderie that people expected on the ship, particularly in the casino.

When Gabe saw them advancing with angry looks, he grabbed Brad's arm and pushed him past several people entering the casino. All they needed was a fight on their hands. They'd promised themselves to remain invisible. A fight inside the casino would make people remember them. The sounds of machines began ringing behind them, and Gabe paused when he heard the group laughing. He grinned absently as he watched them slap each other on the back, congratulating the winner.

As the men navigated through the celebrating crowd of gamblers, the doorway became congested with people. Gabe's face mirrored Brad's disgust. They knew Ash would be gone.

They were right.

Six

Ash's legs trembled as he hurried up the stairs, not stopping until he reached the fifteenth deck. His mind was in turmoil as he recalled the threatening looks on the men's faces. Why did an act of love for his mother have to put him in this situation? Why did his friend's loose tongue set these thugs on his tail? And why did that guy look so familiar? And why did he drag Rina into the mess?

He thought about that last question, and his eyes softened. She is something. I like her spunk. I hope to God I don't get her hurt. His mind drifted back to his mother, and he glanced at his watch. Time to make that call. He found the blind corner under the big screen on the sun terrace and pulled out his smartphone. Connecting to the ship's internet, he pressed the button to buy minutes and then opened his Skype app. Within moments, his mother's gentle face filled the screen.

"Hey, Ma. How are you doing today?"

His mother was approaching seventy, yet she appeared much younger than many women her age. Her tender smile reminded him why he was determined to provide her with what she needed: closure to the regrets of not making the right decision so many years earlier.

"Ashton. I'm feeling good today. Let me look around the ship; I can pretend I'm on the cruise with you. And… Why are you on the ship? Why didn't you fly to Paris?"

Ash didn't respond but turned his phone's camera to show her the tiers of lounge chairs. Sounds from the ball game on the screen above him blared. Several women nearby laughed, raising their wine glasses in a toast to something that must have been hilarious. Their faces creased in smiles as they lifted their glasses in unison.

His mother chuckled at their antics. "Have you met anyone special on the cruise, son?" Her voice had a teasing quality he recognized but thought she'd lost during her illness.

He laughed. "Ma, I'm not here to meet anyone special. You know this is just a way to get me to Paris without…and…she isn't…"

His mother squinted at the phone. "…And she isn't what? You did meet someone," she whispered gleefully.

Ash laughed again. "Which reminds me, ma, I might have to go find her. She's supposed to meet me here, but I'm stuck behind a column. Her name is Rina, and I've shown her the box and all that glitters inside."

Magda's face stilled.

"It's ok, ma. She might be the only one who can help get it off the ship for me. I didn't want to tell you, but you have to know... Some people want this box just as much as you want me to take it to Jacob. So far, I've managed to stay out of their way. That's why I made the detour. I don't want to disappoint…" His words slowed as he watched horror creep across her face, her eyes filling and turning glossy with tears.

"Ash! Please don't put yourself in danger. Your father would never want to lose you over the box or the jewels inside." Her face, which was pale when he first called, began to turn pink and blotchy.

"Ma, I'm a big boy. The only reason I told you is that we promised each other no more secrets. I can handle this." His fingers gripped the phone as he tried to hide his dismay at opening his big mouth.

His mother's face calmed. "Tell me about your lady friend."

I don't think Rina would like being called my lady friend, ma, but she's putting up with me because she feels she has no choice.

Her eyebrows raised a notch. "Really?" Her lips struggled to hold back a smile.

"Ma, don't play Cupid for me. She's helping me for YOU, not for me. I told her a little of our story, and she's a soft touch…"

"Oh, really?" Rina's voice landed beside him like a bag of cement. Ash turned slowly, thinking quickly. When he held out his phone toward her, she saw the older woman on the screen, and Rina's eyes brightened.

"You are Rina?" The voice was gentle. Soft brown eyes looked back at her. She sat up in her chair, and Rina could see a blazing fire in the fireplace behind her. Several paintings hung on the wall, and a lamp glowed, casting shadows across the woman's lined face.

"Uh…yes, I'm Rina." She glared at Ash before turning toward the woman with a smile. "How are you, Mrs. Mahone?"

"Please, dear. Call me Magda. My son was telling me you are willing to help him get my little cloisonné box to an old man in Paris?"

"Not to Paris, surely. I'm just helping him hold on to the box long enough to get off this ship…" Her eyes turned toward Ash as if to say, Aren't I?

Ash's face felt hot for a moment before his eyes swung back to the phone. He laid a hand on Rina's arm. She shrugged it off and scooted onto a chaise lounge beside him. When she pulled her feet up onto the blue-and-white striped cushion, her eyes pinned him to his chair.

"Ma, my time is running out here. Same time tomorrow?"

She grinned, kissed her fingers, and waved them toward him. Then the screen went blank.

Rina and Ash stared at each other.

"I'm a soft touch, huh?" She raised a hand to the waitress, weaving her way between the chairs, and pulled out her Princess cruise card.

"That isn't exactly what I meant, Rina." He motioned for her to put her cruise card away and lifted his own. The blood vessels in his hands stood out as if he'd run a mile. He didn't want to screw this up, so he let out a sigh and brushed aside her second attempt to buy a glass of wine.

"Huh." Rina took a breath and raised a hand to her chest. The group of laughing women moved toward the bar, but several younger men and women filled their spot. One woman had a captivating tattoo across her back, and her hair was a vibrant shade of blue. Rina shook her head.

Waitstaff were attending the Lido Deck's tables, hurrying to take and deliver orders, clear tables, and clean. Now, a server stood beside them. Clearly in a rush, Rina turned toward Ash in silent defiance.

Ash ordered two glasses of wine and stalled for time.

Rina bit her lip and relished his discomfort. She had forgotten how to flirt and wasn't sure if this could be considered flirting, but she hadn't felt her heart race like this in a long time. When he turned to her with a hopeful expression, she felt a smile budding and couldn't stop it from spreading across her face.

She reached a hand toward him as a peace offering. "Okay, let's start over. Did you find the guys? They obviously didn't find you, or you wouldn't have been here for our rendezvous." She tuned out the sounds of the football game that replaced the movie on the Movies under the Stars screen. She craned her neck to see the Packers score a touchdown against the Seahawks. The score was 38-10, and the crowd was going wild. It was far too loud for her taste, but she laughed at their antics.

A glass of Cabernet now sat beside each of them. She tuned out the squealing crowd and game sounds behind her as she lifted her glass.

"I found them." He snickered and raised his hand to his forehead in a salute. He chuckled at the expression on her face.

The wineglass stopped midway to her lips. "What?"

"Found them in Gatsby's Casino among a crowd of gambling passengers. In the middle of so many people, I knew the men couldn't do much to me. I threatened them, and then made my exit in the middle of the crowd, and then hiked up here to call Ma. That's all I know." He sipped his wine while his blue eyes watched her face over the rim of his glass.

"So, you threatened them...does that mean I can give it back to you and we can each go our separate ways?"

"Not sure. Let's see if they get in the way again, and we can decide in the morning when we dock, please? They've spent a lot of money to follow me, so I doubt they give up so easily." His eyes pleaded with her as he ran his fingers through his graying hair.

One more sip.

The football game was over.

The crowd rumbled around them.

Another sip.

Rina saw the young woman with blue hair again. She stood a few chairs away in a skimpy bikini. Men surrounded her, poking at her arm and the tattoo that covered it up to the elbow. An Eiffel Tower tattoo adorned her back, while a bow was inked on each leg just below her butt cheeks. She grimaced before turning to Ash again.

"Why did you pick me? Why not someone else...like that young cutie with the tattoos all over her back, legs, and arms? Why me?" This time it was her turn to watch him. She licked the rim of her wine glass. Her face showed that she was enjoying the look on his face.

Ash was mesmerized and couldn't take his eyes off her tongue as it swirled around the edge of the glass. When he saw her take a small sip of the red wine, his heart twisted. What in the world was happening to him? He hadn't felt attracted to a woman in a long time, and he admitted he was enjoying the time spent with Rina. He shook his head.

"I don't trust anyone with blue hair," he answered simply. He raised both eyebrows, lifted his glass again, and grinned impishly. "Or girls with tattoos."

She rolled her eyes.

Seven

Gabe and Brad grumbled under their breaths as they pushed their way down the tinsel-laden spiral stairs to regroup. They had initially thought it would be easy to grab the box and then hide out in their room until the next port of call. When they first heard about the cloisonné box and jewels, they joked about it; it would be a grand heist. When they couldn't get it out of their heads, they decided it might be their key to a future they could only dream about. The scuttlebutt around the art gallery sent Gabe scampering to follow Ash Mahone, grab the blue beauty, and make it a done deal. But it hadn't been so easy.

When he was face-to-face with Mahone, he wanted to punch him again. His gut tightened as he recalled how that one war article had derailed his army career. If it hadn't been for that jerk's story, he'd still be on track for Captain, not tossed out on his ear. How had the journalist seen him fire into that crowd? Gabe had been terrified and ready to run for his life, pulling his men into that building afterward. They'd agreed to keep the shooting spree to themselves, but Mahone didn't miss it and…

Now, Gabe had a chance to pay him back. They had watched Ash and listened to his phone conversations, thanks to a microphone bug planted by a friend from the security company. When they learned he was taking the fortune to Paris, they followed him. They were prepared for a plane ticket, not a cruise ship. They shadowed him to Los Angeles and then to the San Pedro dock. They purchased tickets on the only available deck, frustrated that the cheap cabins were no longer available at the last minute. When they embarked on the Ruby

Princess, the plan was to grab it before the first port in Puerto Vallarta. Ash Mahone was smart; he knew he was being followed.

The day they saw him on the Lido Deck near the pool, chatting with a dark-haired woman, they wanted to grab it and run. He had it in his hands; they saw it shimmering in the sun. But that hadn't worked out either. Now, the ship would be sailing into Mazatlán within a few hours, and they were no closer to being the new owners of the blue box than they had been at the onset of the ocean journey.

Gabe sat on his bed, staring out of the glass doors toward the balcony. The slight ocean breeze felt warm, and he wished again that he could pretend this was a holiday; a little drinking, women, and all the food he could eat. He glanced over at Brad, who was snoozing on his bed, oblivious to everything. Gabe grunted in disgust and kicked Brad's foot.

"Wake up. We have to make a plan, you ass. I want that guy."

One of Brad's eyes opened halfway. "You make the plan and tell me about it later. I'm tired of chasing him. He can't go anywhere anytime soon. We're on a ship, for God's sake." His arm stretched toward the ocean waves rumbling below as far as the eye could see. The warm air flowed through the open glass doors. The sounds of the ocean lapping against the ship felt like a dream and lulled Brad to sleep.

Gabe shook his head in disgust and gripped the other man's ankle. "We do this together, man. If you think you're just going along for the ride, get ready to have your profits fall below 50%."

Brad's eyes flew open, and he sat up with a growl. "Okay, what do you want me to do?" His jaw needed shaving, and his eyes were bloodshot. He'd been drinking all day, even though he'd complained that the booze wasn't free. Since their cruise ID cards were linked to their credit cards, it was easy to forget, and he'd deal with it later. He'd told Gabe they would be rich when they got off the ship.

"When we sail into port, we need to be down on Deck Four where the gangway is located. Everyone going into Mazatlán has to go that way, and our guy will want to get off this ship. There are two of us, for God's sake. There's only one of him. It can't be that flippin' hard. He will have the box with him. We wait and follow him. And then we grab it." Gabe's voice turned threatening. His hands kneaded his thighs as he considered the plan aloud.

Brad stared at him. "Yeah, that should work. Now, can I go to sleep? Even if we find him on the ship, where do we go with it? He's clever, and we know it's not going to be easy..."

The Italian captain's heavily accented voice blared over the loudspeaker, drowning out Gabe's response. He grabbed his cruise card and shoved it into his pocket. Brad's snoring already echoed through the room.

Gabe walked down the long hallway from his cabin on level ten to the stairs and jogged down to seven. Club Fusion was his favorite bar at the aft end of the ship, and he found comfort there. Music began to play, and the dance floor filled up. He'd seen the daily ship's Princess Patter newsletter advertising '50s & 60s Music Trivia.'

The moment he walked into the lounge, his body relaxed. He wouldn't worry about something he could do nothing about. However, seeing Mahone up close again brought all the ugliness back to his mind. He knew he was wrong to blame Mahone, but he did it anyway. He'd been a good soldier, yet the man's story made him sound like a monster.

Gabe rubbed his temple, found a chair, ordered a scotch, and glanced around the room. When he noticed a woman sitting alone with a glass of white wine in her hand, he smiled. Seeing her head bob along with the music, he decided to turn the evening into a holiday after all.

"Do you want to put some of that energy into play on the dance floor?" His words slipped out as smooth as silk.

The woman's head turned toward him, and he could sense her caution as she contemplated her answer. She shook her head for a moment before pushing her chair back and allowing him to lead her onto the dance floor. He liked how her hair curled around her ears and bounced as she walked. She smelled good, too.

"You're right. It's hard to sit still when music like this fills you up. My name is Christina." Her gray eyes met his as he guided her into a fox trot.

He liked having her in his arms. "I'm Gabe. I like music too, and I'm glad you don't mind dancing with strangers." He smiled at her, suddenly wishing he wasn't on a ship full of so many normal people to steal from a man who deserved to be robbed. The woman moved in his embrace, swaying to the rhythm of the music, and he could almost pretend his life was normal.

He had been avoiding the law since he was seventeen, when his dad died. His mother had left years earlier, so he and his dad had been a team. When Dad was gone, he joined the army. Getting thrown out of the military would have broken his heart. He'd always told him he should be accountable for his actions, and Gabe had listened. Always. But war changes a man, and his stinking job at the art gallery would have embarrassed the old man afterward.

This time, it was different. This time, there was a lot of money involved. Why did he pull Brad along with him? Why couldn't he just let it go? The music changed to a two-step, and Christina hadn't moved out of his arms.

"Nice," she whispered.

"Yes, it is," he responded, trying to keep his mind on the dancing and not on the mess before him. That shiny box would provide him with enough money for a lifetime, and he couldn't mess it up. And he'd pay back the man who took his life away from him, too.

"You are very quiet for such a big man," Christina whispered as her lips lay close to his ear. She patted his back and looked up into his face. Their dance steps were perfectly synchronized, as if they had been dancing for many years.

It surprised him how comfortable he felt with a stranger. "Sometimes I talk so much, I can't shut up." He smiled down into her face, wondering if the evening might be like a real holiday after all. The music and the crowd enhanced their enjoyment until the musicians began to slow down. They danced until the bar closed and the musicians left the stage.

"Will you walk me to my cabin? I'm on Deck Nine." Christina's voice was soft with a touch of a southern accent.

Gabe guided her toward the elevator, but she shook her head and led him to the carpeted stairs. The ship was quiet except for the sounds of the ocean as he brought her to the outer deck. They watched the moon slip across the water like a Spencer Joiner oil painting.

He wrapped an arm around her, and she leaned into him for warmth. "I love the sound of the waves slapping the ship."

"Me too. I love sailing. And meeting you has been special, Gabe."

He grinned into the night and tightened his grip on her shoulder. His mind rebelled against the reason for being on the ship and tried to enjoy the moment, but his stomach was jittery.

After a while, they made their way toward her cabin. She paused in the hallway before turning to him. "Thank you, Gabe. I enjoyed the evening, the wine, and the ocean in the moonlight. I..."

He leaned down to kiss her soft lips. "I enjoyed it too, Christina."

She made a purring sound. "I listen to music each evening." Her eyes were hopeful, still holding his fingers.

"Tomorrow, we dock in Mazatlán, Christina. My buddy and I are going into the city, but we should be back before dinner. I'd like to see you again, so I'll look for you." His hair slid across his brow, and he grinned.

"I'd like that," she whispered.

"Christina, I... Maybe we...."

She grinned and raised on tiptoe to kiss him. "I'm going into the old city on a walking tour. I can hardly wait to see the cliff divers and receive the free margarita that the tour brochure promised. So, I'll see you tomorrow?"

Gabe nodded without making any promises. Who knew what tomorrow would bring? He pulled her into a hug, and she slipped her card into the slot, opened the door, and closed it behind her.

He stood in the hallway, relieved she hadn't pulled him inside, yet feeling disappointed. As twilight settled, he turned to retrace his steps and climbed one more level to his cabin, his mind filled with chattering thoughts. They had to grab Ashton Mahone in the morning. He sighed loudly, as if the burden of thinking weighed heavily on him.

Eight

Rina leaned back in her chair and sifted her fingers beneath the loose hair that covered her ears. She ran her fingers over the fine hair hidden underneath. Her head had been shaved from the nape of her neck to about three inches above her ear. The doctor had kindly left the top and crown of her hair to conceal the buzz cut after her surgery. She usually wore a red hat with her hair tied in a top knot or brushed it out to fall over the shaved area around her ears. When she was at the pool, she always wore her hat; it was there that Ash had first seen her. He almost hadn't recognized her the next day in the bar with her hair down. She grinned at the memory.

She had overeaten again. It felt as if the ship was a floating dining table, with food everywhere she looked. And it was all delicious. She toured the galley and took photos of the vegetables and fruits cut and shaped into animals and flowers. The whole ship was amazing. She stretched out to relieve the pressure from too much food and dropped her fingers to her ears.

Antique silver earrings with embedded pearls adorned each earlobe, a gift from her Uncle James. His antique shop was in San Rafael, California, where he taught her the art of recognizing and understanding antique jewelry. She had just begun to draw and create her designs. She loved spending time with him and learning from him. It was a place where she could be happy without Jenna, who had never been interested. For that, Rina was glad.

Her breath caught as she suddenly remembered with clarity that her Uncle James had died while Rina lay in her months-long coma after the accident and surgery. When she woke from her long slumber and learned of his death, she was horrified, and then Jeff and Jenna... Rina shook the thoughts away.

But the memories came flooding back. She'd been home for only three days when she noticed the text messages on her husband's phone. Flirty messages, intimate messages. A lot of messages. With her sister.

Ash brought her a plate filled with cheese and grapes and set it on the table beside her. She groaned and rubbed her stomach. "Really?" Her eyes stared at the food and then turned toward him. "I am SOOO... full."

"I know we have food coming out of our ears, but this looked good." He sat down and looked at her in surprise.

When she saw his eyebrows ripple upward, she knew he'd seen her scalp. Rina reached her fingers up self-consciously. "I had surgery, and the hair is just beginning to grow out." She lifted her hair and flicked it behind her ear. "I don't have tattoos or blue hair, but my hair is stylish, don't you think?" She swirled her layered hair around her head.

"What was your surgery for?"

"I was in the wrong place at the wrong time. A contractor was preparing for an implosion near my uncle's antique shop to build an apartment building beside the bookshop. He hadn't cleared the area properly. When I got to work one morning, the guy pushed the button and the building fell in on itself as he'd expected it to do. But he'd left tools on a piece of machinery that went flying in all directions. I was in the line of fire and would have died if the surgeon hadn't been able to release the pressure in my brain and operate within the hour." Her eyes glistened as she recounted the story. A sad frown was overtaking her pretty face.

"You don't stumble over words or go blank. You speak very well for someone who's had brain surgery." He stretched his fingers over the pieces of cheese and popped a juicy grape into his mouth.

The doctors are amazed, too. I feel fine. I stumble sometimes when I least expect it. It makes me angry, so I have to concentrate hard when I walk." She flicked her hair again. "I'll be glad when this grows out, but it's nothing compared to the painful headaches I had when I woke up. I was in a coma for months. When I came out of it, my world had fallen into shambles, but I won a lawsuit and my bank account is now smiling.

"Life can throw some bad curves, Rina. You seem to have dealt with it pretty well, though, haven't you?" He sucked on another grape and pushed the plate toward her.

Rina shrugged and avoided his gaze, unwilling to share her personal life with him. She picked up a piece of cheese on a cracker and pushed it into her mouth. "I can't believe I'm eating this when I just told you I'm stuffed."

"Your family?" He was intrigued.

Rina concluded his questions weren't interrogative, but rather interested. She shrugged again. "My parents are both dead. I have one sister. I had one child, a daughter, who died from a lung disease called Cystic Fibrosis twenty years ago when she was three. It nearly broke me in two. I was twenty-three. I never had another child. My husband is an ex-husband. My sister is an ex-sister."

His eyes went wide.

"And I don't intend to expound on the reasons why, Ash." She stuffed more cheese into her mouth without another word.

He was intrigued by her candor and didn't question her further. "Thank you for being so kind to my mother, Rina. I'm worried sick about her because getting this box to Jacob means so much to her. My life went upside down too...when she told me Jacob was my real father. I still cannot fathom how Dan Mahone was able to treat me like his son, but love does that, you know? And we loved each other."

"Jacob knows about you, then." She stated.

"Yes, Ma told me when she left Poland, he eventually went to France. By the time he finally found her ten years later in San Francisco, she was already married to my dad, Dan Mahone. So, Jacob later married a woman and moved to Paris. He became a successful gem dealer."

"And they stayed in contact all this time?" Her face was brimming with emotion. Ash wanted to reach out and run his finger down her cheek.

After he left for Paris and married someone else, he sent Mom a diamond or emerald every year.

Rina's eyebrows rose.

He wanted to fill the cloisonné box with gems. He said that if she needed to sell them, she should go ahead and do that, so I guess it was like an insurance policy. There are thirty-two gems in that box, one for each year of my life, once he could afford them.

Rina was fascinated by his story. "What's Jacob like? Is his wife still alive? Kids? You might have sisters or brothers in Paris." Her face turned pink with interest.

"Sisters. I don't know anything about Jacob except that he loved Ma and she loved him. His wife died ten years ago. He has twin girls. I have two half-sisters, twins who are twenty-eight, named Dora and Laura. They don't look alike, and Ma said one looks a little like me."

"So that means when you find Jacob, you will meet your sisters, of course. I wonder how they feel about all of this." She chewed another grape and swallowed it before he could answer.

"I asked Ma. She wasn't sure if they knew about me." He rubbed the back of his neck and looked up. The Atrium soared three decks high with an expansive open area. The magnificent ceiling was a stained-glass masterpiece, showcasing shades of yellow, green, brown, and red. Glittering lights hung throughout the outer area, illuminating the ceiling and reflecting onto his face. The elevators had a delicate backdrop leading to the Atrium. Ash's gaze followed one as it ascended rapidly.

Rina's eyes followed his, and they smiled at the beautiful area around them. "If they don't know now, they will when you show up, especially since one of his daughters resembles you. Does Jacob know you're coming? Since your mother is so ill, I wonder if he knows that too. I'd love to see their faces when they learn they have a brother." Rina's eyes turned glassy, imagining such a meeting.

Ash processed her statement, choosing his words carefully. "You could come with me." His eyes revealed surprise at his own words, yet he looked at her with an expectant expression. He realized he felt nervous at the thought of meeting the old guy.

She tensed and her head swiveled toward him. "Not likely. I have a book to read and a life to straighten out." Rina raised an eyebrow and smiled shakily.

They shared a confused look before she chuckled slightly.

Ash swallowed, wondering what had gotten into him.

She got up, nodded at him, and left him to ponder their conversation. She strolled past the art gallery and jewelry shops, continuing toward the outer deck. When she pushed against the heavy wooden handles, she blinked against the wind as the ocean's breeze rushed toward her. She grinned. This is what she'd come for, not a wild storm of intrigue.

The sky was vast and blue as far as she could see, while the ocean surrounded the ship like a cozy blanket, ruffled and softly roaring. The beautiful wooden planks beneath her feet were polished to a high sheen, and the reflection of the water danced on the metal ceiling above her. She gripped the railing and felt the wind toss her hair around her face, reveling in her sense of freedom.

Two men jogged past her, grinning and flirting boldly. When one began to approach her, his partner pulled him along. He mumbled, "She doesn't look like she wants company, man."

Rina nodded toward them, but she didn't smile. Looking down at the broad, shimmering waters of the Pacific Ocean, saturated with rich blues, she wrapped her arms around herself and lifted her face to the sun. For a few glorious moments, the pounding waves and giant swells transformed into a silvery path. Rina whimsically fed her daydreams to wonder where they could lead. The air was crisp as she stood there, staring into the beauty of the ocean.

And then she remembered the cloisonné box.

Nine

That night, after he and Rina made plans to leave the ship with the cloisonné box stored in her zippered purse, Ash logged back onto the internet. He found a ticket to Paris from the General Rafael Buelna International Airport, also known as Mazatlán International Airport, priced at $1,600. However, he wouldn't buy it just yet; he wanted to wait until Cabo. It would take him twenty-two hours to reach the City of Lights, where he'd find a father and two sisters he'd never seen before.

He fought against sleep and kept checking the clock. Just in case he wasn't headed to Cabo for the last port of call, he'd already packed his meager suitcase and resolved to go. Now, his mind wouldn't shut off, and he doubted he'd sleep at all.

Between the worry of the men chasing him and the long flight ahead, lingering images of Rina slipped through the haze. He pumped his fist into the pillow for the hundredth time, trying not to think about those blue eyes and short dark hair that fought for space on her head. He certainly never expected to find romance on the ship. He punched his hand into the pillow again. He had to sleep. He had to be ready. He knew the men wouldn't walk away from this treasure. Trying to shake off the tangle of half-formed thoughts, Ash finally fell into a restless sleep just before dawn.

Rina stared at the ceiling in the dark. She listened to the ship's engines purring below her and heard ocean waves slapping against the behemoth ship. She had taken control of her destiny when she boarded the ship. She'd bought the cruise passage; she'd cast aside people she'd once loved and had watched dolphins play in the ocean from her balcony high above the waterline. Now, what was she supposed to do with herself? She had no idea.

She thought again about the beautifully inlaid metal box and wondered if fate would play a part in the next chapter of her life. She hadn't expected a deep-voiced stranger to have any part of her decisions. If she didn't want adventure, she should have stayed home. Sometimes, maybe I should just let the rain fall.

Sunrise. The foghorn woke them early the next morning. A slight breeze ruffled her drapes as she slipped open her glass door to steal a glance from her balcony. She loved the soft sound of waves splashing quietly against the ship far below her.

On another level of the ship, Ash quickly got up and dressed. He didn't spend time enjoying the view from his small porthole window.

Rina took longer than expected, checked her watch, filled her small tourist bag, and took a shower. She dressed in a black and white polka-dot romper and slipped on her sandals. Mazatlán! Once Ash was away with the box in his possession, she had a walking tour planned for the historic area. She'd done her homework; she'd be shuttled to the historic district where small golf cart vehicles called Pulmonias were located, and she knew exactly where to find a fruity, chilled margarita. Although she knew she should hurry through her makeup routine, vanity took over.

The plan was for Rina to disembark first. She tossed her bag over her shoulder, walked down the long hallway, and jogged down eight levels. She had her passport and money tucked snugly into her money belt beneath her dress, hoping she wouldn't need to show them to anyone in transit. She laughed at the thought; lifting her dress to access either would be a memorable experience. She chuckled.

The Italian captain's voice echoed over the sound system, instructing the passengers to disembark on Deck Four. She arrived earlier than many passengers planning their day in Mazatlán. As she reached the doors and passed through the debarkation area, she presented her Ruby Princess cruise card to the man dressed in white. He took his job very seriously, carefully glancing at her card before nodding toward the doorway that led to land. She took a breath and searched for a spot to wait for Ash.

That's when she noticed the two men lurking on the other side of the gangway area. She raised a hand to her throat and counted the minutes in her head. The tour bus was parked with open seats for people to jump on. Tick. Tock. The men hadn't seen her. Maybe they don't know I have the box. Perhaps I can walk away and find Ash later? At the airport, maybe? He'd think I stole it, wouldn't he? Tick. Tock… She spotted him at the top of the gangway, showing his card, a leather satchel in his hands, and a leather bag slung over his right shoulder. He looked straight ahead as planned but was fidgeting.

Rina glanced toward the men hiding in the corner and knew she had to do something. But what? At that moment, a large extended family with children in strollers stood between Ash and the men. She made a lunge toward the crowd and bumped into the teenager. The ruckus was just enough to turn the men's attention to the noise instead of Ash's debarkation.

She caught his eye and nodded her head urgently toward the men.

Ash straightened up and looked toward the shuttle now teeming with passengers. It was a riot of motion, laughter, and chaos. The two back seats were empty. When he saw the men's attention on the noisy family, he jogged toward it, waving his free arm as he ran.

Rina lurched toward the shuttle seat as Ash pitched himself onto it, bruising her hip with the sudden jolt. His leather bag landed in her lap. The two men noticed Ash just as the shuttle driver pressed the gas pedal. They ran toward it, but it was already too far ahead of them. The sun was hot on their backs as they sped past large storage containers. The noisy chatter was deafening, accompanied by the seagulls screeching above them.

Ash and Rina turned around to watch the men's antics behind them. When they jumped onto the next shuttle, they knew it wouldn't leave the dock until it was full, so they had a few minutes. Pressed close together with children's legs dangling on either side of them, they held on, both eager to jump off again.

When the driver stopped in front of the transfer station, they joined the bustling crowd to lose themselves. Small shops lined the brightly lit building as they stepped inside, each with vendors urging them to stop and buy. They followed the blue, yellow, and white azulejos tiles to discover a narrow path where vans waited, eager to take the ship's passengers into Old Town.

Ash briefly glanced behind him to observe the throng of people emerging and slid into the van. It was crowded, and they didn't have a tour ticket. The driver hopped in, looked around at everyone, and sped off without checking anyone's proof of purchase.

"Here." Rina slipped the small package into Ash's pants pocket. When she felt his warm skin through the fabric, her hand jerked as if electricity had pulsed through her body, and she nearly dropped it as her eyes went wide.

Ash touched her freckled arm. "Thank you, Rina. You're in my debt and my mother's. I'll get out first and run for a taxi. There's a plane for Paris leaving in three hours, so I'd better take it before they realize I've left." Without a second thought, when the van came to a stop, Ash kissed her lips soundly. Then he wanted to kiss her again.

She leaned into his body for only a moment, liking the warmth and sweetness the kiss held. And then she heard the second shuttle coming down the street. "Go!"

She saw him jogging around the corner of an old brick building across the street. The small satchel rested under his arm, while his leather bag slapped against his backside. She stared after him, her mind racing with mixed feelings. When she saw the other men jump off their shuttle in pursuit, Rina's heart sank for just a moment. But she was confident Ash would get away.

It was her turn now. She caught her breath and walked into the plaza beneath tall palms and colorful pots dripping with red bougainvillea. The air was balmy, and as she walked over the cobblestones, she felt as if she'd jumped back into another world. Music. A dark-haired man plucked guitar strings under a canopy on a low stone wall. The sounds were the epitome of Mexico. Tour directors were giving spiels all around her, their voices blending together like a choir, and she inched toward one, hoping to learn a bit more about Old Town.

But her mind would not still.

With a disgusted huff, she turned toward the street where Ash had gone. She needed to ensure he was out of the way. She could still feel the warm kiss on her lips as his blue eyes pierced through her afterward. She walked away and entered the streets alongside the plaza, stumbling slightly. She caught herself against the brick building and inhaled deeply. "Damn, I wish this staggering would stop."

Before she could take another step away, a hard push in her back slammed her into the bricks. An urgent voice in her ear said, "I knew you were part of this guy's story," a man whispered harshly. "He likes you, so we'll make him an offer he can't refuse." He laughed at his joke.

Rina's heartbeat quickened as she stomped her foot down. However, he had anticipated her move and yanked her around to face him. She recognized him as the one who needed a shave. She pulled away to break free, but he tightened his grip on her body. When she began to scream, his large hand covered her mouth and pressed into her jaw. His fingers reeked of garlic, making her gag.

"Shut up, lady, or I'll give you something to scream about." The man shoved her along the street and squeezed her right arm. "One more move like that, and you're done."

Her eyes darted around frantically, hoping for a Good Samaritan to appear from around the corner. But she was alone. She thought of the small pepper spray device in her purse, but she couldn't reach it.

The man dragged her down an alley where Rina heard shouting. When they rounded the corner, her heart skipped a beat. The other man stood over Ash, with a large fist pressed against his throat. The satchel was neither in Ash's hand nor beside him on the cobblestones.

Gabe laughed and nudged her forward. "So, it looks like your girlfriend came to help you."

Ash's head jerked toward her. She looked more angry than afraid. "She has nothing to do with this. Let her go!" His voice was low, almost feral. When he attempted to get up, Gabe kicked him in the ribs and knocked him down again.

"You think this is a game? You ruined my life, and now I will ruin yours. Whatever it takes. Where is it?"

Ash glanced between the man and Rina, who remained securely in Brad's strong arms. He searched the area for a weapon to defend himself against the men. "What the hell are you talking about? How did I ruin your life? I don't even know you. Let her go!"

Rina kicked Brad again, only to be met with a punch in the stomach. She fell to the ground. With one eye squinted open, she saw such grief in Ash's eyes that time seemed to stand still for her.

"Hand it over, buddy. One of you has it. And I want it." Gabe almost shouted the words through clenched teeth, no longer able to contain his frustration. He motioned to Brad and jerked his head toward Rina. "You don't remember me, Mahone? You don't remember writing that story about me and stray bullets? You know, where the war changes men and makes them crazy? Do you think you're better than the soldiers who fight for your damn freedom? Bring her over."

Ash's face blanched.

Rina stared at him intensely. "Don't you dare give it to them, Ash!" Before he could respond, she felt a thud in her back, and her world went black.

That was when Ash made his move. When Gabe's foot kicked toward Rina again, Ash grabbed his leg and sank his teeth into his calf. He vaguely wondered why this street was so empty. Were the inhabitants used to seeing people scuffle like this? Were they afraid to come out of their houses? Or was it just freak timing? And what in hell was this guy talking about? He bit down hard.

Gabe let out a harsh scream and fought his way out of Ash's grip. Ash held on and didn't let go, clenching his jaw to keep his teeth in place like a rabid dog. His ribs ached, but his fear for Rina numbed his body.

Brad's arms clamped around his torso, and he momentarily released his hold. But Ash head-butted him and bit down again.

Gabe screamed.

By the time Brad shook his head clear, Ash jumped to his feet to pummel him again. Gabe picked up a piece of wood from the gutter and limped toward Ash with a wicked look on his face. When he swung it, Ash jerked his head to the right and bashed into Brad once more.

Rina awoke to the sounds of men fighting—two against one. Her eyes were drawn to Ash's satchel stuffed behind a large dumpster at the same moment she noticed the large rock. She grabbed it and threw it at Brad with all her strength. Crazy luck sent it right into the center of his forehead, and he went down. Now it was a fair fight. She worked herself into a standing position next to the brick wall and launched her body onto Gabe's back.

Ash jabbed his fist into Gabe's face and then pushed his thumbs into the man's eyes. Gabe jerked his head wildly back and forth to dislodge Ash's hands.

When Ash stumbled, unsure if he could hold the big man, he turned to Rina and yelled, "Run!"

"No way in hell." She struck Gabe across the back with a discarded piece of wood. Now, Gabe was down. His loud groan told her they didn't have much time. She scrubbed her hands together, wondering which way to turn next. "I'm not wired for this stuff, Ash."

An unspoken thought passed between them as they moved as one. Ash grabbed both bags and pulled Rina into the sunshine. "Who says I'm wired for it?" He felt pain in every part of his body and wondered if finding Jacob would be worth it. Sisters? Jewels? He groaned as he lifted one foot in front of the other.

They sprinted like banshees from hell were chasing them back toward the central plaza. When he spotted the Pulmonia, Ash waved to the Mexican driver, and they both jumped into the open-sided vehicle. People stared, some pointed, but nobody intervened.

The driver understood that we craved speed. It was likely a routine situation for him, and he simply went with the flow. She had missed the tour of Mazatlán, but her adventure hadn't stalled.

Ten

Rina sat inside Medas, a café in the Mazatlán International Airport, clutching a ticket to Paris in one fist and a cold Corona in the other. Her almond-shaped eyes gazed at Ash beneath curling eyelashes. Still a bit shaky, her chest pounded erratically from their adrenaline-fueled adventure.

"You're sure you want to come to Paris with me? I have no idea what's waiting for me. I want to get this box of gems to Jacob, but from there, I have no idea what will happen." He scratched his jaw and lifted his beer.

"I guess I do," she said with a burp and lifted the bottle to her lips again. "I said there was too much noise and turmoil in the world, but I had no idea what this side of life could be like…" She lifted the bottle again.

"Why did you come after me instead of going on your tour, Rina?"

"The sense of adventure? Seeing the look on your sister's faces? Meeting your father? Watching your mother's face when she knows Jacob is looking at his son?"

He wrinkled his eyebrows and lifted his bottle again without taking his eyes off her face. This time, he lifted one eyebrow.

"Okay, dammit. It was the kiss."

Ash grinned and ordered two more chilled Coronas.

They took turns snoozing to prevent someone from taking the jeweled box. Both slept fitfully, but during the twenty-two-hour flight, their plane circled Paris before landing at Charles de Gaulle Airport the following morning. The cold December chill in Paris felt daunting compared to Mexico's warm temperatures.

Rina shivered as they passed through customs. "First, we go shopping for warm clothes since mine are still on the ship," she said. She wrapped her thin shawl around her trembling body and shivered. "And contact the cruise line so they don't think I'm floating in the ocean since I didn't embark after I visited Mazatlán. Thank God I had my passport and bank cards."

Ash shook his head in agreement. "I need an international SIM card for my phone. Mom must be worried sick. I notice you don't have a mobile phone or a tablet. What's up with that?"

Rina looked down at her hands. "The cruise was a non-techy trip for me. I wanted to read books without distractions. I was fine without a phone, but now I need one. In this city, especially, we'll need to stay connected, right?" She walked away while muttering the last words, and he had to pick up the pace to keep up.

Later that night, they were settled in two hotel rooms at Le Estudia Hotel on St. Germain. Her newly purchased clothes were packed in drawers, and they had a dinner reservation at Le Petite Zinc.

The sights and sounds of Paris lulled them into a different state of mind as they devised a plan to find Jacob Safra. Ash looked at the map of Paris and traced his finger along the streets until he located 10, Rue du Faubourg St Honoré. He had changed shirts several times. One moment, sweat trickled down his back; the next, chills took over. He picked up the envelope his mother had sealed, wishing he could tear it open to read her words to Jacob. But he wouldn't, of course. He took off his shirt again. At this rate, I'll need more shirts…

The next piece of paper he held listed a phone number. His biological father's phone number. He was fifty years old, and his hand shook like a teenager's. His father was seventy-one. Not that old, he thought. Ash chuckled. The older I get, the older 'old' is…

His phone rang, and the screen lit up with her image. He had taken a photo of Rina on the ship and added it to his contacts. The photo was perfect; her hair floated around her head as she laughed at the antics of a child playing on the curved stairwell in the Atrium. Her face shone like a Christmas tree. In fact, she had been sitting beside the decorated Christmas tree in the photo. He stared at it and then laughed as he answered the phone. He had forgotten she was calling.

"Hey, you. I'm hungry. Can we go now?"

"I'm on my way, darlin."

He hung up and reveled in the laughter she left behind.

La Petit Zinc was located on a corner at 11 Rue Saint Benoît. Its ornate wooden turnstile doors beckoned them inside. He remembered the restaurant from his journalistic days when he interviewed several wealthy businessmen intent on funding the war effort against Syria. When the hostess led them to the upper level, his legs shook. Glad to sit down, he wondered why he felt so weak but dismissed the feeling and looked around him.

Cloth napkins, silver cutlery, and pale-yellow linen tablecloths spoke volumes. His finger traced the words, La Petit Zinc, on his decorative plate. Ash smiled as he listened to soft French voices, which soothed his mind's chatter while he shared this place with Rina. The barely discernible sweet French music floated above the chatter, drawing him into a heady mood.

His father was just a few miles away from where they sat, and he couldn't fathom the thought of meeting him for the first time. His mother's voice kept echoing in his mind. "Just call him, Ash. He will know you when you meet him." Her voice had wavered, shaken with emotion.

He had told himself to get a grip. Jacob was just an old man, after all, and he would find him soon enough. He shook his head to clear his thoughts. They seemed murkier as the minutes passed, so he shook his head again. The cloisonné box was zipped inside Rina's purse. The men they had left behind in Mexico were surely no longer following him.

As he studied the menu, the words began to blur, and he looked up to see Rina regarding him quizzically, her face filled with worry.

"What's going on, Ash?" Rina's voice increased in pitch.

His head hurt, and the chills returned. When Rina's face started to waver before his eyes, he sensed something was wrong. He saw her lips moving and then the surprise on her face. He attempted to nod, but instead, the menu fell onto the table, and he collapsed to the floor.

Rina reached Ash just as the waiter knelt beside him. She opened his shirt at the neck and yanked it loose while the other patrons looked on, forks still raised. Two more men dashed toward Ash, but they couldn't revive him.

Tears began to well up in her chest as the men lifted Ash off the floor. When they carried him toward a small back room, she followed them like a robot. They placed him on the couch and handed her a white towel while another man picked up the phone to call for help.

"Ash. Please wake up," she said as she smacked his cheek and wiped the drizzles of sweat from his forehead and neck. Gripping his hand, she squeezed his fingers, trying to elicit a reaction, but there was none. She placed her ear on his chest. The thumping sound and movement reassured her that he was still breathing. She heard sirens. When she tried to smile her thanks at the men still anxiously standing nearby, she couldn't.

Two hours later, Ash thrashed back and forth in a bed at Pitié-Salpêtrière Hospital. He had a fever, and that was all Rina understood since she didn't speak French. What had she been thinking? Her mind raced as she grabbed Ash's hand again, smoothing it against the bed for the hundredth time. When his eyes seemed to look through her, her chest felt like it had a scampering squirrel inside.

She had been introduced to a young woman, in English, thank God, whose accent was hard to follow, but she grasped the gist of the conversation. "Your husband is suffering from a viral infection, and the doctors have ordered tests to concentrate on specific medications to treat it, but they need to pinpoint it." The woman's red hair fell over her eyes, which she pushed back with an impatient twist of her wrist.

"Oh, he's not my…."

"Where was Mr. Mahone before he came to Paris, madam?"

"We were on a cruise ship. We flew from Mazatlán, Mexico, to Paris." Rina wrung her hands together before grabbing Ash's fingers to soothe her agitation again, her mind clouded with worry.

"Mexico? Ah, madam, that will tell us something." She jotted a note on her pad and left the room.

Rina's fingers pressed Ash's clammy hand to her cheek. A dull ache throbbed in her head as she wondered what would happen next. They had traveled so far to bring this cloisonné box to Paris, a trip that meant more to both of them than the gems inside. In the little time she'd known Ash, she had sensed his anxiety swell after discovering that the father who raised him wasn't his biological father at all, and that his real father was a stranger he hesitated to meet. She, on the other hand, was running from the emotional trauma of relationships and found herself questioning why she felt such a strong connection to a man she barely knew.

Ash groaned and turned his head toward her again. His eyes opened, and they glistened; a small tear slid down the side of his face. Her heart jumped, and her finger prevented the moisture from going any farther. How could she care for this man so much when she'd only known him for a few days? He had a barrel of his own problems, and she didn't want to add them to her own, but she couldn't ignore the attraction. Why else would she fly to Paris like a wanton gypsy? She felt the chuckle freeze in her throat as uneasiness slithered down her spine.

Two nurses entered the room, followed by the doctor who had initially spoken with her, as they placed Ash onto the bed. The man had a bald head with only wisps of white hair flanking each ear. He pulled a chair closer to her and sat down. The nurses adjusted IV bags and positioned a thumb-sized device on his big toe to measure his oxygen level.

The red-headed young woman joined them and translated the conversation. "Your husband is very ill. I think he contracted Dengue Fever in Mexico after a mosquito bit him."

Rina's eyebrows shot upward. "Mosquitos in December?"

The doctor looked up, expecting the woman's translation, and then nodded in agreement. "Did he get off your cruise ship before Mazatlán?"

"Yes, Puerto Vallarta was the first port of call four days ago. I wasn't with him when he explored that city; I stayed on the ship. Maybe he was bitten there? I don't remember mosquitoes in Mazatlán when we were there, but maybe…" She ran her fingers across her arms, looking for raised bites on her skin.

Dengue Fever has symptoms similar to Malaria. Your husband shows signs of this infection. It is transmitted by the bite of an Aedes mosquito infected with the dengue virus. The mosquito becomes infected when it bites a person with dengue virus in their blood.

When he saw the look on Rina's face, he touched her arm and continued as the woman translated for Rina. "The virus cannot be transmitted to others. I want to test your blood to confirm you are free from infection, though."

She rubbed her arms again. "Yes, please do that. One of us needs to be well, and he looks like he's in misery."

"I'm sure you would have had some symptoms already, though. In the next few days, Mr. Mahone will experience a high fever, which he has now, pain behind his eyes, vomiting, muscle pain, nausea, and a skin rash. Now that we know what we are fighting, we can help him."

Rina didn't correct the doctor or the nurses. It felt trivial given the circumstances, and she worried that they would cease to share the diagnosis or treatment with her if they realized she wasn't Ash's wife.

The redhead extended a hand. "I'm Brigitte." She handed a card to Rina. "Please call me if you have questions or need a translator, and

I will help you." Rina smiled and nodded her thanks. Their hushed conversation and the scent of disinfectant trailed them out the door.

When the room was empty, she reached over and smoothed Ash's forehead with the palm of her hand. It felt damp to the touch, and she couldn't draw her fingers away from his face. Her eyes filled with tears, and she swallowed hard to get past the lump in her throat. They were so close to finding his father. It just wasn't fair!

The sounds of hospital staff murmurs and beeping machines filled her head all night as she sat beside him. And she hated it. She had left the hospital only a few weeks earlier, and she hadn't wanted to walk into another one anytime soon. The tangle of clear tubes, the rumble of carts, nurses' uniforms, and machines beeping day and night had been a nightmare. Now, here she was again. Despite sitting in the visitor's chair this time, and the patient being a man looking for answers, she was unnerved by the noises and smells. Yet, she admitted she was drawn to him like a moth to a flame.

What should she do now? The doctor told her he could treat him, but he'd given Rina the impression they were in a wait-and-see mode as each symptom came and went. Should she call Magda in San Francisco? Would Ash want his dying mother to worry? Should she contact his father here in Paris? She was in a quandary and didn't want to make a mistake trying to think this problem through alone.

Within minutes, the nurse returned with a needle to draw her blood. She hated needles, but watching Ash thrash around told her this was no time to be squeamish. The nurse placed two vials of her blood on a tray and left as quietly as she had entered the room.

She wondered how long she'd have to wait before finding out whether a blasted mosquito had taken a bite out of her. It would be a crazy way for her to experience a peaceful change in her life, shifting from reading on a cruise ship to lying in a hospital bed, sweating and delirious. Her mind was racing, so she stopped worrying about what could happen and focused on what was going on right now.

Ash turned his face toward her as she reached over to wipe the sweat from his forehead. He looked vulnerable and soft, and unbidden tears slipped down her cheeks. She gasped a single, wrenching breath and held his hand to her lips for a few moments longer.

Shaking her head to dispel the tears, she left the hospital room, knowing she wouldn't leave his side until she had to. Paris sunshine greeted her through the tall windows as she sat on a bench near the front door. She observed people coming and going, yet her discomfort of being in a hospital lingered. She had spent a long time in a bed, vowing to keep away from them until Ash came into her life. She smiled.

Eleven

Rina took a cab back to the hotel early the next morning. It was a beautiful day, and the scenery was beyond anything she had ever imagined. When she joined the bustling crowd along the street toward St. Germaine, she decided to walk. A stroll through the gritty streets and peering into crowded bars felt preferable to returning to her empty room. Her head was a jumble of nerves, but she was in Paris, and she was determined to make the best of it.

Paris introduced herself. Tourists walked among the locals like schoolchildren; each nationality dressed in distinct attire. Rina peeked into the bustling tourist shops and thought about all the poets and writers who no longer frequented the historic boulevard. She felt the youthful atmosphere that accompanied the Sorbonne's university district, although she noticed the area was not limited to students, bars, and tourists.

"*Bonjour*," she said to a smiling woman.

"*Bonjour, madam*," the woman whispered and walked past.

As a hub for bookstores, design shops, museums, churches, upscale art galleries, boutique hotels, historic cafés, and restaurants, it was nearly impossible to feel disappointed. To paraphrase Samuel Johnson with a twist, if you are bored in St. Germaine, you are bored with life.

It was pure Paris—the place for romance and love. She wondered where the bridge crossed over the Seine, adorned with all the love padlocks. Paris had always intrigued her, but she never imagined she would be walking these historic streets, especially alone. She pulled out the map again, knowing exactly where she was headed. She wouldn't take the Metro. No, she'd walk. A good walk seemed just the remedy for all that ailed her. She knew that a walk could give her fresh perspective, and today she needed that. The lilt of violin music wafted from a nearby café, and she smiled feebly. Impossibly, parked cars shared their tiny spaces with birds, dogs, and motorbikes.

Safra Gems was nestled between a wine shop and a small French bakery. The aroma of croissants and freshly baked bread wafted through the air. Glass cases overflowed with iced petite sweets, elegantly arranged to make a customer swoon with desire. And she did just that. She walked away with a small bag of croissants. Then, she turned to look at the sign above Jacob's shop.

Within seconds, Rina stood before the window. She stared through its depths, using her hands to shade her eyes as she peered inside. Within the sparkling glass display, she saw small raised platforms covered in royal blue velvet. On each tiny dais stood a stemmed wine glass with shimmering gems inside.

Well, I'm here. Now what? She turned back to the bakery and sat at a small table slightly away from the others. It was cold but clear, and sitting outside was exactly what she wanted to do. After ordering a steaming hot latte and a pain au chocolat, she angled her chair to watch the door of the gem shop. She'd found the shop for Ash. Now, she would let the latte soothe her. Happy to be away from that hospital and the smells that lingered to remind her of her pain and tears, she sipped the hot brew.

The latte was frothy and hot. She felt her tongue curl around the croissant, letting it linger as a thousand points of pleasure invited a party inside her mouth. She had just lifted her cup to her lips again when the shop door opened and a white-haired gentleman stepped onto the sidewalk. He glanced around as if he were looking for someone.

When he locked the door, she knew it must be Jacob Safra. Rina sat transfixed for a moment. She thought her heart would stop when he turned to look at her. When he sat at a table nearby, she nearly spit out her coffee. Darn it, what now?

The man had a thick head of white hair and the bluest eyes she had ever seen. His height and physique resembled Ash's so closely that she couldn't help but stare. When she noticed him studying her as well, she smiled and nodded. Magda was right; Ash would recognize this man instantly. They shared the same smile, right down to the small dimple on his left cheek.

He smiled back. When the server placed a cup of something on the table in front of him, he reached for it, but his smile didn't fade. He appeared to be trying to make a decision, and she was intrigued.

Rina dropped her face, but her eyes found him once more. She pressed her hand to her chest to calm the pounding. When she lifted the cup to her lips again, she watched him rise from his table.

And then he wound his way toward her. Her breath caught in her throat when he set his espresso cup down on her table. "I saw you looking in my window a moment ago, madam. I liked your face, so I decided it was time for coffee when I saw you sit down here." His quick smile reached his eyes.

She liked him instantly and saw Ash staring at her through the old gentleman's eyes. "Women like sparkly gems, monsieur. And I am no different. The display is beautiful. Are you the owner, Mr. Safra?"

Jacob Safra blinked in surprise. "Yes. You know my shop?"

She gulped the remaining latte and took a gamble. "I came looking for your shop. It's a complicated story." She took a deep breath. "And I think we need more coffee." She lifted a finger and ordered another latte while watching the man's quizzical face wait for her to begin again. When it was steaming in front of her, she held the hot cup between her palms as if to gain sustenance and courage.

"My name is Rina Silvan." She took a tentative sip.

He moved his head as if to urge her on. She could see he was charmed, and she wasn't sure how to start. When he lifted his hand to her, he said, "*Enchanté de vous rencontrer, mademoiselle.*" I am enchanted to meet you.

She glanced at the man. It wasn't merely an errand at that point; it was more of a mission. The higher the stakes, the greater the reward. "I am a friend of Ashton Mahone's."

Jacob's furrowed face froze. "What?"

Now she definitely had the man's attention, and she suddenly knew where to start. At the beginning.

He listened attentively; both were glad that he spoke English. When she finished her story, she concluded with their arrival in Paris. He quickly looked around.

"Where is Ash? Why did he send you to find me? Is Magda....??" His worried frown displayed emotions skittering across his face so quickly that Rina reached over to cover his wrinkled hand with her own.

"I am here because Ash can't be." She sighed.

His eyes filled. "Oh, God. Do you mean, he's...?"

She realized her mistake instantly. "No...no, no. He is in the hospital because he contracted a virus from a mosquito that was infected with a disease in Mexico. He might not be happy I have come to you without him, but I am unsure if the doctors can heal him, so I thought you should know about...." Her words caught in her throat.

His face calmed for a moment. He finished his espresso and set down his cup. Then he stood, extending a hand to pull her from the chair. "Please take me to my son," he whispered. "I need to make a phone call first. Please follow me."

They entered the gem shop, and he pulled the closed sign over the glass door. Lifting a segmented wooden box, he skillfully removed the stemmed glasses she'd seen in the front display window. Once in their cradle, he looked into her face before inviting her to sit. She watched him take the box into the back room, where he opened the large safe and placed the box inside.

Rina looked around the shop to see advertisements from South Africa and South America. She noticed a calendar featuring the French countryside with large red marks on several of the dates. The spacious room faintly smelled of lavender and spices she couldn't identify. As she tugged at the sleeve of her leather jacket and glanced down, she noticed the floor was free of dust, as were the shelves. She could hear him in the back room talking to someone. She overheard him mention the name Dora. She knew that was the name of one of his daughters.

The air suddenly filled with anticipation as Jacob Safra returned to her side, and he jingled his car keys in her direction. Leading her out the back of his shop, he helped her into his small Fiat. Jacob barely gave Rina time to put on her seatbelt when it rumbled to life, and he stomped on the gas pedal. The sights of Paris passed by her in a blur as he drove through the streets toward the hospital.

Not long after, the last twenty minutes of events caught up with her, and she leaned against the door to his hospital room. Ash was asleep. Rina heard the older man's quick intake of breath as he saw his son for the first time in his life. The expression on his face made her heart race. She knew she'd made the right decision.

She paused at the door. "Would you like to sit alone, Mr. Safra?"

He turned his face toward her, and she saw tears flowing down his weathered cheeks. No words escaped his lips as he nodded.

A slight limp carried Rina away to the waiting room and the inviting couch four doors down the hallway. She pulled her legs underneath her after she toed off her shoes, relieved to be alone in the room. Had she made the right choice? Would Ash be angry with her? Should she have waited it out instead of fearing that the doctors didn't know how to heal him? The hospital's scent took away her questions and left her with an unsettled feeling.

Her phone buzzed in her purse. She stared at the text message. Jenna. It had been challenging to get a new phone with her old number, but the Apple employee had managed it. She'd lied and said she'd lost her phone. Now, she wondered if she should have just bought a new phone with a different number. Redefining herself should have included her new phone, too. There were twenty-two texts from her never-again sister.

Rina blinked back tears and clicked the button to clear them all. Her sister's texts vanished just like the love Rina once felt for her. When she had told Ash that she had an ex-sister, she meant it, but now her mind tugged at memories that drifted back through time.

Jenna was eighteen months younger than Rina. They had been like twins for a couple of years before the competition began with a vengeance. Her mother made Rina promise to always look after her little sister, and she tried, but Jenna wasn't easy to love or protect. It was Rina who needed protection, but her mother hadn't recognized that side of her youngest daughter. Jenna made sure of that.

It was the year Rina turned eight when Jenna hurt her beyond redemption. It was Christmas, and Santa brought her a doll with real hair, not the kind painted on a baby's head. Real hair. Rina still smiled when she remembered her excitement that Christmas morning as she held her baby doll close to her chest, loving her instantly. And of course, like everything Rina received, Jenna wanted it.

Jenna was the baby, after all, her mother told her. But this time, Rina stood her ground. She refused to give in to her little sister's tantrum. Jenna was furious. Rina was not sharing her new baby doll, and she told Jenna her baby was off-limits; she couldn't play with her. Her mother tutted but agreed that it was indeed Rina's, and Jenna had to play with her own doll, not her sister's. Jenna wanted Rina's doll, and that was that.

Rina had prepared a small shoebox lined with a baby blanket, where she tenderly laid the baby each night when the girls went to sleep. She had never owned anything so special, and it was a time in her life when she craved something of her own, just for herself.

One morning, a few days after Christmas, Rina was on the front landing trying to figure out how to use her new jump rope. A sound from the front door distracted her. When she looked up, Jenna was holding Rina's new doll in her arms; the doll's hair had been sheared off nearly to its roots, sticking up in tufts. Rina squealed with anger and ran up the steps to grab the baby doll from Jenna's arms. As she furiously tried to retrieve the doll, Jenna pushed her as hard as she could, shoving the doll into Rina's chest.

"No!" Jenna yelled furiously. "It's mine now. She's ugly, so you can't love her anymore." She hugged the choppy-headed doll to her chest and thrust out her bottom lip, pulling away from Rina.

Rina had lost her footing and fallen down six deep cement steps. The sharp pain in her leg made her cry, but when she saw the white bone protruding from her tibia, her cries turned to screams. She stared up at Jenna, who stood stroking the hairless doll with a satisfied smile on her face. That was all she remembered besides the neighbor's shriek before she fainted.

That marked the beginning of the end of their relationship. Jenna wanted everything Rina had: all of their mother's love, not just her half, Rina's toys, and Rina's boyfriends. Jeff's face flickered across Rina's mind, prompting her to shut her memories away.

Now, here in the hospital, her eyes drifted toward the door, and she let out a deep, troubled sigh. All she'd wanted was a new life free from the encumbrances of a relationship to muddy the waters. She'd decided that living alone was best. Relationships were complex, and she was tired. Then there was Ash pulling up a chaise lounge in the middle of an ocean cruise, disrupting her reading and the careful planning of the new life she'd expected to start in San Rafael. Her heart had skidded in every direction. Damn.

Losing her uncle was so sad that she never wanted to visit the antique shop again. But he left the shop to her, which Jenna had wanted even though she had only been there a few times. He knew it was Rina who loved it. Her shrewd uncle recognized his niece's mischievous antics from afar. He was determined that Jenna would have nothing to do with it and made sure the trust would only include Rina. He had a special clause inserted that would disinherit his youngest niece if she caused any trouble at all.

Now, a successful antique store sat empty, while a furious woman in California couldn't get her hands on it. The store's new owner was in Paris, twiddling her thumbs as a stranger held her captive to his problems. Rina glanced at her watch. Jacob had been with Ash for thirty minutes already. She sighed heavily and tried to imagine having a son for nearly fifty years without ever seeing him.

The reunion between the men must have been overwhelming, and she wasn't sure she wanted to get in the middle of it. She knew Ash had been carrying worries about meeting his father ever since his mother told him about him. How would they connect? After meeting Jacob and knowing Ash, she felt it would be like a thunderbolt. She also understood they would be vulnerable. She'd wait a few more minutes. Then it would be time to join the party.

Twelve

When Rina left him alone with his precious son, the hairs on his arms stood up, and he felt goosebumps prickling. He pressed a hand to his chest to slow the pounding and saw a clone of his own face lying prone, asleep. His old love for Magda rushed back so fast that he was unprepared for its onslaught, and Jacob fell into the chair beside the bed.

Knowing he had a son across the ocean and seeing the man with his own eyes were two different things. His fingers itched to smooth back the hair from Ash's forehead, to touch his hand, to count all his fingers and toes; all the things new parents do when their babies enter this world. He was fifty years too late.

He willed Ash to open his eyes, but he had been told this was the best thing for him, forcing him to rest as fluids seeped into his system. Magda had mentioned that the boy had his blue eyes; she had shared only a little, in bits and pieces. He had always wanted more.

But he had married Sadie. Their relationship had always been strained, and then they had the twins. Life had taken a turn, but he had never forgotten his son born so long ago. Magda had been the light of his life, and poor Sadie had never measured up, and she knew it. He rubbed the moisture from his eyes. He had tried to love the woman; he was sure he had, but Magda was the love that lingered within his heart and permeated every pore of his body. It was Magda's face he saw each night when he fell asleep, Magda's body he held when he made love to Sadie. He knew he had not been fair, but how does a body and mind turn off the love that two people share so deeply?

When he finally found her ten years after she slipped away from him, she was married to a man she assured Jacob truly loved his son. She told him to live his life because she had her own and refused to leave

Dan Mahone for an uncertain life with Jacob. She reminded him that Jews and Gentiles shouldn't marry, but she hadn't stopped him that last night before her parents spirited her away to America. No, she hadn't stopped him from loving her, even though they had no right to love. But then a child was created. Jacob looked at the man in front of him, and the tears could not be quenched.

He allowed the past to wander through his mind as he touched the younger man's hand. The connection to that warm touch wove its way into his very Jewish heart. He knew he could never let this child go.

When visions of his twin daughters emerged, he sat up. They were unaware that he had a son; they had a brother who resembled Dora so closely. He leaned forward in the chair, covering his eyes with his hands. Great sobs filled the room while Ash continued to sleep.

When Rina slipped into the room and saw Jacob bent over in the chair, she hurried to kneel before him. Pulling his hands from his face, she leaned in and kissed his wet cheek.

"Jacob? Did Ash wake?" Her hair slipped over her ears, revealing her buzz cut, but she didn't care. Her breathing was heavy, and she knew something intense had happened.

"No. But…" he broke down again, allowing her to hold onto his hand. "Merci, Rina. Thank you." He reached for her and pulled her close.

She pulled a chair up next to him. The nurse entered the room and lowered the side rail on the bed. "I am giving Mr. Mahone a shot. The doctor must check his pupils and vital signs. Please wait in the lounge. I will find you afterward?"

Her efficient manner ushered them out the door, and soon Rina found herself back where she had been only moments earlier. The sounds of the hospital trailed behind them as she pulled the door closed.

"Does Magda know Ash is here? Sick?"

Rina shook her head. She wasn't sure how much Jacob knew about Ash's mother's illness, and she had already pushed the envelope by bringing Jacob here, so she tried to dodge his question.

He stared at her.

"No, she doesn't know. She will be very worried, though, because Ash Skypes her every day. And they haven't spoken for two days."

"Skype? What is Skype?"

Rina drew in a deep breath. "Have you spoken to Magda, Mr. Safra?"

"Jacob, please. No, no. She and I have exchanged letters only."

Indecision clouded her face. "Do you want to speak with her, Jacob?" Her eyes bore into his.

Jacob glanced at her quickly. "*Oui.* Yes."

"We need Wi-Fi, Jacob."

"In the shop. Can't we call her on the telephone?"

Rina grinned at him, slipped a hand through his bent elbow, and pulled him up. "Wait here, Jacob."

She entered Ash's room quietly. He was asleep. It seemed the fever had broken since his shirt was no longer damp. She caressed the hand he rested on the sheet beside him. Rina leaned down and pressed her lips to his as emotions overwhelmed her.

One hour later, Rina opened the Skype app on her new iPad. She had pirated the address from Ash's phone. When Magda's face filled the screen, the older woman looked perplexed. "Rina? What happened? Ash hasn't called and I've been very…"

I know. I know. A lot has happened. First, I want to tell you that the doctors are optimistic about his progress.

Magda's face paled. "Doctors? What's happened?"

"Please believe me, Magda. He's in good hands. A mosquito bite in Mexico has given him a virus. The fever is gone. I wanted to tell you this to relieve your mind. But I am calling for another reason. But…how are you feeling?" Rina's voice sounded like a child's. She was scared.

"The doctor told me today that I am better than I was a week ago. I have been anxious to tell Ash that we think I am in remission." Her face creased in a smile.

She and Rina grinned at one another. "Magda, there is someone here---a friend---who wants to speak with you." Rina's chest was thumping wildly as she and the older woman stared at one another.

Magda Mahone's face changed, and she brought her small hand to her throat. "A friend?" Rina propped the iPad up on a pile of heavy books by Jacob's desk and then pulled him into the camera's lens.

"Hello, my dear Magda."

Rina walked away when the old woman's face looked into the eyes of her lost love, and the years melted away.

Thirteen

Rina heard Ash's raised voice from the hallway before she entered his room that evening. She had left her iPad with Jacob at the gem shop and returned to the hospital. So surprised to hear Ash talking, she paused in the corridor to savor the sound.

"I want to get up. I feel fine…"

"*Monsieur* Mahone. Please."

"Please, nothing. I want up."

Rina walked into the room and gave him a stern look. "Okay, Ash Mahone, simmer down." His coloring cheered her, and so did his attitude. He must be getting better if he's challenging the nurses.

He was stunned into silence, but then he grabbed the sheet to pull it off his body and get out of bed. "I'm getting up."

She smirked when he realized he was naked underneath. "How long have I been here? I need to shave. I want to brush my teeth, and I have to pee." When he looked down, he saw the clear tubing and rolled his eyes…a catheter.

"Two days." She acknowledged the stunned look on his face.

"Oh, God." He covered his face with one hand. "Of all the stupid-ass things to happen. A mosquito, for God's sake."

Rina laughed for the first time in two days, and it felt good. Unsure how much to tell him, she decided to remain silent for the time being. He had enough to worry about, and she dreaded his response when he found out about her involvement in locating Jacob. She hadn't mentioned the cloisonné box or the jewels to the older man; that was between him and Ash. She hugged her purse tightly under her arm, ensuring everything was still exactly where she'd left it.

"Rina, what's up? I can tell by the look on your face that I've missed something. The doctor said I'm doing well and I should be able to leave soon. Sooner rather than later, I told him. Well, I told him through the young woman who's been translating for me. I can't remember a damn thing from the French I took in high school." He grumbled and squeezed the bed covering before rubbing the stubble on his jaw.

She took a breath, counted to ten, and then started talking. When she finished, his blue eyes narrowed like a biology professor. He stared at her until she felt like a worm under a microscope. She tossed away each justification as the words crept into her head.

He folded his hands in contemplation and didn't say a word.

Rina was the first to break the silence. "I don't need to tell you that I was frightened you might not come out of that fever, Ash." When he didn't respond, she continued, "We knew where the shop was and I hadn't planned to speak to him, but…"

In a voice tight with emotion, he asked, "But?"

She answered softly, hardly more than a whisper. "He is a wonderful man, Ash. Perceptions and expectations rarely add up to reality. And he wants to meet you so much. He's in his shop now…speaking with your mother on Skype." She finished the sentence quickly.

"What? She's too ill to handle this right now. Why would you do that? That should have been up to me to decide, not you… a stranger to all of us. What the hell…?" Emotion enveloped the room like a blanket of fog.

Rina stared at him for only a moment before pulling her leather jacket closed and walking out of his room. She made her way down the corridor, pressed the elevator button, and rode downward as his words echoed in her head. That is all I am, a stranger. He was right. I've been a stranger all my life --- to my sister and sometimes to our mother. Definitely to my husband. Ex-husband, she interjected.

She returned to Le Estudia Hotel and stuffed her clothes into her new piece of luggage. She placed the cloisonné box in the hotel safe, labeled with Ash's name. She quickly wrote a note and asked the woman at the desk to give it to Ash when he returned. The taxi took her to the airport, and she walked away from Paris, Ash Mahone, and all the burdens of a relationship she never wanted in the first place. As she settled into her seat on the plane that would take her back to San Rafael, she remembered her iPad and realized Jacob and Magda needed it more than she did. Then she smiled.

Back at the hospital, Ash knew he had hurt her feelings the moment the words left his mouth. He rolled his eyes upward and then started watching the door, waiting for her to return so he could apologize. He was the one who got her into this mess in the first place. Dammit, why don't I think before I speak?

Just after he lay his head down on his pillow, he heard someone enter the room. He'd organized all the words in his head to tell her he was sorry, so he opened his eyes, expecting her to walk into his room.

And looked into the face of a man that mirrored his own.

Neither man spoke for a heartbeat.   And then both spoke at once.

"Jacob?"

"Ashton?"

The room suddenly turned warm as each man struggled to find the right words. The beeping machine interrupted their silent study of one another, and a nurse came in to turn it off. After she left, Jacob pulled a chair to the bed and sat down.

Blue eyes met blue, and their heartbeats were so loud that surely the other could hear them. The hospital room faded away, and Jacob realized the time had come to answer questions.

He lifted Rina's iPad towards Ash's side table. "Rina didn't come back to get this and didn't answer her phone. So, I thought I'd bring it to her and…" Jacob's eyes grew wet, and he rubbed them with a fist.

"My mother told me about you two weeks ago. It's pretty new to me, so I'm not sure how to act here, Jacob." Ash swallowed. Hard.

Jacob reached out with a tentative hand to cover his son's, lying on the coverlet. "I've known about you for forty years, son. And in all those years, I have thought of you every day, so I've had more time to get used to it. You look like my father. Forgive me if I stare, but it's a dream to see you in the flesh."

Ash felt the man's fingers kneading the top of his hand, and he looked down at their joined fingers. An emotion unlike anything he'd ever felt washed over him. Covering the man's hand with his other one, Ash struggled to swallow around the lump in his throat.

"Please tell me about you and my mother fifty years ago, and let's go from there. Mom told me a little, but I want to hear it from you. I'll tell you about my life, and you tell me about yours since then. Is that a deal?"

The old man nodded, and Jacob began to talk. "In the late 1960s, there was a stigma if a Jewish boy liked a Gentile girl. Your mother and I had been friends in school for a long time, and I knew she was the girl for me long before she did. And then, her parents wanted to take her to America. I had to stop her. Time was running out. However, when I expressed my feelings to her, she said it was important to her parents that she marry within her faith. I was a Jew, and they would never allow it. When I pushed her to see my point of view, she pulled away and wouldn't change her mind."

Jacob pulled a large, white handkerchief from his pocket and blew his nose. Then he wiped his eyes. "When she told me she loved me too, I thought she'd changed her mind. I started making plans. But that's not what she meant. Yes, she loved me and I loved her so much… I was beyond help in those days. Before she left with her parents, she agreed to meet me one last time… and then, we couldn't stop the kisses."

Ash mumbled, "Maybe this is more than I need to hear?"

Jacob's chuckle rumbled in his chest. "Maybe you are right. She sailed away with our kisses still on our lips. And within two months, she knew she was pregnant. But she didn't tell me about that or about her parents throwing her away because they knew I was the father. They told her she would never bring a Jewish grandchild into their home and walked away from her. It took me ten years to find her and learn of your existence. I was angry, furious at her, at her parents, at fate.

He leaned toward the bed and gazed deeply into Ash's face. "And I realized I was angry at you too…for the son I wanted with the woman I still loved. By then, another man was raising you as his own and sleeping with the woman I loved. I was so furious; I married a woman because she was there. Poor Sadie. She loved me, and I loved Magda. It was a horrible burden."

Ash stared at his father.

I moved us to Paris and opened a gem shop. Poland couldn't give me the life that Paris could. And then, Sadie got pregnant with the twins." Jacob looked up again as he said the words. "You have two sisters."

"And what do they think of this situation?"

Jacob's face blanched.

"They don't know about me, do they?"

"No, they don't. I'm not sure how they will react, but I hope they'll be fine. I live alone now, but they check on me often. When you leave the hospital, I would like you to come home with me. Rina is welcome too…Where is she?"

Ash bit the inside of his lip. "I'm not sure where she is."

"But you will ask her?"

"Yes, when I see her, I will…she said you and Mom were visiting on Skype. How did that go?"

Ash noticed the change in Jacob's expression, reminiscent of how his mother had responded when she first said, "My Jacob." "So, you know she's very sick."

"Yes, she told me, and she also said to tell you she's in remission."

Ash's face broke into a wide smile. "No kidding. God, that's good news. I need to tell Rina." He reached for his phone on the side table and dialed her number, but it went straight to voicemail. His eyebrows furrowed, and a sick feeling filled his stomach.

Fourteen

Rina's plane taxied into San Francisco, jolting her awake and causing her to jostle against her companion's shoulder. She had slept fitfully throughout the trip while crafting plans, carefully avoiding thoughts of her last conversation with Ash. She didn't want to remember his voice, his sense of humor, the little dimple in his cheek, or her longing for him. She was focused and prepared for her new reality. Her phone pinged. Jenna again. She deleted the message, grabbed her carry-on, and followed the other passengers off the plane.

Showtime.

Rina was exhausted from the journey, but she had to confront her past before she could truly live in the present. She stashed her bag in her condo and drove her Beemer toward her uncle's shop. His shop. It would always feel that way, not hers. It was such an important part of his life. He had helped her through many emotional crises, yet he had the audacity to die while she lay in a coma. She didn't know if she would ever forgive him.

San Rafael is a city and the county seat of Marin County, California. The city is located in the North Bay region of San Francisco and possesses more history and beauty than places farther eastward, at least as far as Rina was concerned. Uncle James purchased the building when he was a young man, barely thirty, as he had looked ahead more than most young men his age. He knew what he wanted, and he pursued it. He had told Rina many times that she was very much like him. She smiled as she recalled their conversations.

Her phone rang. The car's Bluetooth picked it up, and she recognized Ash's phone number. She pressed the button and said, "End call," and he was lost in the satellite miles away. He'd called several times, but she wasn't ready to talk with him. He didn't need her to get involved in his life, and she certainly didn't want him to be involved in hers. She just wanted to hibernate in the shop. She'd clean it up and honor the memory of her uncle James and the silver jewelry stored in his vault.

Her mind swerved to her sister; Jenna hadn't been able to break their uncle's Will, and Rina felt a wanton satisfaction in the knowledge. She delighted in thwarting her sister, and she'd do it again and again to make her disappear. Jenna was indeed an ex-sister; she vowed never to turn into mush again.

When she pulled into the parking space that belonged to Silvan's Antiques, she engaged her emergency brake and sat quietly in the car. It was the first time she had been here since her uncle died, and the sadness permeated her being. She had loved the man who helped her find her bearings, the man who thwarted her sister's lust to have everything.

Rina grabbed her black leather briefcase and held the shop's keys. Standing in front of the doorway, she gazed at her reflection in the beveled glass door. Her hair was tied in a top knot beneath the red hat. Her gray sweater tunic draped over her thin body, layered above black leggings that offered little warmth against the wind howling down the bay.

When she opened the door, the bell tinkled, bringing back memories of Uncle James calling out, "Is that you, Rina?" She gulped down the last of her coffee and tossed the Starbucks cup in the trash by the front door. Then she locked the door and turned to face the small shop.

"Yes, it's me, Uncle. I'm back to stay," her voice stammered just a little until she walked into the depths of the shop. That's when she saw a fat envelope propped against the back wall with her name on it. R-I-N-A was boldly written in his handwriting. God, she missed her uncle.

After stashing papers and wiping the desk until all the dust motes had vanished, she tackled the front windows. Then she poured soapy water into a bucket, grabbed the mop, and got to work on the floors. This place would come alive again. It was all hers and nothing but hers.

She grinned as she said it under her breath over and over again.
Her phone pinged. Jenna again. She deleted the text and started to hum an old high school tune. She refused to let her sister's betrayal and nastiness ruin her pleasure today. Within a few hours, the shop sparkled like new, the desk was free of papers, a pot of coffee was brewing, and she sat down to catch her breath. She glanced at the fat envelope again. Not yet.

Delicate drawings of intricate jewelry designs covered the back table, many of which she had created herself. She smiled as she recalled how her uncle had praised her artistic talent and encouraged her to work on the pieces of silver with the green stones. She remembered her excitement at his compliments. She had been busy with this work when she was taken to the hospital after the accident. Her gaze lingered. Everything was just as she had left it.

When she saw the pad of drawings, it drew her in. Maybe now she could concentrate again. Although having the shop to herself was overwhelming, she straightened her shoulders and sat down.

Her fingers fiddled with the pad as she lifted a pencil to add some curlicues. Then, she continued adding more until her fingers were flying over the pad, and she burst into laughter. "I'm happy. I feel like I'm free at last." She stood up, hugged herself, danced around the table, and landed in her uncle's chair with a thump. And there was the fat envelope again.

She made herself coffee first and added some pumpkin-flavored creamer. She mentally slapped herself and lifted the letter opener to slit open the envelope. After taking a sip of coffee, she jumped when it burned her tongue. Swallowing hard, she began reading the ink-stained paper.

My beautiful Rina,

By the time you read this, I fear I will be gone.   I have visited you in the hospital every day, my darling, and you still sleep.   I have been sick for a long while, but I could not burden you with my pain.

You are a very talented artist, and I know the shop will grow with you in control. My attorney worked diligently on the paperwork to ensure that Jenna has no rights to this shop, the silver, the contents of the safe, or this building. I leave this to you alone because you are that special girl I love every time you walk inside the door.

Rina, you will find ten felt drawstring bags in a large brown envelope inside the safe. Inside these envelopes are jewels that I have saved over the years to use for my silver jewelry. One week ago, I was offered almost one million dollars for the lot. It is my legacy to you. You must decide what to do: keep the jewels or sell them. I hope you can use some of them in your jewelry line. Both ideas will make me happy. You must make that decision on your own. The buyer's name is inside the envelope. Also, you will find a safe deposit key. Everything inside is yours. I love you, my dearest niece, and wish I could have lasted just a little longer. Please examine your relationship with Jeff closely and remain vigilant. He is not what he appears. You are too special not to have the best of the best.

Lovingly,

Your Uncle James

The tears slid down her face slowly at first, then ran in a torrent as sobs wracked her body. He had been the parent since she lost her own, and he had loved her as his daughter. And he had seen through Jeff at a time when Rina had been oblivious to it all.

Finally, the light faded from the room, and she was all cried out. Her chest ached, and her eyes burned. After rubbing her hands hard across her face and pushing her hair behind her ears, she took a deep breath. She sat down on the floor to open the safe. When she pulled out a large envelope, she squeezed it tightly in her hand. Next, she tucked the safe deposit key into her pocket.

Her phone rang. Ash again. She shoved her phone and everything else into her bag. After locking the shop's door, she got into her car and headed home. Her mind was foggy from lack of sleep, and the jet lag was crippling. Tomorrow, she would go to the bank. The mysteries were multiplying, and the lilt in her belly wouldn't go away. And she missed Ash. Dammit.

Fifteen

Ash tossed his phone onto the bed. He was still in stun mode after he was released from the hospital and walked into the hotel. After reading Rina's note, he'd berated himself so many times for his harsh censure of her actions that he wanted to beat himself silly. He had called her several times and wasn't answering. Now, life was moving at breakneck speed.

Tonight, he was meeting his twin sisters for the first time. Jacob had briefly explained his existence to them. Ash was acutely aware that one of them hadn't taken it lightly. His head felt dazed, and his stomach churned with nerves.

When his taxi arrived at the three-story brownstone, bright lights sparkled from the windows. He paid the driver and dashed through the rain, taking the stairs two at a time. Just before he could slam the knocker against the heavy door, it swung open, revealing a woman who could have been his younger twin.

"Dora." He said simply.

"Ash." She responded, pulling the door farther open to allow him in. Her light brown hair was styled in a chignon with a pearl-studded comb, and her makeup was flawless. He noticed her lips fighting a smile, but when she turned toward him, their blue eyes met, and she couldn't help herself. "This is one of the strangest days of my life. Come in, brother."

And mine. I've known about you for about ten days, so I'm a few days ahead of you. So, it's Laura that...

Her lips quivered. "Come meet Laura. Papa is in the sitting room. She will be harder to befriend than I am." She lifted his coat and patted his cheek. "You are quite nice looking, brother." She grinned at his expression and shook raindrops off his jacket as she sped ahead.

He followed a little more slowly and entered a large, wood-paneled room with a crackling fireplace. His father sat in one chair, while his other sister sat across from him. Jacob quickly rose to greet him, arm outstretched. Laura didn't move her head to acknowledge him; in fact, she pretended he wasn't there at all.

His eyes met Dora's, and her answering look was **I told you**.

Jacob pulled Ash into the room and poured him a traditional Provençale Christmas wine. "*Vin Cuit* tastes a lot like port."

Ash didn't like sweet drinks, hated them in fact, but he sipped it anyway. He wanted to avoid giving Jacob or the ladies anything to gripe about. He knew he was the bastard in the room, and when he looked at Laura, he felt it was written in copper across his forehead.

"Welcome, Ash. I see you have already met Dora. This is Laura." Jacob Safra pointed toward the other woman as if Ash hadn't seen her when he entered the room.

His lips lifted in a smile.

Laura lifted an eyebrow and nodded toward him before taking a generous sip of her drink. "Hello." Her eyes appraised him, taking in every inch of his body. Then she glanced between Ash and Dora. His appearance strongly mirrored the stance and bearing of her father. Her face flushed as she realized he was Jacob's son and her half-brother.

"Laura. Dora." He grinned, trying to break the ice, and was pleased when the housemaid came in to announce dinner. He could have really used Rina's presence tonight and felt angry again that she'd left him in the lurch. How could she have believed his words and just... well... left?

His sisters were very different from each other. Dora was a partner in a fashion design shop in Paris called Boutons et Nœuds. Her clothes fit perfectly, and she walked as if she were modeling the latest creation. She smiled frequently. He liked her. Laura, on the other hand, taught history at the Sorbonne. He hadn't seen her smile yet and wondered if her face would crack if she did. Maybe she looked like their mother? Dora and Ash definitely resembled Jacob.

Dinner was served simply yet elegantly—rice with chicken and vegetables mixed under golden gravy. The soup was a broth that tasted like heaven. He wasn't sure what it was, but he could have eaten more. When the cheese and fruit were presented as dessert, he was already full, but from the looks of things, ignoring it wasn't an option. More wine. More cheese. If he still smoked, he could have used a cigarette right about then.

When the dishes were cleared away, Ash still hoped to see a smile on Laura's face. It didn't happen. Dora took his arm as they left the dining room, and Ash caught a glimpse of pleasure on Jacob's face when he saw them together. She led him to a loveseat.

Jacob and Laura had stayed behind.

"What do you expect from me, Papa?" He could hear Laura's strained whisper so clearly that he was certain she wanted him to listen to her.

"Please understand my feelings, Laura. This is very important to me." His voice sounded strained.

"So, your love child is forced upon us to dirty *Maman's* memory for us? And we are to bend our knees and be happy about it?"

The room became warmer, and Ash's temper flared. He heard Jacob's quick intake of breath and then saw Laura leave the dining room and head straight up the steps to the next level of the house. When Jacob entered the room, he stood in front of the fireplace, staring into the flames, his shoulders rigid.

"Papa, you knew it wouldn't be easy. To me, this is exciting. To Laura, it is as if *Maman* were in the room. You know she is pessimistic, just like she was. I am sorry to say it, but you know it's true." Dora turned to give Ash a look.

Ash felt warmth wash over him again. "I didn't come here to break up a family, Dora. My mother is very ill, and all my life, I thought my stepdad was my father. This is all new to me, too. When my mother told me about Jacob, I was shocked and angry. Angry at her, at Jacob, and angry at my dad for not telling me the truth. I made a promise to my mother that I'd come to Paris to meet Jacob and bring him the…."

"Dora, you know this is as I told you, *oui*?" Jacob quickly interrupted Ash before he could finish his sentence.

"Yes, Papa. And it is delightful to meet you, Ash. It is almost like looking into a mirror. I believe we look more alike than my twin and I." She chuckled. "And I like you. You have kind eyes, and I feel a kindred spirit. For Laura, it's different. You will have to work very hard to turn her around from her persistent protection of our mother's memory. It won't be easy. Me? I'm easy." She laughed.

Ash was enchanted by her, but when he looked at Jacob, he sensed tension in the air. He wasn't sure how to interpret it.

"Jacob, shall we meet for coffee in the morning before I get ready to return to America? My flight is at 4:00 p.m., and I think we have more to discuss. Oui?"

Dora and Jacob shared a look.

"Yes. But the housekeeper has made up the guestroom bed for you. When you were released from the hospital, I hoped you would stay with us for a few days instead of returning to the hotel. Please think about it?"

Dora raised her eyebrows. "Say yes, brother. I have just met you and I don't want to lose you so quickly.

Ash was surprised and grinned at her.

Jacob said, "I will take you to the hotel, and we can bring everything back here. I need more time to be with you. Please say yes."

Father and son stared at one another.

Ash nodded. He would stay under his father's roof and postpone his flight. He knew Jacob also wanted to Skype with Magda on Rina's iPad and couldn't quite wrap his head around it, but felt pleasure in that knowledge.

~

When Jacob drove Ash away, Dora went upstairs to confront her twin sister. Upon opening the door to her room, she saw Laura lying face down on her bed. Her light brown hair spread over the pillow, and her stockinged feet dangled near the floor. Her fingers twisted the sheets.

"So, you are going to act the bitch about Papa's son, are you?"

Laura turned her head and glared at her sister. "I'll act any way I damn well please. He has no right to Papa. If his mother hadn't opened her legs before marriage, this would never have happened. *Maman* would never have done such a thing."

"Holy Jesus. Really? Is that what's got your belly in a knot? Because Papa fell in love and had sex before he married *Maman*? My God, Laura, are you a child? Humans fall in love, and sometimes they have sex when they aren't married. You're just angry because you think Ash will want some of Papa's money when he dies. Is that it?"

Laura pounded the bed with her fist. "Of course not."

Dora stared at her shrewdly. "Did you take a minute to talk to the man? He appears honest and kind to me, not selfish or mean. How can he be when he is Papa's child? Papa has always been kind to us. Always. How can you hurt him so much by treating his son so horridly?"

"I do not have to like him. You can like him for both of us. I want him gone. He isn't part of our family and he never will be."

"So, you will still play the bitch, then?" Dora slammed the door so hard that the porcelain babies rattled against the windowsill.
Laura threw the pillow across the room.

~

Jacob was quiet in the car, but Ash felt compelled to ask. "The girls do not know about the cloisonné box, do they?"

"No."

"And they don't know about the jewels you sent to Ma?"

"No."

"Well, I came a long way to return it to you. Don't you think spilling your past to your daughters would have been a good decision?" Ash tried to keep his voice neutral, but the words flowed out in a torrent.

Jacob pulled over to the curb. "What? You didn't bring the cloisonné box of jewels to return to me, Ash. You brought them to show your mother you cared enough about our love to meet me. They are yours. I saved enough money to send her one jewel every year after I learned of your existence. They are my legacy to you. We were both very poor when we were young, so your mother knew the value was in giving much more than in the box or the gems. My promises were wrapped around each jewel. I knew she would slip the jewels inside the blue box every year and feel the love from me and for you."

Ash couldn't speak. "I thought I was giving **you** the box. That's why I took such good care of it. Ma said if I gave you the box, you'd know I was your son when you saw it in my hands. She also said I'd recognize you and I damned sure did."

Jacob laughed. "Magda always had that insatiable sense of humor. The box was always hers. The jewels were always yours. She wanted you to bring me the box so you could meet your sisters and me. The love was the value, not the beautiful box."

"Well, I had a hell of a time keeping that box safe. Do you have any idea how valuable that little blue beauty is? I've been beaten bloody and chased halfway across the country over it. And Rina was hurt because of it, too. It's very valuable, for God's sake."

Jacob's eyes widened. "I didn't know. When I was nineteen years old, an old man needed to take his family out of Poland, and I helped him. The country was a mess, and I had access to an old farm truck. We made a hidden space under the hay; they crawled under it, and I drove across the border into Czechoslovakia. He didn't have money, but he had his grandfather's beautiful little box...beautiful like Magda. Afterward, when she refused to marry me, I gave it to her. I told her my love was inside the box, and every time she missed me, she could open it and breathe me in. I never put a financial value on it. You say it's worth a lot of money now?"

Ash nodded. "Yes, sir, it is."

"Well, good. You have jewels to sell if you need money." He drove his Fiat away from the curb again.

Ash held the cloisonné box in both hands and snorted. "Sell it? After all this trouble? You must be joking." Ash shook his head and blew out an exaggerated breath.

Jacob shrugged.

Within a few minutes, Ash's hotel room was cleared, he checked out, and the men returned to Jacob's brownstone home.

"I will postpone my trip home only if Ma stays in remission. I'm stunned. When I saw her last, she was pale and weak. The doctor didn't give me much hope, and all I could think about was finding you before she died."

His fists clenched against his pant legs as he gazed out the window, watching the car speed past the lights of Paris. The sights were too beautiful to ignore; he lifted his eyes toward Notre Dame and the gargoyles he knew were guardians of the cathedral. Lights twinkled across the Seine, and boats glided around the Left Bank. The rain had stopped, leaving the streets gleaming from the earlier downpour.

Cafés glowed brightly, and he noticed tables filled with people enjoying late dinners. He shivered, wishing for a heartbeat that Rina sat next to him so he could share the beauty of Paris with her.

"We can Skype Magda when we get home?" Jacob asked, hopefully.

Ash turned to the older man and shook his head. "Sure." He couldn't help but grin, and his shoulders sagged with relief. Now if he could just figure out how to get Rina to answer the damn phone so he could tell her that he felt like crap.

Sixteen

Magda Mahone couldn't stop smiling. Her fingers clung to one another as she squeezed them in her lap after putting on makeup and running a brush through her curly salt-and-pepper hair. When she'd sent Ash to find Jacob, she recalled the face of a thirty-year-old man, which was the last time she'd seen him. Ash was ten years old. She lifted her hands to her mouth and felt the smile there. The giddiness of a young girl bubbled up from her belly, and she laughed out loud.

When she saw Jacob's face fill the screen after Rina had called her a few days earlier, she didn't notice a silver-headed man, the wrinkles around his blue eyes, or the sagging skin beneath his chin. Instead, she saw the young man, her Jacob, because the years had fallen away, and they were children again.

She sniffled and wiped her nose with the lace-edged handkerchief from her slacks pocket. Then, she caught the moisture that slipped from her eyes before tucking it into the cleft of her blouse. She had been wiping away tears for days—happy tears that she had never expected.

The emotions that wracked her body were a blend of anti-climactic joy and anticipation; her son had finally met his biological father, she was in remission from her cancer, and oh dear God, she still loved Jacob. The look on his face that first time with Rina could still warm her from the inside. She was seventy years old on the outside, but on the inside? Younger. He still smacked her heart into slush, and she loved that feeling. She reached for the lace hankie again.

~

Since the Christmas holidays closed schools, Laura Safra decided to stay with her father during vacation. She certainly did not plan to share any part of the house with a bastard half-brother, and she was not pleased about it. She avoided them at every opportunity and grimaced when she heard them come through the door.

Jacob, on the other hand, nearly danced with joy. He took Ash to the gem shop with him every morning, and they had lengthy discussions about life in general, his childhood, Magda, and the gems he lived with daily.

"When did you decide that journalism wasn't the career you wanted anymore, Ash?" Jacob seemed to hang on every word; every part of the life his son had lived without him.

"I was tired of traveling. Each new job took me farther and farther away from home. Then, when Ma got sick, I started turning jobs down, and I realized I didn't miss it. I'm fifty years old now, and it's a little late to change careers, but I am going to do it."

Jacob stared at him thoughtfully.

"I just don't know what I want to be when I grow up…"

Both men laughed.

Ash learned to measure and weigh Jacob's gems while watching him meticulously record the results in his journal. The internet served as a significant source of income for the old man, and he was very impressed by the way Jacob managed his business.

"Have you thought of selling your gems outside France with the help of a marketing agent, Jacob?" Ash had been considering an idea for a couple of days and wasn't sure how to approach it.

Jacob looked up from his desk and pulled the jewelry digital caliper away from his face. "No, I hadn't thought of such a thing. I know there's a market for it. Are you applying for the job?" Jacob chuckled.

Ash thought a moment. "Yes, I may be doing just that."

Jacob's expression shifted from thoughtful to serious. "How could we make something like that work? Even on the internet, there are drawbacks, taxes, different export laws, and such."

Over the next few hours, the men discussed some parameters and concluded it could be a profitable venture. Jacob felt excited when they got home, and during dinner, the men mentioned it to the women.

"What?! That is ridiculous!" Laura tossed her napkin onto the table and stomped out of the room. "First, he wants to be our brother, and now he wants to be part of the business? God."

Dora's eyes grew wide as she looked at her father. "It sounds like a good idea to me, Papa. I believe it would be good for both of you. Ash, since you're no longer writing for the newspapers, it would be an interesting challenge. But, Laura...."

"Is Laura involved in your business, Jacob?"

"No, she's never been interested," he said.

"I don't understand her anger then."

"It isn't anything I can explain. She is not a happy girl. She doesn't like her life to be bumpy." Jacob nodded toward the stairwell and shook his head toward Dora, urging her to talk with Laura.

Dora rolled her eyes and left the table.

After a while, the men sipped their coffee by the fire, and the conversation shifted back to the cloisonné box. The room was cozy and warm as the men enjoyed the camaraderie that quiet words often inspire. Flames danced in the fireplace while the men sat together, each with their heads filled with ideas and exciting scenarios.

"I've been thinking about the box, Jacob. I know it means a lot to you and Ma. And the gems take my breath away, but we should decide what to do with them." Ash had been worried about its safety and wondered again about a plan to safeguard it. After realizing that the beauty was meant to be his, it made his heart tingle with love for this old man, a man he didn't know at all. But he wanted to be part of his life.

The men didn't hear Laura's footsteps on the carpeted stairs or realize she was standing outside the door. Dora had shamed her into apologizing, and she'd finally agreed. It wasn't Papa's fault the woman got pregnant after all. When she began to push into the room, she heard Ash's words, and her curiosity was piqued. She withdrew silently to listen.

"I know the jewels are worth a fortune, Ash, but as I said, I had no idea the cloisonné box was valuable. It's up to Magda. I gave her the box. She should decide. The jewels were always yours. My wife, Sadie, was never aware of the box or the jewels. They were all mine to give to you."

Laura narrowed her eyes and edged closer. She was sure they were discussing that box again but couldn't hear the words clearly. Pressing her ear to the door, she strained to listen. Her body shook with anger.

Ash glanced at his watch and sighed loudly. "Okay… well, I'm beat, Jacob. I think I'll go to bed. We can talk about it in the morning at the shop. A decision should be made. Rina helped me hide the box when those hoodlums tried to rob me, so we can't have them lying around."

Jacob stared into the fire. "You are right. Tomorrow. And when we get to the shop, we can Skype Magda?" Jacob's face lit up with expectation, and he couldn't stop the grin that sparked a smile in his eyes.

Ash smiled indulgently. "Yes, we can."

Laura hurried through the foyer when she heard Ash approaching. Once he had gone upstairs, she entered the den and sat down with her father. The fire had burned low, and he was gazing into the flames.

"I am sorry I was angry, Papa," Laura lied. Her face looked sincere, and she was relieved to see that her father believed her. She patted the arm of the chair while she measured her words.

Jacob lifted his head quickly and came over to pat Laura's cheek. "I know this isn't easy for you, darling. But this is very important to me." I have known about my son for many years, but this is my chance to truly get to know him. He is your brother, and I also hoped you might like to know that.

"It is difficult for me, Papa. He may not be who he claims to be. What can this stranger do for you that your daughters cannot?" Her hands tightened in the folds of her gold-colored skirt. Her jaw was tense, and all the lines around her eyes stood out like a spider's web.

He sat down and drew one of her hands into his. "This stranger is my child, just as you are my child. And as far as him not being who he claims to be? Just look at him, Laura. You and Dora, I love very much, and my heart is filled with memories of our many years together. For Ash, I have no memories. And I want to create some. Let me do that without feeling guilty, won't you?" His eyes begged for her understanding.

"Are you keeping secrets from us? Has he told us the truth about his life and himself?" Her face was blotchy, and her eyes turned hard. "I think you have secrets that you are not sharing with me and Dora." Her fingers tapped the arm of the chair, and she stared at her father as if she were in her university classroom, chastising a student.

"Secrets?" His eyes looked back at her with surprise.

"Yes, does he have something we don't know about? I heard you talking about..." Her lips thinned.

Jacob wondered where she was going with this. "Of course not. He is a man who has just learned his entire life was a lie. I am lucky he didn't turn away from me…us." He lifted a hand to his face, unable to understand his daughter's attitude and irritated that she had eavesdropped on their conversation.

"Well, he must think you can do something for him, then. He's not working for the newspapers anymore. Maybe he wants money...."

"Laura."

"Alright, Papa. But I warned you." She got up, pecked him on the cheek, and left the room.

As Jacob watched her leave, he felt uneasy. She was Sadie's daughter—slightly unscrupulous, self-serving, and sometimes mischievous. He would have to keep an eye on her and warn Ash to be cautious. Once they decided what to do about the blue box, he could relax again.

Seventeen

Rina ran her fingers over the crisp savings bonds and flipped through them like she was shuffling cards. There were 200 bonds, each valued at $500. She wasn't a math whiz, but she knew that at maturity this amounted to $100,000. "Oh. My. God." She struggled to take it all in. Where on earth did her uncle gather this much money? The antique shop did very well, but how could it be? She brushed her fingers over the one-inch fuzz beneath the crown of her hair. Her uncle's business acumen had just stepped up another notch.

When she had gone into the bank, she had shown the woman her uncle's death certificate and a copy of the Will. There was no question about the validity of her ownership. The question was now in her hands. The safe gaped open, and she didn't know the answers.

The velvet drawstring bags filled with jewels were a different matter entirely. She had thought the jewels in Ash's cloisonné box were stunning, and they were. But this? These belonged to her, and she wasn't sure if she could make a wise decision. Should she sell or keep them? Why keep them if they wouldn't fit into her jewelry designs? She could use the money to buy her own jewels. She wished she could discuss it with Ash or perhaps Jacob.

When the phone rang, she took it out instinctively and answered. "Hello?"

"Rina."

Her hands shook. "Hello, Ash."

"Thank God you finally answered the damn phone. I've been going nuts trying to get in touch with you. I wanted to apologize, and tell you...."

"You were right, Ash. I am a stranger and I had no right to find Jacob and...." Her voice shook now in tandem with her hands.

"No. I was wrong. And things are happening here, Rina. I'm getting to know Jacob and my sisters. One sister is open to a relationship. The other definitely isn't. There have been so many times when I wished you were here. I want to talk to you about things..."

She laughed. "Oh?" Warmth tingled down to her toes.

"Where are you?" His voice hitched.

"Back in San Rafael. My uncle left me his antique shop, remember? And I've been disobedient again, Ash. I've been visiting your mother."

"Huh. She hasn't mentioned it to me or Jacob. How is she, Rina? She said she's in remission, and I want to believe her. Her color looks good on Skype, but I wonder..."

"She's doing pretty well, and every time she talks about you and Jacob being together, she gets all mushy on me." Rina felt a warm glow inside as she remembered Magda's expression from the day before.

"How are you doing, Rina? God, I'm missing you."

Rina didn't answer.

"Rina, are you still there?"

"Yes, I'm here. I've had some surprises on my end. I guess you could say my future has been taken care of. I won't have to worry about whether Social Security goes broke or not."

"Huh. Sounds interesting. And have you seen your sister?"

"I told you she's my ex-sister. And the answer is no. When are you coming home? I'm missing you too, dammit." She changed the subject because she didn't want to answer any more questions.

"I'm flying home next week. I want to bring Jacob with me. How do you think Ma will handle it?"

Rina grinned. "Yes," she whispered. "Yes, do that."

"Well, thanks for answering the phone...and you won't ignore my calls, please? You have no idea how much I've wanted to talk to you about everything that's going on here."

"Yes, sir. Bye, Ash." She pressed the end button. Giddiness rose from inside her like a torrent of wind. Darned if she didn't miss the guy. She pushed the drawstring bags back into the safe along with the savings bonds. It wasn't easy to work herself up from her crouched position, so she braced her elbows on the side of the heavy desk. Forty-three years old, pushing eighty.

As she turned off the lights and prepared to leave, she noticed a woman standing at the front door of the shop. She wore black leather pants and bright red knee-high boots, complemented by a matching coat and hat. Her hand curved over her forehead as if the sun were in her eyes.

"Hey, Rina."

"Get out." She marched forward and pushed the woman out the door onto the sidewalk. Locking the door behind her, she started to walk away when she was yanked around like a child.

"You can't just ignore me, Rina. I'm your sister. Why won't you answer my texts or phone calls? It's getting ridiculous. I dumped Jeff, so you don't have to worry about him anymore. We need to talk." Jenna swished long, dark hair away from her eyes. She folded her arms across her ample breasts and stood her ground.

Rina walked toward her sister. They stood nose to nose. "You stay out of my life and leave me alone. You aren't my sister anymore."

Jenna laughed. "Come on, Rina. This isn't funny. You've got the shop and probably all the bills that come with it. I got nothing." Her voice turned to a whine. "I want some of that money. It isn't fair. There must be something you can share with me." She stomped her red boot onto the sidewalk.

When Rina approached Jenna again, she gazed into her sister's face. As Jenna lifted her chin and a smirky smile appeared, Rina slapped her so hard that her red hat flew onto the sidewalk.

Jenna's hand flew to her cheek, her eyes widening in surprise. She pushed her hair away from her face and sputtered in shock.

Rina jerked around and walked toward her Beemer. She had to admit that it felt good, even though her hand still stung. Once inside her car, she glanced in the rearview mirror and saw Jenna staring after her. As she watched her sister lean down to pick up her red hat and stalk to her car, Rina laughed and drove away.

Eighteen

Gabe Pizelli lifted his swollen leg off the couch, cursing Ash Mahone for the teeth marks that had become infected before he returned to San Francisco. Then he gently lifted his head, cursing the woman who had used him for batting practice when she slammed the two-by-four into his back.

"God, I ache all over and I don't have anything to show for it but bruises and a Visa bill from all the booze I drank on the ship and plane fare to L.A." He grumbled as he walked into the bathroom and stared at himself in the mirror. His breath knocked him back, and the stubble on his jaw was black and rough. When he grabbed a towel to ease his body into the shower, he didn't hear the phone ringing.

Harry Dalton dropped his mobile phone onto the Corian counter. The windows of Park West Art Gallery sparkled, and the paintings he'd hung from the rafters had already attracted several people's attention. The art auction the night before at his weekly Art in the Park was very successful, and he'd gone to bed feeling happy.

The only thing that darkened his horizon now was that Gabe had been missing for the past few days. His driver was usually dependable and could be found in the gallery every morning after an auction. Harry had eight paintings to prepare for delivery, some destined for local patrons and others for buyers outside the city, to be shipped via FedEx. And now his deliveryman was nowhere to be found.

The gallery was in its fifth year, and Harry's success stemmed from his strong business acumen and the artists who filled his studio with excellent paintings. He was fair and friendly, and he also knew how to schmooze his way into any social gathering. People liked him.

Gabe Pizelli had been his friend since high school, through his time in the army and after he returned home. But Gabe had always seemed like a lost soul. He needed a job when he left the army, so Harry hired him. He never asked what had happened, and Gabe hadn't shared his history with him. The man did his job, and for that, Harry was happy.

Now, Harry's expression shifted to worry. It wasn't like Gabe to fool around on delivery day. He picked up the phone again and dialed Gabe's number. Before the first ring, a stranger walked into the gallery, prompting Harry to hang up. Putting on his sales face, he smiled as the man approached him. Harry extended a hand to welcome him to the gallery, "Hello."

"Good morning."

"Hello. I'm looking for an old friend named Ash Mahone. He and I used to write for the Chronicle. He said if I were ever in town, Harry Dalton at the Park West Gallery would know where to find him." The man had brown eyes and a big smile. When he reached for Harry's hand, he continued, "You, Harry? I'm Trevor Iverson."

"Hey, good to meet you. Yes, I'm Harry. But I don't know where Ash is off to. I saw him a couple of weeks ago, but his mother is sick and he's probably with her. I can leave him a message with your number, but I'm uncomfortable giving his number to you…sorry." Harry stared into the man's face with a look of apology.

Trevor pulled out a card and laid it on the counter. "Sure, I understand. I'll be in town until the end of the week. I'd love to connect with the guy. It's been ages." They shook hands again, and he left the studio.

Dutifully, Harry called Ash, left a message, and then redialed Gabe. This time, the man answered, and Harry's face filled with relief.

"Hey, you. Where are you? It's delivery day."

Gabe dried himself with the bath towel and sat on his bed, still aching but feeling much better. "Yeah, sorry, Harry. Got a slow start this morning. Someone jumped me the other day, and I'm still nursing my wounds."

"What?! Did you call the police?"

"Nah, you know this happens all the time, and they don't have time for the little stuff. I'll be there in about an hour. That good?"

"Sure. Are you up to delivering paintings today?"

"Yeah, I'm good." Gabe hung up and leaned both elbows on his knees. His hair still dripped, and he shrugged the towel over his head. He inhaled deeply and whispered into his empty apartment, "Where's Mahone and that damned blue box? I can't give up. Sorry, Harry."

When Gabe arrived at the gallery's back door an hour later, he moved slowly. Harry had half the paintings wrapped, with labels slapped on them both front and back. The delivery van waited by the back door as the men worked together, propping the paintings up carefully with a buffer between each one. Sun sneaked through the front windows, lending an eerie light to the packages lining the back wall.

"Come have coffee with me before you take the first load, Gabe." Harry walked back into the studio, pulling his coat tightly around his chest. "That wind goes right through you. I'm sorry to hear you were attacked. Are you okay?"

Gabe laughed. "Yeah, I'm good. You've lived in San Francisco a long time, Harry. It's never going to change. You should be used to the wind by now."

Harry snickered. "You'd think so, right?" He poured two cups of steaming coffee and handed Gabe the creamer, but drank his own black and strong. "Tell me about the attack."

Gabe lifted the coffee to his lips slowly, giving himself time to respond. "I was cutting through the alley behind my apartment, and two kids jumped me. One clipped me on the neck, and I was down. The other jabbed me with something on the leg. I bashed one and rammed the other into the wall, and they went running with their tails between their legs. Unfortunately, I was feeling pretty broken, but I was close to home, so here I am."

Harry shook his head and cursed, "God, I'm sorry, Gabe."

Gabe avoided meeting Harry's gaze and took another sip of the hot brew. He mumbled something, and they began discussing the deliveries and the timelines promised for each one. When Gabe stood up to set his coffee on the counter, he noticed the calling card and picked it up.

"Who's this? A reporter? Or a painter? One of your patrons?" He grinned at Harry.

"None of those. The guy came in this morning looking for Ash Mahone." Harry sipped his coffee, jotted notes on the pad beside him, and counted the remaining paintings waiting to be wrapped.

Gabe swung his eyes toward Harry. "Oh? Why is that?"

"He used to work with him on one of the newspapers somewhere, and he's in town trying to connect with the guy."

"What did you tell him?"

I didn't know where he was, so I left Ash a voicemail.

Gabe thought about how to respond to him. "Didn't you say his mother lives around here?" His black hair fell across his forehead, and he brushed it back with an impatient hand.

Harry's eyes lit up, and he snapped his fingers, "Yes, that's right. She's pretty sick, and he's probably with her. I think she lives over by the old *San Francisco de Asís*...You know, Mission Dolores. Since the mission is the oldest surviving structure in San Francisco and the seventh of the California chain of missions, it is listed on the National Register of Historic Places. She must have big bucks: her name's Maggie or something like that. Well, I left Ash a message, so I'm sure he'll find the guy. Let's get you moving, huh?"

Gabe nodded slowly after he surreptitiously ran his hand across the gallery's counter before returning to the van.

"I'll have the rest of the art ready when you get back after lunch," Harry yelled as the van's back door closed and the gallery fell quiet again.

Despite the delivery list crumpled in his hand, Gabe added one more stop to his morning jaunt. He pulled over onto Market Street, yanked out his phone, typed in Mahone and San Francisco, and bingo. Magda Mahone. Whatever happened to privacy, he wondered. Next to her name were the names Dan Mahone and Ashton Mahone. He scribbled down the address and started whistling.

~

Across the bridge in San Rafael, Rina continued to clean up the clutter in the shop. All the files were organized in alphabetical order. The client list was consolidated in one location rather than spread across a hundred little sticky notes, as her uncle preferred. She shook her head with a sad smile as she remembered how many times she'd told him, "Uncle James, your organization skills suck."

She could still hear him answer, "Rina, I don't like that word. I know where all my client names are, so you do it your way and I'll do it mine." And that was that. Until now.

The silver pieces were now arranged in a pattern based on size, shape, and weight. The gems were nestled inside the velvet box with the glass lid, which contained nearly all of them that she'd taken from the safe to accompany her new drawings. All of them, that is, except for the ones in the drawstring bags. She had no idea what to do with those. Should she keep them or sell?

Her phone rang, and she quickly grabbed it, hoping it was Ash. When she saw Magda's photo spread across the screen, she smiled. "Good morning, Magda."

She heard the older woman's chuckle. "No surprises nowadays, are there?"

Rina laughed out loud with a word, "Nope."

I'm feeling pretty good today, and I thought it would be fun to have lunch together. Are you too busy for an old lady?

"An old lady? That's a joke. What time and where?"

"You are a dear. Why don't you come to my house, and I'll have Pereira's deliver some of that delicious Portuguese soup and fresh bread."

"I'll bring dessert and see you about 11:30. I have an appointment at 1:30. Will that work?" Rina felt a smile tingle in her belly.

"Perfect, dear."

When Rina hung up, she felt Ash's warmth wrap around her.

Gabe had already delivered three paintings across the city and had three more to deliver. He would see the old lady last. He didn't want to hurt her; he just wanted her to tell him where her son could be found. Gabe doubted Ash was in town since he knew the man had planned to go to Paris. He hoped he wasn't too late to grab the blue box.

He would make the old lady reveal where Ash had gone and wouldn't leave until he got an answer. He'd tell Harry he had a personal issue to take care of. He hated lying to Harry, but this was a once-in-a-lifetime opportunity, and he wasn't going to throw it away. Gabe would get rich, and Mahone would pay for writing the story that ruined his career.

At 11:15, he pulled the gallery's van in front of the old Victorian house. He sat there for a few minutes, contemplating the best way to handle her. And then he pulled out Trevor Iverson's card and probed his cheek with his tongue. Yes, it should work.

Magda heard the doorbell, expecting the restaurant's delivery person. When she opened the inner door, her face drew into a frown when she saw the man's hands were empty. "Can I help you?"

Gabe smiled at her. "Yes, I hope so, ma'am. Are you Ash's mother?"

She smiled back at him cautiously. "Yes?" The storm door was locked securely between them.

He pulled out Trevor's card and held it up to her. "I used to work with Ash. He said if I'm in San Francisco, he'd buy me a beer." His expression was warm and friendly.

Magda hesitated a heartbeat but unlocked the door to invite him in. "Can I get you something to drink?"

He rubbed his jaw. "No, I just need to find Ash."

She clucked her tongue. "Sit down, young man."

When she pointed to a chair, he sat down. The pale woman seemed to weigh barely a hundred pounds. He noticed the artwork hanging on her walls and the heavy curtains at the windows, which impressed him.

"Where did you and my son work together?"

His head snapped toward her. "Oh, several newspapers. It was years ago. When he went overseas, I stayed in the States." Gabe squirmed, wanting the information so he could leave.

Magna's eyes seemed to look through him as she processed the information before responding. "I see. I'm glad he's given it up to change careers." She busied her hands in the folds of her woolen dress.

Gabe's face changed, and he sat up. "Changing careers?"

She grinned before continuing. "Yes, he's working with his father in Paris, but he'll be home soon. Nowadays, with computers and the internet, people can work from anywhere, at any time. I think it's amazing." Her eyes sparkled.

"In Paris." His heart thudded inside his chest.

"Yes, Jacob Safra's shop is in Paris and…" Her face turned pink.

Before she finished her sentence, Gabe stood up. "I better get going, Ms. Mahone, I have an appointment across town and I can't be late."

"I'll tell my son you stopped by. I'm sure he'll be sorry he missed you." She rose to walk him to the door.

He shook the hand she extended toward him. "Thanks, ma'am." He left, whispering Safra, Safra, Safra. His fingers tightened around the steering wheel. He needed to find an internet café. He had some work to do.

Gabe's delivery van had just turned the corner when Rina's Beemer pulled into Magda Mahone's short driveway. When Magda opened her door, her mind was on lunch, her son, and the father he had met for the first time.

Nineteen

The next morning, Ash Skyped his mother. The time difference was a little challenging for them, but they had managed to maintain their daily calls. Sometimes, he would share the call with Jacob because Ash knew he was the person his mother really wanted to talk to. He still felt uneasy about the relationship, but he could see how beautiful it was for them.

When his mother's face filled Rina's iPad screen, he felt that everything was right in the world again. "Hey, Ma. How are you feeling today?"

Magda blew her son a kiss across the miles. "Good. I had a wonderful lunch with your Rina yesterday." She smiled when she saw her son's face. "And I hope your friend got in contact with you? Trevor, somebody."

"Yes, Harry called me from the gallery early yesterday morning to say he'd been in the studio asking about me. I haven't called him back yet, but I plan to do that today."

Her face appeared thoughtful. "That's funny. When he came to see me yesterday, he didn't mention going into the gallery or leaving you a message. In fact, he left suddenly after I told him you were in Paris with Jacob. That was at lunchtime…"

Ash was stumped. "What did Trevor look like, Ma?"

"Well, a big guy. Black hair, and he was limping a bit."

"A big guy? You mean tall or heavy?"

"Oh, very tall."

Ash stood still. "How did you know it was Trevor?"

"Why, he showed me his card, dear. And he told me you'd worked together at the newspaper and magazines and…." She noticed the expression on his face and paused. "What?"

"Don't let him inside the house again, Ma. My friend Trevor is about five and a half feet tall, and he has blonde hair."

Magda stared at him. "Who was it then?"

"Don't worry about it, Ma. I'll call Trevor right now. I love you to pieces. Keep your doors locked. How was your lunch with Rina?"

Her expression shifted again, and he felt relieved. She didn't need to worry, and he knew that spending time with Rina made her happy. Suddenly, he wished he were with Rina too—just four more days.

"Do you have time to speak with Jacob, Ma? He's hovering…" Ash chuckled. When he saw the look on his mother's face, he handed the iPad to his father.

~

Rina Silvan knew it was Jeff the minute he walked into the antique shop. Gritting her teeth, she didn't move from the desk, nor did she acknowledge him when he walked toward her.

"Hello, Rina. Can we talk?"

His puppy-dog look made her angry. How dare he waltz in here as if he were the victim? He wore his good jacket; his hair was freshly cut, and a charming smile was pasted across his face. He looked good, but she was happy to admit it didn't faze her one bit.

"What do you want?"

"Uh, well, I thought we needed closure. It will make us both feel better if we have a long talk." He smiled again before placing his hands on the edge of her desk. He sat down, uninvited.

She peered at him over the rim of her reading glasses.

When she didn't respond, he looked uneasy. "I've left Jenna."

"Oh? She said she dumped you."

His nostrils flared.

"And she said I didn't have to worry about you anymore."

His eyes narrowed.

"What do you want, Jeffrey?" Her voice was steely and firm.

His face drooped. "We were still married when you got that insurance settlement, Rina…"

The light dawned, and her eyes held his like a butterfly under a microscope. "Get out."

"I'm just saying…"

"GET OUT!" When she jumped up from her chair, he moved so quickly that he nearly fell off his own. When she picked up Thor's Hammer, an antique replica her uncle always kept on the corner of his desk, he turned and fled. He slammed the door behind her with such force that she was surprised the glass didn't shatter.

Her body shook violently, causing her to fall against the desk and drop heavily into the chair. Her hands flew up to her trembling lips, and she buried her face in her hands—the ass.

She instinctively lifted her mobile phone and sent a quick text to Ash. "When are you coming home?!" She wasn't playing games anymore; she wanted him, and she wanted him to know it.

She lifted the paper toward herself, which listed the man's name and phone number, and dialed the phone. It was time to sell those gems and claim this shop as her own. Uncle James said she was talented and should use the money to create her personal line of jewelry. And by God, that is precisely what she was going to do.

When Ash saw the text from Rina, a smile rushed up from deep within him. He had just spoken with Trevor and knew the man had not visited his mother the day before. Ash had changed his airline reservation to the next day instead of four days from now. Something was happening. The thugs were still on his trail. He knew that if they touched his mother, he would kill them. Simple as that.

He answered Rina's text, "Tomorrow, darlin."

His phone pinged immediately with a red heart emoji.

That night, Ash pushed open the door to his father's empty house. He hung up his coat and crept up the carpeted steps to the second floor. The light was on beneath his door. Had he left it on? He listened and heard a faint sound from inside. Moving cautiously down the hallway, he inched toward the door and pushed it open.

Laura spun around quickly, her face filled with shock.

"Well, sister, did you get lost, or do I have the wrong room?"

A look of disdain crossed her face, replacing her shock with anger. She lifted the felt bag and held it tightly against her chest. "I knew you and Papa had secrets, and this is what you were talking about. Whatever's inside this belongs to us…and my mother." She shook the small, heavy bag at him.

Ash tried to control his anger as he entered the room. Placing his hands on his hips, he whispered, "Laura, you don't know what you are talking about." He raised his palm toward her.

Laura glared at him, her fingers clenched around the bag.

Ash breathed in deeply, reluctant to argue with her. He raised his hand to pinch the bridge of his nose. What could he say to help Laura understand the complexities of their family history? He couldn't find the right words. "You don't want to do this, Laura. This has nothing to do with you."

"Yes, it does. If my father gave this to you, it is my business and..." Her eyes darted behind him. She lifted her sullen face and attempted to slide past him. Her breath hitched in short, angry gasps.

When he moved toward her, she attempted to sidestep him once more. Reaching out a hand, he gripped her upper arm with his fingers. "That does not belong to you." His other hand clamped over the felt bag.

Laura whipped around and yanked herself free. "You have no rights in this house! You have taken my Papa's kindness, and now you want to move into his business. I won't have it! You don't deserve to be part of this family. Just because your mother couldn't keep her panties on..."

Ash tossed the bag onto his bed and grabbed her by both shoulders. He shook her so violently that he thought he heard her teeth rattle. He leaned in close to her face and whispered angrily, "That was a bitchy thing to say, sister."

"And I meant it! You're a bastard son. Did you think you could march into the Safra family and take over? As if you have rights? You're a bastard!" She was shouting by now.

The hiss from the door froze her in place. She pivoted on one foot to face the sound. Her hair was disheveled, and Ash could see she was trembling.

"Laura! Leave my house now." Jacob's mottled face was so angry that his lips were nearly blue. He raised his arm and pointed to the exit.

She slumped toward the doorway. "But, Papa, I...."

"Go now, daughter. I do not want to see your face until I am ready to talk with you." His usually kind face was shattered, and his eyes were glassy with pain.

When Laura angrily stormed out of the room, he turned to his son.

"I never expected this from her.   I thought…I hoped…"

Ash walked over to his father and put his arms around his trembling shoulders. "Let's go somewhere quiet and eat dinner. This house no longer feels welcoming. And there's something I need to talk to you about anyway."

His father lifted a hand to squeeze Ash's fingers that were splayed over his shoulder. He sniffed and kissed his son's cheek. "Good idea."

Twenty

The men sat at a corner table by the wall in Le Petit Zinc. Ash sensed Rina's presence. Jacob remained pale from his encounter with his daughter, and Ash wished he had confronted her more forcefully. What was wrong with her? She was old enough to understand human frailties, and she claimed to love her father. He was certain she did, but why did she persist in this conflict with him? Dora had welcomed Ash, and he had enjoyed their long conversations. He was eager to know her better; they had even talked about her bringing Jacob to America one day.

He thought about his delight in one sister and his anger toward the other when Jacob ordered whiskey for each of them. The menu was in their hands, and he noticed the old man's fingers were shaking.

When their whiskey arrived, Ash said, "Jacob, cheers." He tapped the rim of his short, thick-necked glass against his father's.

"Santé. I am sorry for Laura's outburst, Ash. I don't know what she said to you before I heard the last part, but I'm sure it was not nice. She and her sister are very different from one another. Their mother was…tough. Part of that is my fault because I could never love her as I should, and she recognized that. She was also shrewd, always testing me. I'm afraid I could never quite trust her. She is what you Americans call a loose cannon."

Ash felt relieved when he saw the man's shoulders relax and heard a laugh. "I know Laura feels I've disrupted your lives and she feels threatened as if I've taken some of your love from her." His dark eyebrows shot up as he lifted the whiskey to his lips. Sip. The fiery liquid burned going down his throat. It was delicious.

"Laura is exactly like her mother. After living with Sadie for so long, I have come to expect her tantrums and grumpiness. Dora, on the other hand, has always been a joy. The girls spark off each other. Dora has fallen back, always apologizing to her sister. But I must tell you that yesterday, the girls had a loud argument, and it was Dora who walked away the winner. I stayed out of it, but I was happy to see her standing tall without allowing Laura to bend her to her will."

Ash nodded. "I like her spunk, and we get along well. We're both surprised to discover that we share many of the same interests. Why don't you come to America? Laura told me she'd travel with you, and she wants to meet Magda." Ash noticed the surprise on Jacob's face and wondered if he'd already considered such a trip.

"It would be a dream."

Good, that's settled. Now, for the other thing I wanted to talk about. Two things. First, I'm flying home tomorrow.

Jacob's face fell. "So soon?"

"Well, the second thing is to tell you why. There's something I didn't tell you before, but it's time I did."

His father's eyes glimmered in the lights above them. He grasped his whiskey glass tightly. Before taking a sip, he placed the glass down on the table next to his empty plate.

"When Ma told me about the cloisonné box, she didn't know how valuable it was. I was so enthralled with it and the idea that you sent the gems inside that I foolishly shared the information with my friend, Harry, at an art gallery. And Harry shared the news with others. That's how I met Rina."

The old man's white eyebrows shot up. "Go on." He picked up his glass and sipped slowly, his eyes never leaving his son's face.

I knew I was in trouble when two men attacked me. I'd already promised Ma I would bring it to Paris. I knew these men wanted the cloisonné box...they told me so. I fought them off and needed to hide. I couldn't fly straight to Paris because I knew they'd follow me. So, I boarded a cruise ship. The only one leaving was from Los Angeles, sailing to Mexico, and I got on it. I didn't know until after we'd left Puerto Vallarta that the men were also on the ship. I was stunned. So, I tossed the box to a woman who looked trustworthy so they wouldn't find it on me… His face was flushed.

"Rina?" Jacob was fascinated. By now, his fingers tapped the rim of his whiskey glass, and his eyes twinkled.

Ash grinned. "Yes, and I fell for her like a ton of bricks when she told me to get lost. When she heard our story, she agreed to help me. Then the men found us when we left the ship in Mazatlán. After that, we bought tickets to Paris, and you know the rest.

"So, now you are leaving tomorrow because…?"

Because one of those men wormed his way into Ma's house yesterday, and she told him I was here. He's still after the box.

Jacob gripped the glass. "Did he hurt Magda?!"

"No. He impersonated one of my old journalism friends. Ma had no idea until I spoke with her this morning that the guy was lying to her. That's why I need to leave now."

"Of course. Of course, I understand. My God, I never thought that a Polish man's cloisonné box would have such an impact on so many lives. You must keep Magda safe, yes, yes…you must go."

Jacob was agitated again, but Ash had no idea how to ease his worries while he felt as upset as his father. All he could think about was those men getting their hands on his mother.

His mind stumbled. "Rina is there for her. I told Ma to lock the doors and keep everyone out. She knows I will be home soon and…"

"…And you want to get back to Rina?" Jacob's eyes sparkled.

"Well, there is that too, you old coot."

Jacob laughed, raised his glass again, and drained it.

The next morning at dawn, Ash was on a plane back to San Francisco. His stomach was still in knots, even though he felt helpless until he arrived home. Rina would pick him up from the airport. It would be a new chapter in his life, and he felt his stomach clench at the thought of Rina on the other end.

As Ash's plane flew west, another plane carried Gabe Pizelli east. The internet revealed several Safra names in Paris, and he sent emails to each of them; when he mentioned Ash Mahone's name, one woman expressed a desire to meet him and seemed eager to learn about their connection. Gabe felt suspicious, but she was the only lead he had.

Laura Safra sat in her office at the Sorbonne grading papers, but her mind wasn't on her students. Her thoughts were on the man whose email had surprised and delighted her. She focused on devising ways to derail the relationship between her bastard brother and her father. She wondered how she could trick this man, Gabe something, into helping her do just that. He had found her through the university website's email. When she had read his note the day before, she had started scheming.

A student knocked on her door, and she growled at him. He shook his head and mumbled, "Later," and sped away. She leaned her chin on her hand and balanced her elbow on the stack of history tests. When she envisioned her half-brother's face and how closely he resembled her father and sister, disgust hit her stomach like a boxer's glove.

She and Dora hadn't spoken for several days, and she didn't like it. Dora had always doted on Laura, and their twinship had always been solid. Laura enjoyed being the leader over Dora, the weaker twin. She sat back in her stuffed chair and swiveled to look out the window. The trees were bare, and the wind blew harshly against their beauty, which she loved. Maybe she should call Dora and shame her into apologizing for being so nasty. But then she shook her head. "Let her come to me." Laura's angry lips spit the words into the room.

Across town at Safra's Gems, Dora and her father faced each other. Jacob leaned against his large display table, listening to his daughter.

He could see that she'd dug in her heels. Dora didn't want to take sides against her sister, but she was firm. "Papa, you've been alone for a long time. Don't you think it's time that you make life decisions without thinking of your daughters? We are both adults. Even though I wonder about Laura sometimes…"

Jacob clucked his tongue. "Yes, we both know that. But she feels threatened, like always. Only this time, she stepped over the line. She tried to steal something that belonged to Ash, and I don't want to talk about it." He lifted his hand to the back of his neck and closed his eyes for a moment before he turned to his daughter again.

"I know I'm being wicked, but she makes me so angry. And now Ash has left us, and I already miss him. I'm amazed at how close we have become in less than one week. He is a good man. Why can I see it and Laura does not?"

Her father shook his head and didn't answer.

"So, when do we go?" she asked him impishly. "I've wanted to go to America for years, and now that the shop is doing well, I know Chloe won't mind if I spread our wings. She has contacts in New York and Phoenix. I think it might be time to expand into the San Francisco area."

Jacob smiled tiredly. "I agree, but right now Ash and I are working on a new idea. He thinks I should expand. I hired him as my marketing agent in the United States. He's going to talk with Rina. Her jewelry business could use my gems." His voice became more animated. "And if you can open a link for your shop there too…well, that's icing on our cake." He was thoughtful for a moment before Dora broke in again.

"Is Rina his girlfriend? Every time he mentioned her name, he got a silly look on his face. So do you, Papa."

Jacob laughed. "We talk about a new marketing plan for my gems and your clothing shop, and you only ask about Rina?" He chuckled. "She is a wonderful girl. I wish you could have met her. She is the woman who introduced me to Skype. The one who brought Magda's face on the screen of the iPad…when I saw Magda and talked with her." He grinned as he remembered, placing his hands on both cheeks.

They exchanged a glance, and then both of them burst out laughing.

Twenty-One

Jenna Silvan turned the corner just as she spotted her sister's Beemer backing out of its parking space in front of the antique shop. She slowed down so Rina wouldn't notice her and then parked discreetly around the block. Unsure of how long Rina would be gone, Jenna's plan was now set, and she felt anxious to get started.

The two young men she had hired stood on the corner. One had his foot braced against the brick wall of the diner, and the other was squatting beside him on his haunches. She shook her head as she thought about how easy it was to hire them. Once she had her share of the shop's sales, she would give them a bonus. Easy, easy, easy.

As she approached the shop's front door, she inserted her shiny new key into the lock and stepped inside. The locksmith had not questioned her ownership once she showed him her Silvan ID. Less than five minutes later, the young men joined her.

"Did you bring gloves?" she demanded.

They nodded and rolled their eyes skyward.

"I don't want you to steal anything. Just mess this place up real fast so she thinks she's been robbed, and then get out of there. Got it?" Jenna's eyes gleamed in anticipation, and then she walked out. "Fast!"

The men jumped as if they had been spun from a coiled rope. Five minutes later, each of them left with a hundred-dollar bill stuffed inside their pockets. They laughed all the way back to their motorcycles.

An hour later, Rina waited in the mobile phone lot at San Francisco airport for Ash's plane to arrive. When her phone rang, she became sentimental at the sound of his voice.

"I just landed. No checked bags. I'll be outside waving my arms."

"I am absolutely on my way this minute. Don't move."

"I won't move as long as I know I'll see you in a few minutes."

She caught her breath with a smile and hung up.

Ten minutes later, he opened the passenger door, and she flew into his arms. His gentle lips took her breath away, and she pressed against him. "Mmmmmmm… so nice."

Horns began to honk behind them, prompting them to pull apart unsteadily.

"Guess I'd better drive." She chuckled and shifted her gaze to the man she hadn't been able to stop thinking about since leaving him alone in that hospital room.

"Before we drive to Ma's, I want to see your shop. She promised to keep her doors locked, and I want you all to myself."

His words motivated her as she made her way to San Rafael. She was eager for him to notice the new lettering on the front glass door. Even though the name was Silvan Antiques, she had hired a company to add her name below in curlicue script, Rina Silvan. Her new logo featured a swirling bird on a cobalt blue background, reflecting his cloisonné box. She hoped he would approve.

She was near the Richmond-San Rafael toll bridge when he reached his finger over to slide it along her cheek. "Don't do that, Ash. I'll drive us over the edge." She turned toward him for a moment and noticed his dimple creasing a hole in his cheek.

Rina sped through the Fast Track Lane and pulled into her parking spot a few minutes later. She turned to him, and their eyes met. "I missed you so much, Ash. Suppose I'm embarrassing you, too bad. I say what I feel."

He reached for her hands. "I've missed you, too, and your honesty is one of your best features. Let's go inside." The air felt brisk, and a slight wind blew the hair off his neck, reminding him that he was home again, winter in San Francisco.

When they reached her front door, they stopped, and he gazed at the logo on her glass door. Turning toward her, he lifted his fingers to outline the blue entwined logo. "I love it."

She stepped closer to him while he wrapped his arm around her. As she opened the door, they entered together.

And then they stopped.   Both of their faces were studded with shock.

"Oh no! I've been robbed." She hurried inside the shop and began searching through everything on her desk. Then she ran into the back room to check her safe. Luckily, it was closed tight as a drum.

Ash followed her and held up his hand. When he confirmed they were alone, she checked all of her valuables and then sat down at her desk. "There doesn't seem to be anything missing. What do you think they wanted? Do you think it's the guys from the ship? How could they know who I am or where I...? We need to call the police." Her eyes grew round.

"They can't possibly know about this shop. It must be something else, Rina." He got up and locked the front door. When he returned to her, he opened his arms, and she launched herself into him.

"I don't like it."

"What?" He reared back to look down at her.

"Not you, the mess." She burrowed back into his chest.

"Call the police first. Tell them nothing's missing, and then I'll call Ma. I'll help clear up this mess, and then we'll see her. Is that good?"

Rina's eyes told him yes when the words wouldn't come. She couldn't imagine what the vandals were seeking. Her silver, drawings, and jewels were all intact. Her files remained in the cabinet. It was merely a mess scattered as though a tornado had swept through the room. And she was fairly certain nothing was missing. Her stomach tightened with anxiety, but seeing Ash in the room with her as he purposefully rearranged her shelves full of antiques eased some of the tension.

She dialed the police. "No, just make a note of it. Don't send an officer over, just be aware that this happened in my area. Yes, thanks." Rina sighed as Ash dumped the last bit of trash into her bin.

~

Jenna sat hunched over her steering wheel when she saw Rina and a tall man emerge from the antique shop. Her eyes narrowed. Who was he? She was certain she had never seen him before, and she liked what she saw. She pursed her lips between her teeth and studied them. She noticed the man's intimate touch on Rina's back and the way he tucked her hair behind her ear as he opened her car door.

"Interesting. Big sis has a new boyfriend. Jeff might be interested in knowing about **that**." Jenna sent a text to Rina's ex-husband and laughed. "Oh yes, he will not like that one bit.

Jenna started her Volvo and inched out, trailing a few cars behind her sister's Beemer. When she saw them heading toward the Richmond-San Rafael Bridge, she veered off. There was no way she was going to fight that horrendous traffic. She glanced at her watch and sped up. She didn't want to be late for Rina Silvan's appointment with the realtor at one.

Twenty-Two

Magda slipped her fingers behind the curtain to watch her son and Rina walking toward her house. Their hands were linked, and Magda's heart did a jig. She liked the young woman and had yearned for her son to find someone after his disastrous marriage so many years ago. His way of life in those days didn't contribute much to a successful marriage, but the woman he chose was wrong from the start.

The doorbell rang and she hurried to let them inside.

"Hey, Ma. You look great." Ash leaned down to wrap his arms around his mother. "The last time I saw you, you didn't look so good, and to be honest, I wasn't sure if you'd ever get out of that bed."

"Now look at her. Makeup, hair, nails, and smiles." Rina squeezed the older woman's hands, and their eyes met.

Magda grinned and led Rina and Ash into the large sitting room. "I have a new lease on life. Doctor Lomax says the tests came back negative, and he's still shaking his head. I think it was because I knew you would find my Jacob, Ash." She blushed.

"That reminds me, Rina." He rummaged through his backpack and took out her iPad. "Dora bought Jacob his own iPad the day before I left so he can Skype his girlfriend whenever he feels like it."

"Ash!" Magda's pink cheeks made her look healthier than he'd seen her in months. "Now tell me what's going on. You said that man who came to see me was probably one of the bad guys, but you promised to explain…" Her brow furrowed.

Rina leaned forward.

"I know it wasn't Trevor. I called my friend Harry at the gallery because Trevor said he'd gone there first and left his card. Harry said he couldn't find the card after he left me a voicemail message. After a little more conversation, I learned that his deliveryman had been there. He told Harry two people had attacked him in an alley. He was limping and his neck hurt. Sound familiar?" he asked Rina.

"Oh no…It was the man after the cloisonné box?"

He nodded and stared at his mother. "He's dangerous, Ma. He could have hurt you. Why did you let the man in the house?"

Rina and I expected a lunch delivery from that Portuguese restaurant I like so much. I thought it was the man with our food. I didn't unlock my storm door until after he showed me the calling card and told me he was your friend. I won't be taken in so easily next time," she said staunchly.

"There better not **be** a next time," he answered stiffly. "What did you tell him?" He reached for his mother's hand.

She hesitated for a moment before whispering, "I told him you were in Paris with your father and mentioned the name Safra."

"Oh." He pulled out his mobile phone to call Jacob. Jacob answered on the first ring. "We have a problem, Jacob. Ma told the man your last name is Safra. He wants the box and the gems. He may come after you. Maybe you should call the police. His name is Gabe Pizelli, and his employer said he left for a while. I have a terrible feeling he's headed for Paris because he thinks I'm there with the box."

He heard Jacob's resigned sigh. "What does he look like, Ash?"

After Ash described Gabe, Jacob asked if he could talk to Magda. He handed the phone to his mother and reached for Rina's hand. When he heard his mother's voice change, he grinned and pulled Rina into the kitchen, where he quickly drew her into a long kiss.

"Do that again, Ash. I haven't caught up yet."

He obliged, and they stood close for some minutes before they heard Magda's shoes tapping toward them.

"Okay, you lovebirds, let's have some lunch."

"Who are the lovebirds?" Ash asked and winked at Rina when he saw his mother blush again.

Magda had a pot of white chicken chili on the stove. While Rina laid out the bowls and spoons, Ash sliced the olive bread and took out the butter from the fridge. As they sat down to enjoy the hot soup, they discussed the mess in Rina's shop, her new logo, and his new job as an agent for Safra's Gems. Before finishing their meal, he brought up his idea regarding the complex business arrangement between Safra Gems and Silvan Antiques.

Both women's mouths hung open for a moment before they exchanged a long glance. Rina reached for Ash's hand. "I like it. I'm reinventing myself in more ways than one now, and being part of Jacob's life would be so special."

She turned toward Magda. "What do you think about a business arrangement with Jacob's gems for my jewelry line? I haven't told either of you about my Uncle James' gems."

"And?" They both said in unison.

"He gave me several little bags of gems along with his buyer's contact information. He told me I should sell them and create a personal line. The gems in the velvet bags are not the kind I want to use. And I'm meeting with a buyer in two weeks," she finished smugly.

Ash pulled her hand into his. "I'm glad to hear this. You'd be making a fresh start with new money. I imagine adding Parisian gems may even add a special allure to your jewelry."

She nodded, feeling even more relieved that she'd accepted the buyer's offer. Since Ash was now Jacob's agent, she would ask him to accompany her. Despite her concerns about her shop being damaged, her mind was swirling with new possibilities.

~

Across the bridge in San Rafael, Jenna Silvan walked into Latimer Properties. The bell above the door chimed, and a blonde woman glanced up with a quick smile. "Hello, I'm Sylvia Latimer. You must be Rina Silvan, the owner of Silvan Antiques?"

Jenna smiled back at her. "Yes, I am." She pulled papers out of her briefcase and handed them to the realtor after shaking her hand. These are the blueprints for the shop, along with the most recent appraisal. I'd appreciate it if you could begin showing the shop as soon as possible, as I'm planning to move out of the country. Also, please call this number to contact me instead of the shop number; I'd appreciate it."

"Of course." The woman took Jenna's card and taped it to the blue file on her desk. After she slipped the papers inside, she was surprised when Jenna stood, shook her hand again, and left without another word. The blonde's face reflected her confusion. However, Jenna was sure the woman wouldn't ask questions when she considered the commission on the shop's sale.

Jenna laughed as she drove back to her condo, wishing she had the forethought to install a video camera to capture her sister's reaction when the first prospective client arrived to buy the shop out from under her.

In Paris, a world away, Gabe Pizelli sat down for a *café au lait* next to Laura Safra. He was surprised by her beauty but wondered why she seemed so morose. He was grateful that she spoke English; the only French he knew was oui, yes.

The café was situated near Sorbonne University, and everyone inside knew her. Whenever the owner saw her walking toward him, he always had her café au lait waiting at the table by the time she sat down. She didn't have many friends, which she attributed to her role as a history professor. As she toyed with the cup, she waited for the American to explain why he wanted to find the bastard son.

"Thanks for meeting with me, Ms. Safra. I'm looking for Ash Mahone. As I explained in my email, I heard he was in Paris with someone named Safra, and I'd hoped you could...." He saw her mouth go tight.

"Who told you that? He isn't with me. He's with my father, Jacob Safra. He owns *Safra Gems*. His shop is not far from here."

His mother. Seems to know a lot about what's going on here with your father and Ash Mahone.

Laura's eyes narrowed. "I'll just bet she does. That son of hers tried to weasel his way into my father's business. She's the one who put him onto my father in the first place." She sipped her steaming coffee and quickly pulled her tongue back, surprised when it burned her.

Gabe's brows shot up. "Really? What could he want with your father? I wonder if he's trying to sell those..." He wasn't ready to share his information with the woman, but his curiosity buzzed in his mind.

"What? Sell what? Did he bring Papa something in a small, heavy container?" Laura sputtered, her eyes drilling into him.

Gabe watched her white-knuckled grip on the cup's handle, waiting for it to explode into pieces. He studied her a moment before picking up his cup. Her reaction and words startled him, but they also raised more questions than answers. He watched other Parisians and some tourists seated, sheltered from the cold. The sounds of soft French conversation were soothing. He leaned forward. "You don't like him. Why?"

She pressed her lips together. "No, I don't like the man, but I don't have to tell you why. Why do you want to find him?" When her light brown hair snagged beneath the curlicue clip that held her scarf, she jerked it free in annoyance.

"He has something I want. And I guess you know exactly what I'm talking about." He gripped his knee with one hand, and the other wrapped itself around the small coffee cup. Again, he noticed the way her brown hair floated around her face and the way she held her head as if she were a celebrity.

"Yes, but not exactly. I heard him and my father talking about something my father has hidden from us for years." She pouted.

"Years? He knew your father for years?"

"No."

His head lifted quickly, eager to learn more. He waited for her to elaborate on her response, but she didn't seem inclined to add anything. "Where is Ash Mahone now?"

"The last time I saw him, he was in my father's house. Just before my father threw me out, I thought the man was taking advantage of him. And he chose Ash Mahone over his daughter!" she snarled.

"Really? So, where's your father's house?"

Laura looked up quickly. "Don't you dare contact my Papa. I'll help you find Ash Mahone on one condition. And that is, you must make him disappear from our lives. Make him gone."

"Make him gone?" He wasn't sure he understood.

"Yes, gone, completely gone." Her voice rose with each word.

Gabe was shocked. She was serious. She wanted Ash dead. What had the man done to her? Gabe had never killed anyone except in war, and he certainly wasn't going to start now. Yes, he wanted the blue box and jewels, but murder? No way. He stared at her.

And she stared back. "There's a lot of history with him and my father that my sister and I just learned about. Our lives were fine before he jumped into our family. Now I want him out. When he also tried to slip inside my father's business, I tried to stop him. If you want the little bag of goodies, I'll help you. You know what I expect in return." Laura lifted a hand to open her blouse and tugged it just enough to show cleavage.

Gabe's eyes lingered there, but he knew she was playing him. "No. I've done a lot of stupid things, lady, but murder isn't one of them. Find someone else. I'll find the damned man myself." He pushed his chair backward.

Her eyes went wide. He realized she thought he was a stupid American, and he had surprised her. The box was important, and he had already spent too much time and money, but this was a whole new ballgame. He wanted Mahone to suffer for ruining Gabe's career, but not to die.

Laura tapped her nails on the table and moved her cup in circles. The steam had vanished from the coffee, and she made no move to drink it. She pressed her lips together and took a deep breath. When he didn't say anything more, she lifted the cup to her mouth.

Gabe had watched the emotions play across the woman's face, and he didn't like what he saw. When he got up from the table and grabbed his jacket to walk away, she followed him out onto the sidewalk.

"Please, Gabe. May I call you Gabe? I over-reacted. Of course, I don't want him dead, not really. I want him...away from us." She stared up into his face.

He turned toward her. "I'll find your father's shop. I can talk with him there. I don't need his home address." He walked away from the café and headed toward the Metro. More determined than ever to put this behind him, he wasn't wasting another moment with a woman who was willing to kill someone. He thought fleetingly that he shouldn't turn his back on her.

Laura scrambled after him. "I get off at 3:00. Come back to the café about half past and I will take you to meet Papa. I know we can work together," she said to his back.

He raised his hand in agreement without breaking his stride and continued down the crowded street. Horns blared from every direction, and a smoke-belching bus nearly knocked him off the sidewalk. He had never been to Paris before, and he marveled at the historic stone buildings and wide sidewalks.

He wished he had time to enjoy it, especially after spending all his money to get there. He fiddled with his street map to guide him back to the hotel, but changed his mind and started walking toward Notre Dame Cathedral instead.

His thoughts turned dark, and he exhaled heavily as he saw the Seine and the stone bridge leading to the small park. He stuffed his hands in his pockets and sank onto a bench to watch the boats floating along the water. He needed to think. Working together was one thing; killing was definitely another. And the woman had to understand that.

Twenty-Three

Jacob Safra never imagined the cloisonné box would be so valuable. He also never thought he'd see it again. When he had given it to Magda over fifty years ago, it was empty. And then across the miles and over the years, he'd poured his love into it for a son he hadn't been able to watch grow into manhood.

Now thieves were trying to steal it, injuring his only son and his new friend, Rina. He shuddered at the thought that the man might have incapacitated Magda, too. He knew she was in remission from cancer, but who could say how long that would last? He had to do something, but what?

Ash took the cloisonné box and jewels back to America with him, as he should. Jacob encouraged him to hide them in his bank safe deposit box. Ash agreed. Until they could figure out what else to do, that was the plan, and he couldn't think of a better one.

Jacob turned his thoughts to Ash's innovative ideas, an American envoy, and the possibility of becoming Rina's gem distributor—his first American client. His heart skipped a beat as he imagined creating gems for her new creations: silver jewelry.

"I hope Rina likes the idea," Jacob whispered. He glanced at the clock above his front door across the room. Ash was likely discussing it with her and Magda right now. His chest felt tight. Talking to Magda was the highlight of his day. Thank God Dora understood. But how could he ever accept Laura's reaction to the whole situation? Jacob wasn't sure she could. Yet why should he have to choose a daughter for his long-lost son? He rested his head in his hands, and his shoulders trembled.

It was 2:30, and he wanted to go home for the day. He had suddenly lost heart in the shop and thought a nice nap would do him good. He pulled the shade down on the front door and locked it. Strolling outside, he found his Fiat wedged between the alley and a dented blue Volkswagen. The wind had picked up again, so he held his coat tightly across his chest.

When he got home, his bed looked so inviting that he dropped his shoes onto the floor and climbed in without taking off his clothes. He was tired, so very tired. He pulled the coverlet up to his chin.

Ten minutes after Jacob fell asleep, Laura and Gabe arrived at his gem shop. When his daughter saw the closed sign hanging on the door, she became concerned. She was also worried; usually, when her father left his shop during the day, his manager was at the counter. However, today the shop was dark inside.

"This is his shop?" Gabe asked her, clearly disappointed.

"Yes, and he doesn't close until five. I don't know what's going on. I told you our lives have changed dramatically since Ash Mahone entered our midst. This is just one more thing."

"Can you call him? All I want to know is where to find Mahone." She huffed beside him and paced back and forth in front of the shop. Still undecided, she took him to the café and ordered another coffee. He followed suit. She yanked her mobile phone out of her purse and held it to her ear. When her father didn't answer, she bit her lip. Then she called her sister, Dora.

"*Halo?*"

"Dora. Where's Papa?" she demanded.

"It's 3:30. He is at the shop, I should think." Her voice was frosty.

Laura knew Dora wasn't going to add anything. "He's not here. Do you think I'd call you if I wasn't worried about him?"

Dora hesitated. "Did you call him at home?"

"Yes." Laura hissed.

"I am just now leaving the dress shop, so I'll check on him...at home."
She was quiet for another moment. "I'll text you when I find him
and call you back if I don't." Dora hung up.

Laura's eyes blurred.

Gabe watched her and was surprised to see tears from the woman, who
seemed so stoic and tough. When he noticed her looking at him, she
lowered her head as if to hide her vulnerability.

"Now what?"

"My sister is going to the house now. Drink your coffee. We wait."
Laura tapped her fingers on the tabletop. While watching other
patrons, she glanced at her watch every few minutes, but the phone
didn't ring. She'd waited.

Dora found her father's car in the garage across the city. She slipped
into the house and listened. Nothing. As she quietly walked up the
steps, she leaned against the door to his bedroom, pushed it open, and
saw the lump in his bed.

Suddenly, she felt frightened. Papa rarely napped during the day
unless he was unwell. She hurried to his bedside and leaned down to
listen to his chest. He was breathing. When she lifted her head, his
eyes popped open, startling both of them.

She reached for her heart, and he grabbed his bed covers.

"Dora?"

"Papa?

"What are you doing?"

"Why are you sleeping during the day?"

"Why shouldn't I take a nap if I want to? I'm not a child, I'm an adult."
He noticed the hurt look on his daughter's face and reached out a hand.

"Forgive me, Dora. I am not myself." He swung his legs to the edge of the bed and allowed her to help him up.

"Let's get a drink, Dora. I need to talk to you."

A few minutes later, they shared glasses of red wine while sitting on his oversized couch. The afternoon darkened as the wind whipped against the windows. He turned on the gas fireplace, and they enjoyed the flames dancing behind the glass.

"Laura called me because you weren't at the shop."

"She hates the shop. Why would she be there in the afternoon?" he asked curiously.

"I don't know, Papa, but she sounded worried. I should tell her you are fine." She took out her mobile phone, texted her sister, and then tossed it back into her purse.

He sighed deeply. "I do not know where to begin except at the beginning." He gripped the stem of his wine glass and stared into the dark red depths, taking his mind back more than fifty years. His daughter, not yet forty years old, a young widow without children, was studying him when he finally pulled his eyes away from the wine.

"Papa," she said as she leaned over to touch his arm gently. "I know this is important, so just begin. I will try not to interrupt." Her warm brown hair slid across her face as she readjusted herself next to him and sipped her wine. "I may need to pour more of this, though." She smiled deeply into his eyes and heard him chuckle.

"I told you and Laura only part of my story, only about Ash. Now, you need to know the rest. When I was around twenty years younger than you, I fell in love with a young girl I had known for many years. She was a Gentile, and we were friends despite her parents' dislike for Jews. In those days, it wasn't easy to be friends when parents drilled it into their heads at a very young age that we don't mix. For Magda, our love was impossible. I was so sure it wasn't…" He sipped more wine. And then he thrust his fingers through his tuft of silver hair and made a soft sound, remembering.

Dora didn't move.

"When she told me her parents were going to emigrate to America, I panicked and begged her to marry me. To stay in Poland. But she was adamant and said it was too important to her parents. Two days before they left, I tried once again, and she said that she loved me, but…" He looked up at Dora and swallowed. Then he whispered, "But we made love without marriage. For that, I was sorry, but it was the most beautiful time of my life. I am sorry, Dora. Your mother and I just never…" His breath caught.

"I know, Papa. I knew your marriage was not happy and often wondered if it ever was. Go on." She sniffed, got up, and poured more red wine into her glass. She held up the bottle to her father and grinned when he raised his glass in response.

"After they took Magda away, I promised myself that I'd save my money so I could find her in America. I couldn't get her out of my head or my heart. Before she left, I gave her a blue cloisonné box and told her I'd poured my love inside for her to keep it always. I knew she would touch it, breathe in my love, and remember me. It took me ten years to find her, and when I did, I learned she had a son— my son. And she was married to a man who was raising him as his own."

Dora gasped but did not say a word.

"Magda wouldn't divorce him. I didn't ask her, but I knew this to be true. I did not see Ash, but I was so heartbroken that I left her in anger." He looked into his daughter's face. "And I married Sadie, a woman who was kind to me, but I did not love. I was sorry for that, and she recognized it, becoming hardened and very unhappy. And so was I. My greatest happiness was the birth of you and Laura."

"And for *Maman*?" Her eyes lifted to his, and she held her breath.
He looked sad and pursed his lips. "Nothing made Maman happy, not even you girls, Dora." His lips trembled as he lifted the glass to rest them against the rim until he could drink from it.

"You see, when I moved us to Paris and my shop became successful, I began to send Magda a gem every year to put inside that box for my son. She sent me a letter telling me she would one day give him the blue box filled with the gems. She also promised to send the boy to me with the box when he was ready or if she couldn't keep the secret of his birth inside her heart any longer. I knew when he arrived that something urgent had happened."

Words finally escaped Dora's lips, "What happened, Papa? All you told us was that you had a son before you married *Maman*. Maybe if you'd explained this to both of us when you told us about Ash in the first place, Laura would…"

"Magda has cancer."

Her face fell. "Oh, no. Poor Ash."

"But she is now in remission. I know you and Ash have discussed my traveling to America to see her, and I would like to do that. But before we talk about that, I need to tell you what the problem is now." He took another breath and gripped his knees with his hands after placing the wine glass on the table.

"You mean Laura?"

He laughed a little. "I wish it were only that. No, some men are aware of the cloisonné box and the jewels. I had no idea it was so valuable until Ash mentioned it to me. They have tried to take it from him, and I just found out one of the men approached Magda. He even got into her house! Thank God, he didn't hurt her…" He wiped his face with his hand. "…but he could have. That's why Ash left Paris early this morning."

Dora hadn't expected that. Again, she kept silent, and he smiled at the sweetness on his daughter's face. If only Laura were more like Dora; however, as quickly as the thought entered his mind, he chastised himself.

"Ash is now my agent for *Safra Gems* in America, and I may have Rina as my first client. She helped Ash save the blue box from the bad guys. Rina is a jewelry artist and has inherited an antique shop near San Francisco. She may want my gems for her creations, which would make me happy. She is a thoughtful and loving woman, and I'm hopeful she and Ash…" He chuckled.

Dora was fascinated by the story of her father's life. She leaned toward him, and her eyes spoke the words before they fell from her mouth. "When do we leave, Papa?"

He pulled his mind back from the thought of seeing Magda and wasn't sure how to respond. "I must get Laura to change her mind about Ash before I leave the shop for a little while, Dora. You can understand that, can't you? I can't leave with the awful feelings between us. She ransacked Ash's room and was stealing the little blue box of gems when he caught her last night. I made her leave the house."

Dora's hands twisted around her glass, one finger gliding up and down its length as she processed this news. "Oh, God. No wonder Laura was so upset today when she couldn't find you." She lifted her phone at the sound of the ping, her face contorting with anger.

He glanced at her mobile phone. "What did she say?"

She read the text aloud and felt bile rise from her stomach. "He must tell us next time he leaves early. I am sitting with an American who is looking for your brother."

Jacob shook his head and made a sound with his tongue.

"Your brother, not our brother. I think if you wait to get her mind right, Papa, you will be in your grave before you can see Magda again. I know we aren't going to San Francisco to see Rina about your gems. I wasn't born yesterday, was I?"

He blushed and finished his wine. "One more glass and I'll be off to bed," he said impishly. "You are right. I must call Andres to tell him he will be managing the shop for the next few days or weeks. Can you leave your dress shop for that long?" His face was hopeful, reflecting a much younger appearance than his seventy-one years.

"I will make it happen, Papa. I want to meet this mystery woman. If she is anything like my brother, I will like her. And if you still love her after a lifetime, maybe she will be the mother I always wished I had." Her lavender scarf slipped from her neck, and she wrapped her fingers in its folds. Her face told a story that Jacob already knew; a heart that had never known the loving arms of a mother or the kind words a child needed to hear.

"Yes. Make the reservations, and I will Skype with Magda tonight to share our plans with her. And she can tell Ash we are coming." He glanced at his watch, trying to calculate the time difference. His expression turned inward, and his lips formed a small smile.

Dora laughed and stood up to purchase their airline tickets.

Twenty-Four

Laura had just finished her second glass of Cabernet when her phone pinged to alert her of a text. When she read her sister's message, her lips thinned, and she responded without thinking. After the angry words slid across her screen and she pressed the send button, she felt a moment of unease.

"Your father?"

"No, Dora, my sister."

"And?" Gabe's face mirrored her impatience.

"My father went home early. We will have to wait until he returns to the shop tomorrow. Ash should be with him. He and Papa are joined at the hip these days." She made a disgusted sound with her mouth.

"What time does he open the shop? I want to be here when they arrive." His head tilted toward the bakery, and his eyes scanned the area, searching for a place to wait in the morning. It was getting colder now that it was dark, and he felt anxious to leave.

"I don't want to know how you make him go away, Gabe. Just make it happen."

He looked at her as if she had grown horns. "I told you already---I will not kill the man. I'll hurt him if I have to, but it's the box I want…and the jewels."

"Jewels? There are jewels inside that damned box?" Her eyes suddenly changed, and she crushed the napkin in her fist. "Whatever is inside belongs to our family." Her voice turned dark.

Gabe pulled back and stared at her, mouth agape. Something was off about the woman. He didn't care what it was because he had too much money invested. She could go elsewhere. The ticket to Paris cost a fortune, and the cruise hadn't been cheap either. He thought of Brad and the lie he'd told him about visiting his sister in Virginia, but his guilt over cutting him out only lasted a moment. Now, this woman wanted her share of the pie or maybe even all of the damn pie.

He pushed back his chair and zipped his heavy jacket up to his neck. "Cold here, I'm going back to the hotel. I'll be in touch with you tomorrow." His long strides carried him down the block and out of sight before Laura could argue.

Laura grabbed her purse and slung it over her shoulder after checking her phone again. No response from Dora. When would she learn that her father and Dora spoke the same language? Papa and Dora. Laura and Sadie. It had always been this way throughout her life. With her mother gone for several years, she felt as if she were drowning in loneliness. She and Dora weren't close anymore, and her father had never been her confidant.

After a slight hesitation, Laura dropped her purse onto the small table, looked around at others in the café, and pulled out her phone once again. She shot Dora another text and decided afterward that she didn't have to be lonely. Gabe was a good-looking man, and he'd stirred feelings she hadn't felt in a while. Her body was tingling for a man.

"Merde." After scrolling through her contact list, she pressed the call button, and within seconds, a man's voice came through on the other end.

"*Halo*, Laura."

"Can I come over?"

The man chuckled. *"Oui."*

~

Across town, Jacob's wrinkled hand held the airline itinerary, and his brows shot up. "Not much time to get packed, is there?"

Dora's smile matched his. "No, Papa, so you better get started. I'll go home to get everything in order and return in a couple of hours. I'll order a taxi to arrive here at 6:30 in the morning. What about the shop?"

Jacob scratched his chin. "I'll wait until morning to call Andres to tell him he has the shop on his own while I'm gone. No sense in bothering him at home tonight. He always opens the shop early, and I'll call him from the airport. He always asks to work more hours so that he will be happy."

She nodded and blew him a kiss as she opened the front door.

~

Gabe Pizelli sighed loudly as he unlocked the door to his hotel room that night. He wasn't thrilled about spending an extra day in Paris, but he'd do what he had to do. He'd come too far to fret about the additional money it was costing him. "In the scheme of things, this is peanuts," he whispered as the door shut behind him and he entered the dark room.

His mind was riddled with worries. He was betraying Brad. He'd lied to Harry and him about a sick sister in Williamsburg. He let out another sigh. The guys accepted his story without a second thought. Gabe switched on the lamp and sat down on his bed. With his shoes in a pile along with his shirt and pants, he lay back on the bed and stared at the ceiling. Why did life have to be so messy? When had he decided it was okay to steal this damn box? Why couldn't he just be happy working for Harry? When he thought of Mahone, his expression hardened as questions surged through his mind.

Visualizing a confrontation with Ash Mahone didn't slow his racing thoughts. Laura Safra's face kept interfering with the plans he devised and then discarded. Damn that woman. She was a tough cookie. And he liked tough ladies. But he focused on the cloisonné box and its contents.

"Why does she think it belongs to her family?" His words sounded strange in the empty room. He clasped his hands together and laid them on his chest, mulling over their earlier conversations. No, he'd stay away from her. Crawling beneath the covers, he fell asleep within minutes as jet lag took over and his mind stopped reeling from the mind-bending chaos.

Two hours later, Laura quietly let herself out of Andrés' apartment. He had fallen asleep afterward, as he always did. She shook her head, thankful that he didn't expect anything more from her. And her father remained unaware of their occasional sexual relationship. Her mind began to slow. She knew he'd be upset, and their relationship was barely held together by chewing gum as it was. She had always wished it could be different, but since her mother died, the die had been cast. She was her mother's daughter, while Dora was her father's daughter. It wasn't going to change overnight; she doubted it ever would.

As Laura left Andres's house that night, Dora loaded her car. She called her partner, Chloe, at the dress shop and told her she'd be gone for three weeks. She threw on play clothes. At the last minute, she added fancy clothes for the elegant realms of San Francisco.

The lure of America had fascinated her for years, and after talking with Ash for hours, it was now more than a dream. The dress shop already had contacts in the United States. Why not add San Francisco to the list? She chuckled as she parked in front of her father's house. "Why not?" Her voice startled her. *Oui*, why not? *Boutons et Nœuds* in Paris would be Buttons and Bows in California.

Twenty-Five

Magda heard the computer chirping while she put away her late lunch dishes. The wind had calmed, and the sun shone on the fir tree outside her kitchen window. No clouds disturbed the bright blue sky, and she was feeling good. The computer chirped again. Wiping her hands on the nearest towel, she hurried into the alcove where her computer stood on the antique desk. She grinned and sat down quickly.

When Jacob's face filled the screen, they smiled at each other like schoolchildren. His blue eyes sparkled with that special look she'd never forgotten, and he appeared as if he'd just won the lottery.

"Magda, how are you feeling, my dear?"

She nodded, afraid that her thoughts would turn into words and spill out. Her nervous fingers clenched tightly into fists, and she licked her lips. "Jacob. I am fine. You?"

"I'm better than fine. Do you have two empty guest rooms?" His eyes twinkled like the sunshine she'd just enjoyed out her window.

"Yes, I do…" she said slowly. Her heartbeat sped up, and she placed a hand across her cheek with excitement. "When are you coming?"

"Our plane leaves Paris in the morning. Dora has already ordered a taxi, and then poof. We will be there. Please tell Ash to pick us up. Dora will send him the timetable and… I will see you soon, Magda." The last part of his sentence dwindled into a whisper, and his blue eyes pooled.

Magda saw him lift a white handkerchief to his nose and sniff. She shook her head in wonder. "I will prepare your rooms. And make food. Lots of food. Do you still like that special sausage, Jacob? I will get some at the Polish market and..."

Jacob laughed. "Do not overwork yourself, please."

"I will do whatever I **want** to do." She sat up straight.

Jacob shook his head and couldn't stop grinning. "You are still the same Magda as always, aren't you?"

She smiled at him and ran her fingers through her short hair, which was now filled with silver strands.

Without another word, he waved two fingers goodbye to the woman across the miles. Once in bed, her answering smile was the last thing he remembered when he fell asleep.

Magda called Ash. When she hung up, she burst into tears. The thought of having Jacob in the same house with her was almost too much to bear. Just a few weeks ago, when she thought she was at death's door, she thanked God for this extra time. To see this man again and to be held in his arms felt like a dream she had wished for forever. She stood up, covered her face with both hands, wiped away her tears, and rushed toward the kitchen. She had shopping to do and meals to prepare.

When she pulled her Audi out of the garage, her face wreathed in smiles, and a long grocery list rested on the seat beside her. "Don't overwork myself? I've waited a long time to cook that sausage for you, Jacob. A very long time."

~

A few miles southwest of San Francisco, in San Rafael, Rina stared at the woman. She must have heard her wrong. Golden sunshine streamed blissfully through her freshly washed windows. Brand-new valances complemented the bright red cushions on the chairs she had arranged in a new seating layout. She had been working on the ambiance, altering the feeling when customers peeked into her window or wandered into her shop. She was not only reinventing herself but also Silvan's Antiques. New glass display cases showcased four new jewelry pieces created by Rina Silvan. She felt giddy.

She had been standing, admiring her display when a blonde woman and two men walked into the store a few minutes earlier. She seemed to be explaining or instructing them on something.

Rina heard the woman discussing the architectural features of her shop. As their conversation progressed, Rina's mind seemed to go blank as the woman's voice outlined her antique store for the men.

"Why are you showing these men my shop?" She was sure she'd misunderstood the woman. Her muscles tightened, and her stomach had butterflies clamoring for release. Shock lit the woman's features.

"Oh, I am so sorry. The owner must have forgotten to tell you she's put the shop up for sale. I met with Rina Silvan two days ago and..." The woman looked guilty and fanned her face, looking between her clients and the woman she assumed was an employee. She lifted a file to thumb through it. "...here it is, it was early Tuesday morning."

"You met with Rina Silvan?" Rina laughed, and the butterflies flew away. She braced herself against her display case and crossed her arms over her chest.

"Yes, I'm sorry she didn't mention it to you. I assume when she sells the shop, you will have to...." The woman faltered and took a few steps back when she saw Rina's angry face.

Rina's eyes glittered. "When she sells the shop...?" At that moment, her phone rang, and she nearly spluttered out her words.

Ash's face illuminated the screen. When Rina answered "Silvan's Antiques" in a clipped tone, her eyes remained fixed on the woman's face. She stood rigidly beside the men, who now appeared more than nervous.

"Hey, you. I have news." She knew he would use any excuse to call her, but this time, it sounded different. She heard excitement in his voice, but she couldn't think about that now.

"Oh? I do too. And I'm mad as hell." She gripped the phone tightly and watched the threesome back up again. One looked ready to run out her door, and she wanted to use her foot to boost them along their way.

"Uh-oh. What happened?" Ash was quickly alerted by her tone.

"Are you coming to San Rafael anytime soon?"

"On my way." Ash hung up and turned his car toward the bridge. The traffic was snarled, but that was nothing new. She needed him, so he ignored it and took a deep breath as he headed toward the bridge.

Still standing stiffly in Rina's shop, Sylvia Latimer's face reflected her discomfort upon overhearing Rina's conversation, and she turned to her clients, who were now fidgeting. She pulled her purse strap over her shoulder and stood tall. "We should come back when Ms. Silvan is in the shop or after hours. I don't want to cause you any problems, Miss."

Rina spread both hands across the top of her display case, where just moments earlier, she had gazed inside to admire her first artwork for sale. She straightened herself as tall as she could and examined the blonde woman closely.

"**I am Rina Silvan**. I don't know who you are trying to sell the Brooklyn Bridge to, lady, but you picked the wrong woman." Rina's elbows tightened as she saw the shock on the three faces before her.

The realtor was dumbfounded. "But… the woman identified herself as Rina Silvan. I'm certainly not making this up. Latimer Properties has a stellar reputation, and for you to suggest that I…" Her mouth formed an O, and she shook her head as her face flushed pink.

The men had already left before the realtor could stop them. She glanced between Rina and the men, opting to follow her clients outside instead of facing the wrath of the woman in front of her.

Rina was so rattled by the encounter that her legs felt like jelly. Her head felt so heavy that she had to raise her hands to hold it onto her neck. What in the hell just happened? What was this woman talking about? It just didn't make sense. The shop was in her name, she was licensed with the State of California, and everything was in order. Her attorney had assured her that all the legal paperwork was appropriately recorded.

~

Ash tried to untangle the knots in his belly. Now what? Their relationship was so much more than friendship, so he knew by the tone of her voice that this was no small thing. They'd talked for hours before he took her home to her condo the night before, and she'd told him life was sweet. He'd ached to stay but hadn't wanted to disrupt their fragile relationship. Yet, he thought. Not yet.

When Ash rushed into the shop, he found Rina still standing beside her glass display case. He pulled her over to her desk and sat her down before she could fall. Her face was pale, and her body trembled beneath his hands. As he pulled up another chair to sit knee to knee, her eyes lifted toward him in confusion.

"Tell me."

"When I…the woman came in…and the men wanted…"

"Rina. What the hell happened here this morning?" Ash leaned in toward her and placed a hand on either side of her face, drawing her gaze into his. He noticed the confused expression on her face and saw her lips quiver, so he pulled her close and pressed them to his. She allowed him to hold her and let the kiss deepen. When she pulled away abruptly, he nearly dropped her.

"Jenna! By God, I know it was Jenna." Rina pressed her hands against her cheeks, pushing them upward so her eyes were just a slant on her face. She bit her lips fiercely, then slammed her hands down on the desk. "Damn. Damn. Damn!"

"Okay, I give up. Was it your sister who did this to you? You said a woman and some men…" Ash couldn't grasp her disjointed statements, clearly confused. He recognized she was aggravated and annoyed, unsure of who he was supposed to be angry with. The sister? Strange men with her? Vandals?

"Jenna is playing her dirty tricks again." Her eyes narrowed, and she pulled her hair up and away from the shorter strands that had grown long enough to curl. When the story bubbled out of her, she leaned back in her chair and crossed her arms tightly.

Ash laughed.

Rina's eyes glared. "It is not funny, Ash." Her cheeks puffed out as she shot another glare in his direction.

"Isn't it? Your sister has a wild sense of humor, and for her to come up with this ridiculous joke is one thing. To see your reaction is another, and I'm sure she would have loved to witness the look on your face when this realtor came into the shop to sell it out from under you. And for her to instigate that stunt… to pretend she was you…" He laughed again.

Rina's lips tipped up just a second before she burst into laughter, too. Her stomach smoothed out. When she laughed harder, she reached for a tissue to wipe the tears as they streamed out of her eyes.

His laughter joined hers, and his body eased.

"That snarky rat. She's angry that Uncle James left me the shop. She tried to make mischief a few days ago, and I kicked her out. She is no longer part of my life, and this puts the nail in the coffin. It's funny now, but when it was happening…Holy crap, I was so mad I nearly hit the poor realtor. I thought she was trying to scam me with these guys and…God, she must be in a pickle with her clients now. Now that's funny too." She doubled over with laughter again.

He grinned and shook his head. He reached out to take her hand and squeezed gently. When his fingers moved toward his lips, she leaned in and touched them with her own, letting out a moan that promised more.

"You said you had news? Not sure how much more news I can handle." She tossed her head back so her hair covered her ears again.

"They are on a plane as we speak." The skin around his eyes wrinkled, and the dimple in his cheek deepened.

"They?" Rina was confused.

Jacob and Dora. They are arriving on Air France at 12:30 tomorrow. He called a little while ago. I should have the itinerary on my phone by now, but I didn't check it before calling you. And then, when I spoke to you, my news flew out of my head. He was laughing again as he slapped his hand on his thigh.

She chuckled and clapped her hands. "Excellent! It will be wonderful to see Jacob again. And I'm sure Magda is over the moon with excitement."

"Yes, she sounded like a kid when she called me."

"I'm anxious to finalize our new business arrangement. I told one of my old customers I might use gems from Paris in my jewelry, and you should have seen the look on her face. This is going to be fun, blending all of us together. It will be like having a family…"

"Yes, just like a real family, Rina." He sat there, looking at her with a silly grin on his face. Then, he inhaled deeply, stunned by the implications of having the family he had longed for after all.

She saw that her words struck him like a bucket of cold water. He meant it. It would be like a real family, one he had never imagined, which she had helped bring together. She watched his face and appreciated what she saw. She realized it was a face she couldn't envision living without. The look of understanding on his face made her exclaim, "Now that I'm an only child, you can tell me what it's like…but oh wait! You aren't an only child anymore, are you?"

Two sisters. One likes me. One doesn't. I'm not sure if I even want Laura in my life. I don't like how she treats her father. My father. Our father…" he stuttered and shook his head again as if the facts were still too astounding for him to believe.

Rina covered his hand with hers. She saw pain and disbelief etched on his face. She wondered what it would be like to wake up one day and have a sister she never knew existed—and actually liked her. She'd never know; she certainly didn't want the one she already had. And this recent debacle was just one more reason to avoid her. One day, she hoped to stop all her antics completely so she could live her life without wondering what she would do next. For Ash, though, it was a fantasy come true.

"It seems like you're still dreaming, huh?"

"Yeah, like that."

Twenty-Six

Gabe huddled at a table in the corner of the bakery with his back against the wall, giving him a good view of the comings and goings on the street. He'd rather watch from across the street, but he knew the old man would be there soon, so this was good enough. He'd wander into the shop a few minutes after it opened. He pulled back his sleeve to check his watch. He had twenty minutes to wait.

"May I get you more *café au lait, monsieur?*"

"Yes, and one of those curly bread things with cheese and ham inside, too?" He raised an eyebrow and smiled.

The girl grinned at him and hurried away.

A few minutes later, Gabe bit into the hot croissant and groaned with pleasure, wondering when he'd ever tasted anything so buttery and delicious. The coffee was different, too. He could get used to it. Thinking of all the cafés in the San Francisco area where he worked, he dismissed them one by one. Nope, he'd never tasted anything like it or the coffee either.

His watch reminded him it was time to get moving, but the coffee and croissant kept him glued to his chair. The guy wasn't going anywhere, and now that he knew Mahone was next door, he wasn't in a rush to show his face. He doubted he had the little box with him. Hmmmm, maybe he left it at the house? Laura hadn't given him her father's address, but it shouldn't be too hard to find. He had managed to find the mother in San Francisco pretty easily, hadn't he?

He finished his croissant and ordered another one. Maybe he should rethink this plan. He didn't want to leave empty-handed this time or feel Mahone's teeth again either. He sat back and leaned his head against the wall before lifting his coffee cup to his lips. Yes, he needed to get to the old man's house.

Andres let himself into the gem shop with a little dance in his step. After raising the door's window blind once he was inside, he prepared for business as if by habit. When Jacob called earlier that morning, he'd been surprised but not unhappy. He hoped Laura might visit again now that her father was out of town. His brow creased, wondering why she hadn't mentioned Jacob's leaving the night before. But, of course, she'd had other things on her mind. Yes, she certainly did.

Whistling, he cleaned the new inventory and placed gems into crystal wine glasses in the front display window. Jacob always thought of ways to entice his customers, and this certainly did the trick. Before noon, he had more customers than he could count. He knew Jacob would be happy. Andres whistled some more.

~

Gabe found Jacob Safra's address within an hour of leaving the bakery. When the taxi driver dropped him off in front of the beautiful brownstone, he exhaled in surprise. "Nice," he said to himself. "Very nice."

The windows were dark, clearly indicating that the house was empty. He glanced around and, realizing he was alone on the street, slipped between the house and its neighbor. The French doors at the back of the house were locked, so he pressed his face against the glass and peered inside. Afterward, he checked all the windows and smiled when the one near the dining room slipped open. He listened for an alarm, looked around to ensure he wasn't seen, and pulled himself up into the house.

~

During Laura Safra's lunch break at the university, several hours later, she called her father's shop. When Andres answered, she spoke brusquely, "Andres, I need…"

"Well…*Halo* to you, too, Laura. Do you feel better this morning after our late-night dessert?" His voice dropped a notch intimately.

Laura rolled her eyes. "Yes. I need to talk to Papa. It's important."

Andres's eyebrows rose. "You are joking, right?"

"Now, why would I do that? Of course, I'm not joking. Let me speak with Papa, please."

Andres was getting annoyed. "He's not here."

"Is he away for lunch?"

"No," Andres answered tersely.

"Well, where in hell is he?" She tapped her manicured nails on top of her desk and moved a stack of test papers to the corner.

"He's gone." His voice was now as clipped as hers.

"What do you mean he's gone? Where has he gone?"

He called me from the airport this morning.

"What?! Why is he at the airport? Where did he go?" Her voice rose a notch with each question, and her fingertips danced a jig on her desktop. Her impatience with Andres was at an all-time high.

"He said he was flying to America."

"What? That man talked him into it. I know it. So, he and Ash are headed to San Francisco? What on earth for? Huh. Probably to see that woman. Did he tell you anything else? Ash must have taken him!"

"Ash? He left two days ago."

"What?! Why didn't anyone tell me?!   What else did Papa say?"

"Only that he was going. And I don't like the tone of your voice, Laura. Who do you think you're talking to?" He hung up.

Laura wrapped her fingers around the phone and then called Dora's number. She reached a voicemail. After that, she called the dress shop.

"Halo? *Boutons et Nœuds*.   How can I help you?"   The young woman's voice was too sweet for Laura to stand.

"Please call Dora Safra to the phone.   This is her sister."

A pause before the young woman's voice said, "I am sorry, madam. Ms. Safra is not in the shop today."

"Oh?   Where is she?"

The young woman remained silent. "Would you like to speak with Ms. Cahuzac, madam?"

"Yes, if that's the only way I'll get answers!" Her fingers were now scrolling furiously across her desktop, and she stood up to pace the room. The trees outside her window swayed in the wild wind. She wrapped her sweater tighter around her shoulders.

"*Halo?*" Chloe Cahuzac answered breathlessly, as if she had been pulled away from an important meeting, which also angered Laura.

"Chloe.   Where's Dora?   Out to lunch?   Sick?   What?"

Dora's partner sucked in her breath.   "Gone to America."

"What the hell?" Laura's voice was seething with frustration.

"Yes, Dora is making connections for the shop, and she left this morning.   I'm surprised your sister didn't tell you, Laura. Would you like me to ask her to call you when she checks in with me tomorrow?"

Laura heard laughter in the woman's voice. She'd never liked her. She took a deep breath. "Thanks." When she hung up, she slammed her hand on the desktop and sent all the papers crashing to the floor as if a cyclone had swept through the room. The anger on Laura's face matched the force of the onslaught, in sync with the wind tearing across the lawns outside.

~

Across Paris, Gabe Pizelli dropped his feet to the floor. The house was large, with many places to explore, and he was methodical. After about an hour, he finished on the first floor and headed up the winding staircase. The second floor consisted entirely of bedrooms and bathrooms. He found nothing. The home was filled with antique furniture, floor coverings, and beautiful curtains the likes of which he'd never seen before. The old man was wealthy.

He slapped the bottom newel post as he jogged down the stairs again to find the kitchen. By the time he reached it, he was hungry once more, so he peered into the refrigerator and pulled out a piece of chicken. Now thoroughly disgruntled, Gabe stopped being careful, no longer caring if Jacob Safra knew he'd been there. When he sat down to chomp on the chicken, he noticed a small doorway off the living room and jumped up to investigate.

A den. Why hadn't he thought of that first? How had he missed the alcove? Of course, he would have hidden the box in a safe. Behind the large, antique desk hung a massive Pinot painting. He slid the frame aside, grinned, and wiped his greasy hands on his wool jacket. He began to play with the combination. Click. Turn. Listen. Click. Turn again. Listen. He heard the last pin drop into place, and then he pulled open the door to the safe.

When he reached inside, he found papers and small boxes. He turned on the desk lamp and stretched the cord to use it as a flashlight. Peering inside, he was furious; there was no blue box. He threw the lamp onto the floor, where it dangled from the receptacle in the wall beside him. He yanked out the cord, causing it to crash onto the carpet and scatter broken ceramic pieces everywhere. He kicked the leg of the desk, and the matching lamp met its end beside its counterpart.

Inhaling an exasperated breath, he pulled out his mobile phone and entered Laura's number. "I'm at your father's house. He's not here, and neither is the box. I'm going back to the shop."

"It won't do you any good. He's on his way to America. And I learned that Ash Mahone left two days ago. He's already in San Francisco. I have a feeling my sister is sitting beside Papa on that plane right now."

Gabe was speechless and hung up on her. He had drained his savings to buy the plane ticket to Paris. He had told everyone lies, and now he had missed Mahone. He shattered everything breakable. He walked out the front door and left it ajar. The mess mirrored his mind, dark and angry. He wished thieves would come in and take everything. Three hours later, he was on a plane, too furious to sleep in the cramped Air France seat.

Laura sat in a bar, finishing her third glass of Cabernet, contemplating how life can slap you in the face and then laugh about it. Gabe was in a rage. Who knows what he left behind? She cradled the empty glass.

Andres had stopped whistling. When he closed the gem shop, he wondered why Laura was so angry. She had shared his bed for months, and she had never treated him like that before or after sex. And he didn't like it.

Jacob and Dora's plane was approaching San Francisco Bay. Groans of satisfaction filled the cabin as passengers began to collect their belongings.

Magda had been up at dawn preparing food. Her apron was splattered with sauce, and she couldn't remember the last time she felt like singing. So, she did.

Twenty-Seven

During that same night, she kicked the covers away from her feet. His fingers gently massaged her back in all the right places and encircled her waist. He spooned against her. "Mmmmm…you feel *so good*," Rina whispered into the dark and pushed her body against his. She felt his body warmth seep into hers, and she stretched languidly toward him, trying to feel every inch of his skin.

Dawn was still hours away. She moved closer to him, smiling as she enjoyed the exquisite feeling. She had wanted him for days, fantasizing about his kisses in all the right places. Her eyes drifted toward the dark window. "Oh…yes." Her whisper was urgent as she turned toward him, yearning to feel his chest against hers. She couldn't recall the last time she had been so tormented with longing. She relished his intimate touch.

"Do you like it?" he whispered into her ear.

She smiled into the dark and twisted around to move toward him. "God, yes." When his palm cupped her breast, she was sure she couldn't stand another moment of anticipation.

When his fingers squeezed so hard it hurt, her eyes shot open. His arm tightened as she jerked away from him, and he tugged at her hair until she whimpered. Suddenly, she knew it wasn't Ash in bed with her. How could she have thought it was? They hadn't gotten this far in their relationship. She'd been dreaming. Kicking outward with her foot, she encountered warm skin and heard a loud yelp in the dark.

"Dammit, Rina."

Her body stilled. "Jeff? What in the bloody hell are you doing?"

He twisted the loose hair above her buzz cut with his hand, pulling it around her ear. He leaned into her neck. "Does he kiss you like this?" He dug his fingers into her jaw, dropped his lips to her nape, and trailed wet kisses around and down until he reached her right breast. "Does he hold you like this?"

Rina lunged away from him, driving her elbow into his neck. "Get off me!" Her heart was pounding so hard that she had to press a fist against her breast to keep it from bursting out of her chest.

"I'll bet you don't tell your new boyfriend that, Rina. I heard you were right chummy with him, and you know what? Our divorce isn't final yet, so I still have sex privileges, so let me show you how good it can still be for us." Jeff's words came in rapid breaths as he tried to hold onto her twisting body.

"Jeff, get off me! We aren't ever going to have…stop it!" She felt his hot, panting breath on her body. She tried to move between the blankets and his body, but his hands drifted between her legs. When she squeezed her knees together, she attempted to head-butt him.

He threw her down and climbed on top of her. When he stared into her face, the gleam from the streetlight cast a golden shadow onto the bed. His eyes glared, filled with malice. His palms dug into the soft flesh of both buttocks, squeezing hard. "If we have sex before our divorce is final, the decree could be voided and you'd still be Mrs. Sebring."

She laughed tightly. "I was never Rina Sebring. I was always Rina Silvan, and I still am. What is wrong with you? You're so full of…" Jeff kissed her to stop the flow of words spilling toward him.

She jerked away from his wet lips and continued, "The big man who decided my sister was more appealing, more beautiful, sexier…more everything than I was? You chased her. You never realized the only reason she wanted you was because you were mine? Did you forget that I read all those sickening texts and the words that slut sent to you? And I read every intimate response you sent to her?"

Jeff Sebring tensed. "It wasn't like that. I never meant to turn to her, but we hadn't had sex in months. You didn't want me, and she did. Did **you** forget? You hadn't wanted sex since Lizzy died. And that was years ago. Twenty? I had to fight for it all the time. You didn't want it. I did. And Jenna was…"

"You dare mention her name to me?" Rina pulled her arm away from him and stretched her fingers toward the bedside table. She found the small device next to the lamp where she had left it. Thinking quickly, she moved sensuously against her ex-husband to catch him off guard just long enough to wrap her fingers around the faux flashlight. She smiled in the darkness, pushed the lever to the second notch, and brought it around to his ribs.

The zap blast knocked him off her, sending him sprawling onto the floor, writhing and screaming. "Aaarrghhh!" The whimpering that followed sounded like an animal as he scuttled away into the dark.

When she sat up on the side of her bed to pull the chain on her lamp, the light temporarily blinded her. She held the pink device in front of her and pointed it at her ex-husband, shaking it back and forth.

He saw the taser in her hand and jerked away from her with disbelieving eyes. His dark hair fell across his forehead, and he crossed his arms tightly in a protective gesture, still shaking with guttural groans. "My God, Rina."

"Get out of my house and never come back. Go back to Jenna and tell her I'll use it on her if she plays any more tricks on me. I don't know what you're both trying to…" Rina's heart beat so hard inside her chest that she had to hold it still with her free hand. Still pointing the Taser at Jeff, she got off her bed and reached for the phone. "Leave this minute or I'll call the police now!"

He inched his naked body toward the door, still on his hands and knees. When he looked at her, their eyes locked in a silent battle that shocked them both. "The police can't do anything when I haven't laid a hand on you except as a husband for a wife. Just try it, Rina. I had every right to get angry because you're sleeping around." His laughter was cynical. "And we're still married. Remember that."

Rina rolled her eyes and shook her head. "You are out of your mind. You and your screwed-up values make me sick. The divorce is final in one week, and it can't be soon enough for me. And if you think for one minute you have rights to my bed or my insurance money, you better think again. You signed off on that to get rid of me. Don't you remember? Since we're talking about memory here, that should be a big one. What's the matter? Did Jenna decide she wanted that money, too? I don't want either of you in my life!" When Rina yelled those words, a rush of relief surged through her body, and the last remnants of sadness from her lifeless marriage drifted away.

Jeff stared at her. "Jenna and I are through."

"Really? That should make this okay?" She found it hard to swallow. Raising a hand to her neck, she realized she had never actually told him off, and maybe that's what she needed to do.

"I hoped if I came over here to show you that I still loved you... that you'd listen. I went crazy when she told me you were with another man. You can understand that, can't you, Rina? I never knew how sick I'd feel when I imagined you were letting another man touch you, make love to you...have you naked...when you wouldn't give it to me." His voice changed to sweet talk within moments.

Rina was thoroughly disgusted; she lifted the Taser, and without consciously aiming, she pointed the device at Jeff's crotch. "If you aren't out of here in ten seconds, you get this again." Her eyes squinted toward him, and her arm straightened out steadily.

"Okay, okay!" Jeff yelled, lifting his hands, palms outstretched, to shield his body from the pain her weapon could inflict. His eyes narrowed as he stared between the Taser and her angry face. When he realized she was serious, he pulled himself up by the bedroom doorframe, stood with his legs braced, and attempted to button his shirt and pull on his pants.

She nodded sharply toward the door. He struggled to walk a straight line, and she smiled. The taser had done its job. Rina tried to suppress the grin that was eager for release.

"This…this… isn't over. We're still married, and what's yours is half mine. Don't forget it. I'll see my lawyer in the morning. I am not stupid. You owe me. I'll tell the courts I was forced to sign it away."

Rina's taser hand shook slightly with the emotion she was trying to suppress. She didn't put it down until she watched him limp out of the bedroom, hands shaking and covering his ribs. When she heard him slam the back door, her entire body began to tremble. She got up and deadbolted the door, wondering how he had gotten into her house after she'd changed the locks. Moving across the room, she checked the locks on every window. Everything was secure, but how did he get inside? Her hands shook so badly that she had to press them against her waist to hold them still.

A silent scream moved upward from her belly, and she slumped down on the bed again. She glanced at the clock—two o'clock. Chills swept over her after her fury dissipated. Rina pulled the covers up to her neck and stared at nothing. She blinked back blinding tears. She turned off the light and lay there for a long time, trying to unravel the knots gathered in her mind. She vowed to get a restraining order against Jeff. Isn't that how you do it? What about all the women she'd read about with restraining orders whose husbands or boyfriends still got to them? Hurt them? Killed them? Was Jeff capable of killing her for the insurance money? Would he?

Rina jabbed her fist into her pillow and rubbed her fingers over her body, trying to erase the sensation of his disgusting hand. It was then that she remembered she had been imagining Ash's arms around her when Jeff had woken her up, imposing his nastiness on her.

It was Ash she wanted. And she knew Jeff was right. She hadn't wanted him to make love to her for years. She had stopped loving him long ago. How could she blame him for falling into another woman's arms? She hadn't cared, except that it hurt her ego. She felt relieved that it gave her the leverage to see an attorney. She had better call hers the next morning to see if Jeff was right about the money. And to tell her Jeff had broken into her condo and ...

Even though he had been unfaithful and she had a strong argument, the divorce was already set in stone and was final.

But one thing wasn't finished, and it was time to put an end to it. Jenna. She told Jeff she had seen Rina with Ash. That meant her sister had been watching her. Her wicked antics were one thing, but now Rina had two people to fear. And she couldn't ignore it any longer. She wiped the tears from her cheek and reached for her mobile phone. It was time to bring Ash into the equation, time to stop resisting the attraction and admit they were a team. And teams worked together.

Rina took a deep breath and whispered his name as the phone rang. Once. Twice. She closed her eyes. "Ash."

"Rina? What's wrong?" His voice sounded urgent.

She sniffed. "I know it's late, but…"

"I'm coming over."

She hung up the phone and felt the burden of fear fall away.

Twenty-Eight

Dora's head throbbed. The airplane trip had drained her, and she marveled at her father's ability to walk through the terminal as if he'd just had his first cup of coffee. As she trailed behind, her laptop and purse slipping off her shoulder, she noticed his knuckles were clenched around his carry-on bag.

"Papa. Slow down. We have plenty of time to catch our next plane." Her brown hair curved towards her jaw, and the purple and black shoulder scarf hung askew. Striped leggings peeked out from beneath a black tunic, and she yanked the scarf onto her shoulder again.

The loudspeaker blared above them, "…if anyone approaches you and asks you to take their bag or…" Dora snickered and shook her head. The lights were bright, and other passengers rushed by them, each focused on another plane or walking toward baggage claim.

Jacob stopped and turned to his daughter. He lifted his wrist to check his watch. "You're right. Sorry, I guess I'm just…"

She laughed. "I know, Papa. But have a heart. I'm not as young as I used to be." Her shoulder ached from the heavy bag, and her head hurt.

"Ha-ha," he muttered and reached for her arm. "Here, old lady, let me help you along."

She chuckled, and they hurried toward the boarding gate. They had an hour before boarding the next plane. "I need an aspirin. Let's find a seat, and you can watch everything for us. Do you need to…?"

"No, I'm fine."

After he settled into the chair and gathered their small pieces of luggage around him, she hurried down the corridor. She'd been concerned that he might not be up for the trip, but he was behaving like a man half his age. She reflected on the past few days, and it hit her that he wasn't acting like an old man at all. She acknowledged that his seventy-one years were now more like the new fifty. She chuckled and couldn't suppress the smile that crept across her lips. Then, she laughed out loud.

His new hopefulness had added a layer of the same to her. She'd been lost in a fog for months, even years, since her life took such a drastic downward spiral. Ash made all that change. She couldn't understand her sister's unflagging anger when she learned about Papa's son. Why couldn't she see how Ash had brought the dance back into Papa's step? Couldn't she notice the difference in his face, his voice, and when he spoke of Magda? Dora's lips turned down. Of course. That was it. Laura had always been Maman's shadow, and she'd transferred that animosity toward Magda's son. She wasn't just jealous of Ash; she was protecting Maman's rights.

Her head pounded by the time she swallowed the aspirin, fluffed her hair, and looked into the restroom mirror. Her blue eyes stared back at her with a new awareness. She wondered if Laura knew she was reacting so harshly to their brother because of her misplaced loyalty to their mother. She splashed cold water on her face and blinked away the droplets that had slipped into her eyes.

Another woman stood nearby and splashed water on her face. "It helps to wake us up, huh?"

Dora smiled at her, nodded, and wiped her face dry. "Oui." When she returned to the boarding area, she smiled. Her father's head was thrown back, and his mouth was wide open as snuffling snores filled the space around him. When she nudged him, he jerked awake and grinned impishly.

"You caught me. When do we leave?"

"Soon, Papa." She glanced at the boarding monitor. "Thirty minutes. And then we have five and a half more hours to fly toward San Francisco." Her body sagged with tiredness, but her mind snapped awake. She would soon see Ash again. The instant connection between the siblings was stronger than her twin bond with Laura. It was almost as if she and Ash were the twins, and Laura was the older sister.

She leaned her head back against the seat cushion, pleading with the aspirin to work its magic. Soon she'd be with her brother, possibly making exciting connections for Boutons et Nœuds in Paris, and… meeting her father's childhood sweetheart. Her body responded to the thought with a smile. Yes, this was going to be an adventure. Her headache began to ease just before the loud boarding call echoed over the PA system.

~

When Ash arrived at Rina's condo an hour later, he hadn't even knocked on her door before it swung open, and she threw herself into his arms. The house was dark except for a lamp in the back bedroom. He wondered for the hundredth time what had led her to call him in the middle of the night.

"Rina." He held her close to his chest, smoothing her hair with his hand as he calmed the trembling in her body.

"Thank you for coming, Ash." She pulled him along beside her and turned on the stained-glass tree lamp next to her creamy leather couch. The light filtered across the room in shades of red, yellow, and green, giving the room the appearance of a church window. Scents of lavender and thyme wafted from the candles she had burned earlier.

When he sat down beside her, she took a breath and blew it out loudly. "I know you must think I'm a nutcase, but I was scared. I'm usually so together and independent, but Jeff scared the hell out of me."

"Jeff?" His eyebrows knit together as he tried to follow her.

"My ex-husband broke into my house a little while ago and tried to…well, get intimate."

"Did he rape you?" Ash's nostrils flared.

"That was on his mind, yes. I tried to talk him down, but he was focused and deliberate. I thought… Well, I thought it was you for a few seconds. But of course, it wasn't. It shocked me to find him in my bed."

This time, his eyebrows shot upward into his hairline. "What?"

She laughed, embarrassed to admit it, wondering why she had said anything about that at all. "I was asleep, and when he woke me, I was imagining that…well, that…"

Rina bent over toward her knees and tucked her hair behind her ears. Her face was flushed, and she felt a tightness in her lower abdomen. She closed her eyes, leaned back to lift her head, and took a deep breath. When she turned to look Ash directly in the face, he was smiling and shaking his head from side to side.

"Sounds like you were having a nice dream." He reached over and pushed her hair back behind her ear again. "Tell me what happened after you and I…" He chuckled and put his hand on her knee.

"He wants my insurance money. Jenna must be watching me because he said she told him I was with you. He wanted to know if you…If you and I…well, let's say he took it badly. He pretended he still loved me and said some things that I have to admit are true. He felt cheated. The man is out of his mind. He said he was going to call his lawyer to get his fifty percent. I know he can't do it, but it frightened me." Her fingers danced back and forth along her thighs, and her white nightgown fell in soft folds around her calves.

"You're afraid he might get his hands on the money?"

"No, I'm afraid because he didn't break in. My locks are new. The windows are locked tight. I don't know how he got into my house so quietly that I didn't hear him, and he crawled into my bed. He must have a key to my condo." Her voice shook, and her lips wobbled. When she sniffed, she let him pull her onto his lap.

"How did you get him to leave then?"

He felt her laughter before he heard it.

She pulled the pink flashlight off her table. "It looks like a flashlight, and when you push the first notch, it **is** a flashlight." When she saw his questioning face, she pointed it toward the door. "But when you push the second notch, it changes..." The loud buzz streamed across the room.

Ash reared back and stared at her. "Remind me to make noise when I come in and to **never, ever** get into your bed without your knowing it. And to **never, ever** get on your bad side."

She lifted her head and looked at him steadily, holding back the snicker that wanted to find its way out. "I think that's an excellent idea, Mr. Mahone." She lay her head on his shoulder and let him rock her back and forth. And she wasn't afraid anymore.

"It doesn't make sense for me to go home since I'm picking up Jacob and Dora from the airport in..." He looked at his watch. "...in a few hours. Any chance I can stay here and you can come to the airport with me?"

She nodded and pulled him toward the light. When she pulled him down onto the bed beside her, he whispered, "I'll be a gentleman and wake you in time...but if you want to cuddle..."

Rina's heartbeat slowed as she snuggled into his arms while he pulled the blanket over them. Although she was sure she'd never be able to sleep so close to his warm body, the next thing she knew, he was tapping her on the shoulder. The aroma of freshly brewed coffee filled the air, and he was grinning at her.

"You have thirty minutes, darlin, so drink this and get moving. It will take us about two hours, and we'll have a long wait, but I can't trust the traffic between here and the airport."

She nodded. Their fingers sparked when she reached for the mug, and they both knew he might not be able to remain a gentleman for much longer. They didn't say a word to acknowledge their steamy attraction to one another because words were unnecessary. Instead, they sipped their coffee as the sky began to brighten in the east.

She was dressed and ready before his deadline, but her encounter with Jeff still shook her. Rina couldn't get the question out of her head. Where did he get the key? She made a mental note to change the locks again. Trying to keep the quaking in her belly at bay, she drank the rest of her now-cool coffee and followed Ash outside.

Ash pulled her hand into his after he started the car and turned toward her. "Rina. I won't let anyone hurt you again. I promise."

She smiled at him, attempting to ease the tightness in her throat as he navigated the car toward San Francisco Airport, 31 miles south of San Rafael near San Bruno. The traffic was already terrible, and congestion kept them on the bridge longer than anticipated.

"Glad we left early. The plane is probably flying over the mountains toward us about now." He shifted the car into second gear as the vehicles inched their way south like ants toward honey.

Rina scrunched down in her seat and laid her head back. She turned her face toward the window to watch the misty fog and inhaled his scent. Moments later, she closed her eyes as he navigated the wild San Francisco traffic and admitted that his intensity had knocked the breath out of her.

Twenty-Nine

Magda hadn't slept all night. Her nerves were frayed, and her stomach was having a party inside. What would Jacob think of her wrinkles, her black and silvery hair, and her jiggling skin? She wasn't a young woman anymore. Sure, they'd seen each other on Skype, but it wasn't the same as flesh-and-blood bodies touching one another. She would hug him, kiss his cheek, and maybe rub his shoulders. It had stunned her when she'd laid her head on the pillow the night before. Memories from their time together when they were young pulled her back in time, reminding her how she'd loved him. But that was a long time ago. They were adults now. They'd lived their lives and shared a beautiful son, so of course, they would feel a bond.

Her breath caught as she looked at the clock beside her bed once more. About six minutes had passed since she'd last checked it. Making a sputtering sound, she tossed aside her covers and swung her legs over the edge of the bed. After she had shoved her toes into her yellow slippers, she slipped her arms into her fluffy robe, wrapped it around herself, and tied the long sash as she walked toward the kitchen.

It was still dark, but she could see flickering lights across the neighborhood from her kitchen window. A secret smile split her face once more. I'm not a young woman anymore, but he's no spring chicken, either. She filled the coffee pot with water, dropped coffee beans into the grinder, and chuckled. God, she was excited. Her hands shook as she dribbled the coffee grounds into the filter, snapped the lid shut, and pressed the start button. It was five o'clock.

Several hours later, the jumbo jet taxied onto the San Francisco tarmac. The Golden Gate Bridge appeared as a small peak in the fog near Angel Island, where the sun would soon cast its golden shadow. It was windy and cold, but the passengers in seats 13-A and 13-B remained oblivious. Their thoughts were on the man waiting to gather them up.

Ash and Rina had been sitting in the mobile phone lot discussing their ambitions for Jacob's shop and her jewelry ideas for hours. It felt like they could talk about anything—time flew by. Just after noon, Ash's phone pinged. When he read Dora's text, "We just landed," he grinned and showed Rina the message.

"How does it feel to no longer be an only child? I know I asked you before, but has it really hit you yet, or does it still feel like a dream?" Her face was filled with soft points of pleasure and she rubbed her hand over his fingers where it cupped the transmission knob.

Ash shook his head in tandem with his grin. "I love it."

He sent a quick response to Dora: "Text me again when you pick up your bags." When he put his phone back into his pocket, he lifted his hand to the nape of his neck and turned his head. Thoughts ricocheted through his mind like bubbles in a champagne glass.

Sitting beside Rina had made him so warm that he was ready to remove his coat. Now, waiting for his father and sister, he added goosebumps to the mix. He reached for her hand and pulled it to his mouth, running his lips along her palm. When she arched toward him, he wrapped his arms around her, and she melted into him. He kissed her deeply and heard her groan.

"I know," he said.

Overcome with emotion, she touched her tongue to his lips. "Ash."

His phone pinged again, and they exchanged a look that conveyed more than words ever could. Both were breathless, their eyes promising what their bodies recognized. But now, they had a family to meet.

From the shadows, an hour later, Magda watched as Ash parked his car in front of her house. She had just finished her fourth cup of coffee to wash down the egg she had forced herself to eat, and her belly was jumping around like jelly beans in a basket. Pulling back the lace curtain in the front hall, she saw Jacob get out of the car with a young woman she knew must be his daughter, Dora. She was delighted to see Rina with them as Ash pulled the luggage out of his trunk and hustled everyone toward her door.

Holding her hand against her chest to calm the frantic beating inside, she opened the door and came face to face with Jacob Safra. When he stepped into her foyer, she found herself wrapped so tightly in his arms that she could barely breathe. Well, so much for the hug and kiss on the cheek. When he pulled back to look into her eyes, the years melted away, and they smiled at each other. She felt tears swell in her eyes.

"Hey, Ma. Can we come in?" Ash's voice was filled with laughter as he watched his parents embrace for the first time. Magda noticed her son's happy reaction, hoping his stepdad could forgive him for it. She shook off the discomfort of knowing that Dan Mahone might not have appreciated these moments. She wondered if Ash would have understood her choices when he was younger. And she wished Dan hadn't made her promise to keep Jacob away from their son. But that was then, and this is now.

Rina stepped forward and touched Magda's arm. She embraced her and then kissed Jacob's cheek, who held onto her after a quick hug. "Ah, Rina. It is splendid to see you again. I couldn't get a nice hug in the car." He chuckled.

When Dora walked into the house, Magda turned to her. A heartbeat later, she opened her arms, and Dora stepped into them. The house seemed to take a breath. She pulled back and gazed into her eyes, seeing Jacob and Ash in their depths.

"We need food, Ma. And we need to breathe here." Ash led Jacob, Dora, and Rina into the kitchen, where they gathered around the table, ignoring the formal dining room.

Magda moved gracefully to arrange cups, coffee, milk, and sugar, along with a kuchen she had prepared for the occasion. Jacob gazed at the sweet cake before turning to her. He extended his hand, and she sat beside him, taking his hand in hers. Everyone began talking at once, wiping away tears and sipping their hot coffee.

Jacob and Magda stole glances at each other, barely tasting the *kuchen,* and everyone noticed. As their children looked on, Rina's hand crept into Ash's. Both hoped their troubles were far away, but they could not have imagined how wrong they were.

By mid-afternoon, the group was trying to talk over one another, and Magda couldn't remember ever feeling this happy. She watched her son laugh at something Jacob said, then turned to see Rina's eyes shining at Ash and Jacob as well.

"Your home is so beautiful, Magda," Dora said quietly beside her. "And I am so glad to finally meet the woman whose name puts a pink tinge to my father's face every time it is mentioned." She reached for Magda's hands and pulled herself closer to peer into her face.

Magda couldn't find the words, so she squeezed the young woman's hands that rested softly over hers. How could she possibly tell her that her heart was too full to respond? When did her heart expand to hold so much love beyond that which she felt for her only child? She'd loved Jacob and kept his memory tucked away in a tiny pocket of her heart for so long that she couldn't believe it had seeped out to include his daughter.

Dora appeared to understand and enveloped her in an embrace. When she whispered, "Thank you for loving Papa. He needs it so very much," Magda burst into tears.

Jacob pulled away from Ash and joined the women on the couch, clearly worried and frowning at Dora. When the women saw his expression, they both laughed shakily.

"Go back to your man talk. We are just fine." Magda smiled at him, and his expression brightened. She looked at Rina and winked, nodding toward the kitchen while pulling Dora along with her.

When the women returned to the kitchen and the men still huddled together, deep in conversation in the other room, Magda said, "Rina, Dora wants to connect with ladies' clothing shops in San Francisco. I know there is a large shop in San Rafael. Do you have any ideas on how we can get her linked with them for her dress shop in Paris?"

Magda's eyes twinkled. She hadn't felt so young or vibrant in so long that she nearly collapsed with excitement. Walking across the kitchen floor toward the coffee maker like a teenager, she noticed the younger women shaking their heads.

"I'm told you may know people who might help this collaborative effort, and I suspect you are as highly motivated in this venture as I am. My partner has some contacts in New York City and Phoenix. Adding San Francisco would be perfect." Dora grinned.

"Dora, I'd be happy to help you. Let's ask Ash to bring you and Jacob to my shop tomorrow because there are so many irons in the fire that we have to take one at a time." Rina patted her hand where it lay on the table.

"I'd love to see your antique shop and look around San Francisco. I studied the map on the plane and I noticed that San Rafael isn't far away." Dora's voice was animated.

Rina nodded and touched her arm. "It's not far away, but sometimes the traffic is so ugly, it takes much longer than necessary to get there. But I like the way you think, and it's a good plan. Let's tell Ash and Jacob." Rina stood up, and the other women followed her into the living room. The curtains were pulled back to allow the sun to stream across the hardwood floors, making them shine like new.

Magda tut-tutted. "And I'm coming too. After all this excitement, you can't leave me out. I've prepared two guest rooms, but I need a little help with the finishing touches. Help me, girls, won't you?" Magda led the way past the men, who hadn't come up for air since they'd arrived except to eat lunch and *kuchen* with their coffee.

Outside Magda's home, a small Toyota Rav4 Hybrid slowly drove by. When it pulled around a black van and maneuvered into a spot across the street, the driver turned off the engine. Gabe Pizelli pulled a hat down over his forehead, unsure how long he'd have to wait or which of the people inside the house he'd follow first. The trip had exhausted him, as he'd sat beside a crying baby most of the way from Paris before changing planes at New York's JFK Airport. He had very little sleep, and he wasn't a happy man. He hadn't shaved for two days, his hair was disheveled, and his head ached. Yet his anger toward Ash Mahone hadn't lessened; it had now escalated from aggravation to undiluted anger.

Movement behind the curtains in the woman's house caught his eye, confirming that they were inside. The sun warmed his face as he rested his head against the headrest and closed his eyes. Sleeping was exactly what he wanted, but he shook his head to remain awake. Street noises transformed into a cacophony around him. He leaned his head back for just a minute, battling jet lag, and then he fell into a deep sleep.

Thirty

Jeff Sebring stomped into his apartment just after dawn. He threw himself down onto the sofa and slapped his knees. "Damn the woman. There must be a way to get some of that money. I should have compensation for all the mental trauma I went through when she got hurt. I wasn't in my right mind during that time. Why else would I have turned to Jenna?" He ran his tongue along his teeth and lay his head back on the couch, where he slept for three hours. When he awoke, he stretched the kink out of his neck. Then he took a breath, lifted his phone, and hit speed dial.

"What happened, Jeff? Did you shake some sense into her?" Jenna's voice put him on the defensive. She often did that, and he was getting tired of it.

"Not exactly. She knows what I want, though," he said cautiously.

"Did you have trouble getting inside? The key cost me too much money for you to fail." She snorted.

He felt his stomach tighten again. "I told you I'd work it out. You were supposed to get her anxious from the other end. Get her worked up with all the little surprises you have up your sleeve. I, on the other hand, was only supposed to scare her into letting loose with some of the money. Since we are still technically married, I'm calling my lawyer again today to find out how I can legally get some of it." He lay back down on the couch. As he pushed a pillow under his head, he lifted his feet and stretched his aching body while protecting his sore ribs.

"Legally? That will slow you down. I will talk with someone today about Rina. She needs a bigger scare, and there are no legal thoughts about it. She owes me, too. Uncle James should have given me money or at least a percentage of the profits from that antique shop. I'm pissed and she knows it." Jenna's voice held a timber that Jeff hadn't heard before.

He sat up again and pressed the phone harder against his ear. "What are you talking about? You aren't going to hurt her, are you?"

Jenna laughed. "It sounds to me like you don't like the idea. She kicked you out, remember?"

"She had good reason, and you know it."

Jenna laughed once more. "I won't allow her to have everything."

Jeff let out a loud sigh. "I'll talk with you later. I'm going to see what I can do. You always hated that old shop. I doubt it's worth much anyway; drafty, dusty, and dark. She'll probably sell it and move on to something else. You know she's never stuck to anything very long."

"But she loves that old place and everything in it. For a guy who was married..."

"...still married..."

"...to her, you don't know her very well, do you?"

He tapped the end button.

Two hours later, he looked disheveled and had already downed several cups of hot, black coffee. He had thrown his jacket to the floor and was scribbling on the tablet beside him. When he snapped his laptop shut, his expression dimmed.

The only option he found to get Rina's money was if she died before the divorce was final. And that was uncertain if she left a Will, leaving it to... who would she leave it to? Not Jenna, that's for sure. He looked at the calendar on his phone. Six days. In six days, he'd be divorced.

He lay down on the couch again to think. When his face turned dark, his stomach hurt. Jeff groaned. "Why must she make my life so miserable? Maybe if she had an accident…I couldn't hurt her. But an accident…" He snuggled deeper into his pillow and closed his eyes. He needed more sleep.

When the sun slid behind the southern district of San Francisco near Mission Dolores, Gabe shook himself awake. He was getting restless. Laura had texted him on WhatsApp so many times that he turned off his phone. The woman was getting on his nerves. Could he do her bidding, killing a man for money? No, he could not. The woman was dangerous, and he wasn't a killer. He just wanted a life where he didn't have to worry about where his next dollar would come from to pay the rent. Delivering art pieces didn't cut it. That cloisonné box was the answer, even if it meant hurting Mahone.

Now that he had both men in his sights, he wasn't going to lose them again. One of them had the box. He wasn't sure what the connection was among all these people, but he'd damned well find out soon enough.

He massaged the softball in his hand, rolling it around his palm with his fingers. Whenever he felt worried, he always thought more clearly when the ball worked its magic. This situation was different. He was alone, without Brad's constant reminder that Mahone hadn't fabricated the story about Gabe. He was tired of hearing about the shooting, the lies, and the hiding. He'd ignored his friend's messages just as he'd ignored Laura's. He had every right to confront Mahone for what he'd done to him, and Gabe refused to be sidetracked.

When Magda Mahone's porch light turned on, his head jerked up. When the front door opened, it caught his attention. Ash Mahone and the woman from the cruise ship stood on the porch. Everyone hugged each other. He hunched down in his seat and focused on the woman. Maybe that was the way to go.

The moon peeked over the fir trees where he sat, its reflection gleaming in his eyes. When he saw Rina get into Ash's car, he started his engine. No, the man wouldn't get away this time, and it had nothing to do with Laura Safra. He could feel the gems in his hand instead of the softball. He tossed it into the back seat and slowly pulled out into the late evening traffic to follow the couple. He snorted when he noticed they were focused solely on each other.

As they drove away from his mother's, Rina turned to him. "I like your sister, Ash. She's delightful, sweet, and funny. I loved seeing her with your mother, and she looks so much like you. I had trouble not staring at her. She's excited to meet Simone Fraix. She's been my friend for years; we grew up together, and while she studied modeling, I was picking through dusty antiques and watching my uncle make jewelry. Simone's dress shop will be a perfect foothold for Dora. I'm excited to help her. And Simone surely has connections in San Francisco."

Ash chuckled. "I like her too, and I loved seeing her and Ma's reaction to each other. It could've gone either way, you know?"

Rina nodded. "Well, it isn't every day a woman learns she has a grown brother and her father has a secret past that impacts so many people."

It was Ash's turn to nod, and he looked at her with a quick smile. "How about stopping at Lola's for a glass of wine so we can unwind? I know you've had a rugged night and it's nice to see that smile again...and I want to be alone with you."

"I'm up for whatever you're selling, Ash Mahone," she whispered as she let him pull her hand into his. "And wine sounds good too."

They didn't notice the SUV following two car lengths behind them. They pulled into a spot by the laundromat near the bar where Ash often met friends. When they entered Lola's, they heard Faith Hill singing, "It Matters to Me" as they were led to a small table near the bar. He nodded to Sam, the bartender, who winked at him when he saw Rina.

"Order me a chardonnay? I need to go tinkle, but I'll be back in a heartbeat." She traced her fingers across his palm and gave him a smile that promised everything he had envisioned over the past few days.

~

Gabe couldn't believe his luck. He had managed to wander into the bar unnoticed and saw the woman leave the table for the restroom. He quickly glanced around and then leisurely made his way in the same direction. It was noisy and too busy for anyone to notice him.

When Rina opened the bathroom door to return to the table a few minutes later, a hairy arm wrapped around her neck. She was yanked backward forcefully as Gabe held her in a sleeper hold. As her consciousness faded, he realized she was going out when she went limp in his arms. In the army, he had learned to incapacitate others, so the technique of cutting off someone's oxygen wasn't new.

He pushed open the door to the alley with his foot since he had wedged it open just moments earlier with a broken brick. He couldn't believe his luck; there was nobody in the back by the restrooms, and the hallway was still empty. He looked outside and pulled her into the darkness. The pavement was wet. Several men walked between the buildings, arm in arm, singing "Danny Boy" so off-key that he grimaced.

"Hey, did your girlfriend have too much to drink?" The men laughed and looked at Gabe expectantly. Their shirts hung out of their jeans as they shuffled along the alley, clearly drunk.

"Yeah, she drinks wine like it's water, and I tell her to slow it down, but does she listen to me?" Gabe smirked at them and joined in their laughter. He watched them out of the corner of his eye, hoping they didn't get any dumb ideas about jumping him. He didn't trust anyone, especially wise kids in alleys who thought he had enough liquor to slow him down.

"Women never listen to their men, man. Good luck. Doesn't look like you're going to get laid tonight." Again, they laughed at their wit and began singing again. Gabe struggled to keep Rina's limp body upright. He didn't drag her but continued moving, pulling her along the street. The car was farther away than he'd hoped, but he'd get there. Focusing on everyone on the street, he acted like the playful boyfriend with the drunk girlfriend. Several snickers followed him down the sidewalk.

"Hey, buddy. You got a live one there, don't you?"

Gabe pulled Rina under his arm and laughed loudly. "Yeah." He didn't slow down but maintained the limp, pulling stride and felt relieved when the sidewalk cleared and his car came into view.

He lifted her into his back seat and wrapped duct tape around her wrists. His head swiveled back and forth to ensure none of the passersby showed interest. Securing the seat belt around her waist in the back seat opposite the driver's, he jumped in and turned on the ignition. She hadn't moved, and he was worried he might have done more than cause her to black out. Muttering under his breath, he pulled away from the curb and headed for his small apartment across the bay.

"There's more than one way to skin a cat," he said under his breath. He would get Ash Mahone's attention this time, along with the little blue box. His breath began to hitch, clearly agitated as he watched the traffic behind him. His eyes darted back and forth between the rearview mirror and the back seat. He knew he didn't have much time to get her out of the car and secure her in his home. In twenty minutes to an hour, she'd be fighting like a wildcat.

His fingers gripped the steering wheel as he followed the bustling street onto Market. The traffic was heavy and loud. Headlights blinded him as they swung around from the opposite direction, and his nose began to run. Sniffing loudly, he wiped his nostrils with the back of his hand. The scent of fear and sweat filled the air. A thick mist covered the streets, and he knew it would soon start to rain because his joints were aching. He was nearly out of the city when he heard her begin to moan weakly. Gabe stepped on the gas and accelerated, sped across the Oakland Bay Bridge, and turned toward Richmond, northeast of San Francisco.

~

Back at Lola's, Ash was fidgeting. He checked his watch again and noticed the condensation was almost gone from the stemmed glass of chardonnay beside his beer. He twisted in his chair once more to look down the hallway where Rina had vanished. He pursed his lips.

When Sandy the barmaid passed by on her way to get more drinks, he lifted a finger. She came over to him with a jaunty shake to her hips. "What can I get you, Ash?"

"Would you do me a favor? My girlfriend went into the restroom nearly ten minutes ago. I'm worried. Would you go check on her?"

Sandy grinned and spun on her heels. Within a few seconds, she returned with her hands on her hips. "Sorry, Ash. Nobody is in the bathroom. Maybe you made the little girl mad and she hightailed it out of here?"

Ash was speechless. He looked around the room carefully before turning toward the restrooms again. Pushing back his chair, he shot the woman a frustrated glare and headed in that direction. The men's restroom was the first door on the left, while the women's restroom was across the hall on the opposite side. He jiggled the handle. "Rina?"

Silence. He saw a door at the end of the hall and pushed it open. It led to an alley behind the bar where the screams of a feral cat echoed. The wind tossed a stray newspaper across the brick walkway. The sounds of singing could be heard from the next doorway.

By now, he was more than worried. He pulled out his mobile phone and dialed her number. When it went straight to voicemail, he returned to his table and sat down again. He didn't want to leave, but he didn't know what else to do. When he heard his name called, he jerked his head and saw Jack, an old friend who often shared a beer with him.

"Hey, Ash. Good to see you."

When Jack Frey saw Ash's face, he took a seat in Rina's chair and stared at him. "Hey, what's up, man?"
Ash's chest was tight. "I brought my girlfriend in here a little while ago; she went to the john and then went missing."

Jack laughed. "Well, what did you say to her?"

Ash's eyes turned dark. "Something's wrong. She wouldn't just leave without telling me. Besides, I drove us to Lola's. She'd have to get a taxi, and why would she do that? She and I were just…"

"Okay. Okay. Maybe you should call the police?"

"Right? Their reaction would be the same as yours and Sandy's. Rina would not just leave." He pulled out his phone again, redialed her number, and slammed it onto the table in frustration. The hairs on his arms stood up, and his fingers angrily massaged his knees.

"Well, I don't know what to tell you. You can either go to her house to see if she shows up, or I can help you look for her...?"

Fighting off panic, Ash stared at Jack for a minute before nodding. He placed a twenty on the table, grabbed his cell phone, and got up. Jack had to jog after him to keep pace. The traffic was heavy, and a fine, drizzling rain poured down on them.

Thirty-One

Two hours later, when Ash entered the police station on Valencia Street, it was nearly midnight. The precinct was quiet except for three prostitutes sitting along one wall. They had greasy makeup smeared across their faces and skirts hiked up to their butts. One was crying, another looked ready to hold her own in a bar fight, and the third appeared almost normal. After a quick glance, he turned his attention to the woman at the front desk.

"My girlfriend went missing tonight from Lola's Bar. I need help."

The woman on duty pulled a pad toward her. "Name?"

"Rina Silvan." His voice was louder than he'd intended.

"No, your name." The policewoman held a pen in her hand, poised above a pad as she observed the women across from them. When she turned her gaze back to Ash, she lifted her head and nodded impatiently.

One of the prostitutes heard Rina's name and leaned forward, tilting her head to eavesdrop. Spellbound but unable to hear the entire conversation, she discreetly lifted the phone hidden in her bra. After sending a quick text, she tucked it back where it wasn't visible. Then, she inched away from the prostitute beside her and moved toward the wall.

It was the start of a long night, and Ash had been right. Rina had to be missing for twenty-four hours before he'd receive any help from the police. The policewoman shook her head. "I'll keep this information,

Mr. Mahone, so if Ms. Silvan is still missing this time tomorrow, we can look into it. For now, there's nothing else I can do. That's San Francisco for you. Sorry." Her expression didn't convey any remorse at all, but he had no choice but to head home.

He checked his phone again. No texts or calls. He redialed her number and reached voicemail. He had sent Jack home hours earlier, and he had wandered around asking questions. Nobody had seen her. She couldn't just vanish into thin air. He had doggedly chased down alleys, walked into dark corners, and finally gave up. Then he turned to the police.

When he got into his car, he leaned his head on the steering wheel. Could her ex-husband have followed her? He'd been hell-bent on accosting her the night before. Maybe he'd found her and he'd missed him? Ash snorted and slapped the wheel. He didn't even know what the man looked like. He could have walked right by him without knowing it. Why hadn't he thought of that before?

He returned to the police desk. If the man touched a hair on Rina's head, he'd have hell to pay. Five minutes later, he realized he was on his own. He didn't know the ex-husband's last name, and there was no way he could find one in a thousand named Jeff in the San Francisco area. Plus, he didn't know how to reach Rina's sister.

"Kiss my grits. The sister is out for Rina, too. What an awful family." He turned the car toward his condo, trying to think of a way to tell his mother, Jacob, and Dora that their rendezvous tomorrow at Rina's antique shop would probably not happen. Ash's contemplation was interrupted by the sound of a loud horn and squealing brakes.

When the car suddenly struck him from behind, his head collided with the steering wheel as the airbag deployed. His Audi was propelled forward and wedged against a small pickup truck parked on the street just three blocks from the police station.

He tried to lift his head, but blood dripped into one eye. His neck felt like he had been sucker punched, but his head was worse. "Shit." By the time the driver of the pickup truck pounded on his window, he had already lost consciousness.

Sirens blared around him as a policeman directed traffic. When the EMTs pried open his door, they carefully wrapped his neck in a collar and lifted him onto the gurney. The driver assisted them in loading the man into the back of the ambulance, which had swallowed him.

The policeman hovered. "Did you smell alcohol on the driver?" Raindrops threaded their way into their uniforms, and a mist lifted into the air. Each time the policeman wiped the water from his face, another batch whipped toward him with the wind.

The EMTs were busily pushing him into the ambulance, hooking him up to oxygen, and covering him with a soft blanket. The ambulance radio squawked, and garbled voices blended together. The men moved quickly and only paused briefly to answer a question, focused on getting their passenger to the hospital.

"No. He doesn't reek of anything. I do not think alcohol is involved in this one. It looked like a hit-and-run after listening to the onlookers when we loaded him up. You can talk to him later. We have to get him to San Francisco General." They quickly closed the back doors of the ambulance and drove into the night with sirens blaring.

Detective Rom Brady kicked a rock on the street and approached the bystander who had called 911. When he reached the woman, he said, "Please tell me what you saw, ma'am." He pulled his raincoat tighter around himself and scanned the street for the other driver.

"Did you see the car that smashed into this one?" He pointed to Ash's car and glanced at the gathering crowd. No other car was damaged or smoking. A hit-and-run accident, then. The only vehicle on the street beside the injured man was a pickup truck. The driver looked dazed while the other policeman questioned him.

The woman was wringing her hands. She pulled her hat down over her forehead, clearly uncomfortable. Batting away the rain, she hunkered beneath her umbrella and sniffed loudly. "I saw one of those little station wagons driving fast. I was coming home from work, and it scared me. After it hit this man's car, the driver put the car into reverse and drove away fast. It was seriously damaged, and there was steam coming out of the hood. I tried to see the license plate, but it was so dark and the rain..."

"I know you're cold, and I'm sorry to keep you, but just a couple more questions. "Could you see inside the car? Was it a man? A woman? Was there more than one person?" Edginess triggered an increase in volume and intensity as he urged her to share everything she could remember.

The woman stepped back from him. "I saw only one person. The windows were dark. When the car drove away from the street light, I couldn't be sure of anything. I think the car was gray…" She was now jumping from one foot to another to stay warm.

"You said it was a small station wagon. Do you mean an SUV?" Rain was now running down inside his collar.

"Yes, that's it—an SUV. I can't tell you anything else, officer. It drove away, but I don't know how with all that steam… Can I please go home now?" Her patience had run thin, and she looked ready to bolt.

Detective Brady nodded, closed his small notebook, and stuffed the pen into his coat pocket. "I have your name and phone number, so if I think of anything else, I can call you. Thanks… He flipped open the tablet again… Ms. Shay." He smiled through the drizzle at the woman, grateful for the little information he had received from her. He hated hit-and-run accidents, especially when the victim was injured and taken away in an ambulance. At least the man wasn't dead on impact.

The rain intensified, and the crowd scattered. When he returned to his car, he noticed the wrecked pickup truck being towed away from the injured man's Audi. The crunching noises were muffled when he shut the door. He yanked open the buttons at the wet collar of his shirt.

~

Several miles away, Ash lay in the Emergency Room at San Francisco General Hospital, a soft collar brace encircling his neck. As raindrops pounded against the windows, he remained unconscious. The storm intensified, and lightning illuminated the night sky.

A doctor walked into the room after a nurse had inserted an IV into his arm, and blood had already been drawn. He lifted the notes to scan them and put his fingers to Ash's carotid artery.

Doctor Richard Muñoz said, "I am worried. I know this patient was jolted hard, and we won't know the extent of the injury until he wakes up. The concussion worries me. Mr. Mahone could be out for hours or even days. We need to find his family, but until then, we have nobody to contact. He probably has a wife and kids who wonder where he is."

The doctor touched his wrist as he left the room. "Tell me when he wakes up. Being alone and unconscious doesn't help us right now. But, get that catheter inserted before he makes a mess."

The nurses rolled their eyes at him. It was unusually quiet in the Emergency Room that morning. When they turned toward Ash, they saw his fingers fidgeting with the bedcovers despite his unconsciousness.

Ella Rice was an RN, and her assistant was an LPN. Both women were skilled at their jobs. The catheter was inserted efficiently, knobs were adjusted and the room was dimmed. They had Ash cleaned up and the monitors connected to the IV tubes before the doctor left the floor.

The rainstorm intensified, and the windows were awash with rivulets of water snaking down like ribbons. Some of the glass rattled under the force. In addition to Ash's neck brace, a thick bandage was wrapped around his head. As lights twinkled outside his hospital room, nurses hurried back and forth in the emergency area in triage mode.

Suddenly, the loud strains of the Mission: Impossible music theme filtered toward them, announcing the arrival of another patient. Another ambulance was on its way. Everyone on the floor heaved a heavy sigh, rushing through their standard procedures. When the music stopped, their shoulders seemed to sag in tandem.

The rain had caused a maelstrom of accidents, throwing the night shift into action. The music theme played intermittently throughout the night as nurses and doctors rushed from room to room, trying to keep pace with the patients in their care.

And all the while, Ash slept deeply.

Thirty-Two

When Dora set her empty coffee cup on the quartz counter in Magda's spacious kitchen, she turned to her father. Despite attempting to appear unconcerned, there was an elephant in the room, and the caffeine surging through her body couldn't hold it back.

"Where is Ash? He said he would be here by 8:30 this morning, and now," she lifted her wrist to stare at the small star-shaped watch that sparkled on her wrist, "…it's 10:00. I've only known my brother for a short time, but I know instinctively this is not like him."

Magda's eyes met hers in solid agreement. She turned toward Jacob, anxiously staring at his face. The coffee in her cup had grown cold, and her uneaten breakfast was congealing on the china plate in front of her.

"I have called him three times, Magda, and he doesn't answer," Dora said. "We need to find out what has happened." She wrapped both hands around the back of her hair and pulled it into a chignon, then let the light brown strands fall back onto her neck. When she scratched her forehead, they could almost hear her fingernails against her skin.

"Where do we begin?" Magda whispered into the room.

Jacob drummed his fingers against his chin and looked at Magda. "Call Rina again. If she still doesn't answer, we'll call the hospitals. I know how important this is to both of them." He swallowed hard and exchanged an intense look with his daughter.

Magda tapped her phone and listened to the ringing. "Rina doesn't answer. It went straight to voicemail." Magda's voice caught on a quiet sob. When Jacob came over to her, he pulled her into his arms. "Do not worry, *ma petite*. I'm sure there is a good answer to this," he whispered urgently. He lifted her chin and stared into her eyes until she nodded uncertainly.

"You said the hospitals. There are several. I'll get the book and call them right now."

When Magda left the room, Jacob and Dora exchanged worried glances. "Something is very wrong, Papa. You and I both know it. Ash would never do this without calling. And now that Rina isn't answering her phone either, I am getting frightened."

"You too?" Jacob had no other words.

Magda rushed back to the kitchen, shaking a small tablet in her hand. Two local hospitals were duds, but San Francisco General provided her with all the information she needed about Ash.

Within five minutes, they ran to her car and were on their way. Traffic was heavy, and the streets were slick. When they arrived at the hospital, Jacob held Magda's arm to prevent her from running into the nurses and patients near the information desk. "Magda."

She turned frantic eyes toward him.

When Dora reached for her hand, they went to the desk together. Nearby, beeping machines echoed, and a fancy lounge called them to sit. But she wouldn't have any of it. "I'm here to see Ashton Mahone." She blurted the words out like a woodpecker against an oak tree.

"Are you family?" The young man was friendly but cautious. "The attending physician's notes tell me he is not awake, and the doctor left strict instructions that only family is allowed in."

"Yes, I'm his mother." She pointed to Jacob and Dora. "This is his father and his sister. Definitely family." The group huddled together like a tightly bound bouquet of flowers. The camaraderie was palpable as the man handed them three visitor passes with the room number scribbled across them. He directed them toward the elevator.

Minutes later, Magda held Ash's hand, trying to keep it still on the bedcovers. The nurse explained that agitation caused his fingers to continually dance over the coverlet. Despite being asleep, his mind was active.

"What happened?" Magda's voice was small as Jacob's fingers squeezed hers. They both stared into their son's face. Dora stood on the other side of Ash's bed.

Everyone was mentally urging Ash to wake up when the doctor walked into the room. When he extended a hand to Jacob, he said, "I am glad to see we've connected Mr. Mahone with his family. Are you his wife?"

Dora smiled. "No, I'm his sister. Please tell us what is happening." She gripped the sheet where Ash's other hand lay as she watched his agitated movements.

"Why don't we go into our private lounge for a few moments, and then you can come back to keep vigil. We can talk more easily there." He patted Ash's arm and lifted his eyelids, shining a small beam of light into each eye. When the doctor hummed, the family's panic grew. He then led them down the hall into a small room, where the four sat on a couch. Several easy chairs surrounded by elegant paintings and a tall rubber plant went unnoticed by everyone.

"Mr. Mahone was in a car accident about 9:30 last night. He was rear-ended, and the other car fled the scene, an obvious hit-and-run. His head hit the steering wheel and he has a whiplash injury. We hope he wakes soon, but in these types of cases, it could be some days."

She turned to face him, her eyes locking onto him. "He will wake up, though." Magda's voice was low and steely.

The doctor looked at her and touched her white knuckles as they gripped her purse. "Yes. We are monitoring his every breath, heart rate, everything. There is nothing we can do but ensure there is no pressure on the brain. Right now, there is not. It's a clear sign that his body sleeps to get past that trauma. The neck could give him more pain. Until he wakes, all we can do is watch and wait."

Jacob's lips moved, but no words emerged as the internal conflict tore him apart. Dora shifted from the chair to the couch beside her father, wrapping her arm around his shoulders. He trembled beneath his coat. "Papa. I refuse to lose my brother when we've just found him."

Jacob managed a faint smile.

"You're welcome to stay in here for some time to gather yourselves before you go back to Mr. Mahone's room. But to be honest, there's nothing more I can tell you except that this concussion may affect his memory and perhaps his speech. You can talk to him as if he hears your words." He smiled at the group and then left the room.

"We have to find Rina, Jacob." Magda's eyes swung to his. "They have feelings for each other. It's obvious. If she won't answer her phone, she's in trouble. You can drive my car over there." She dug inside her purse. "I have her shop address. I'm not sure what you can do here until Ash wakes up. Do you have GPS on your phone, Dora?"

Dora's eyes glistened as she nodded. She doubted Jacob would leave Ash. Within seconds, he shook his head at the suggestion.

"Okay. I'll go alone. The traffic can't be that bad. I can drive around Paris, right?" She tugged at her hair again, swept it up, and pulled it off her neck. When she extended her hand for the keys, she noticed the older woman's hand was shaking.

One hour later, Dora's stress level had crept past a ten out of ten. Paris traffic was nothing compared to that of San Francisco, and crossing the Bay Bridge before heading south on the I-5 toward the Richmond-San Rafael Bridge was intimidating. She pulled over once she crossed the bay and took out her phone. When Rina didn't answer again, her stomach felt like it was ready to explode.

"Where is she?!" She had left with Ash the night before. Did he drop her off at home? Had she been with him when he was rear-ended? Was she wandering around needing help? If she had still been with him, maybe she would have been hurt. When that thought entered her mind, she froze. Why didn't they check the hospitals for Rina, too? She grimly watched the cars swarm around her and heard the horns honking as she tried to come up with the correct answers.

Before her GPS directed her to Rina's antique shop, she pulled out her phone and searched for hospitals. After contacting the three most plausible hospitals, she dropped her phone into her purse and carried on.

Silvan's Antiques was dark, shuttered, and closed. She parked and approached the glass door and display windows. As she peered inside, shading her eyes with her hands, she saw rows of items on tables and a glass display case near the door. However, she did not see anyone, especially Rina.

She didn't know where Rina lived, so she was stumped. What was next? Should she return to the hospital with Papa and Magda? Start wandering around until she was hopelessly lost? What would Laura do? She was the academic in the family. She moved back to her car and slumped over the wheel. "What would Laura do…?"

There was a bookshop next to the antique shop on one side and a small restaurant on the other. She glanced at both establishments and made a decision. Grabbing her purse, she exited the car again and walked toward the bookstore. The bell rang above the door, and an older woman with pewter-colored hair emerged from behind the counter to push a heavy book onto the nearest shelf.

"Good morning. Can I help you find anything?" The woman's voice was friendly, but quite loud. Glasses hung around her neck, and her fingers played with the beaded necklace that held them there.

Dora walked toward her and cleared her throat. "I am looking for my friend, Rina Silvan…the owner of the shop next door? She isn't answering her phone, and I'm worried. Do you know where she lives?"

The bookshop owner bit her lip. "Well, I don't feel comfortable giving out that information, miss. If you're her friend, you must know her sister, Jenna. Did you call her?"

Dora's face fell. "No, I don't know her sister. I only met Rina recently. We had an appointment this morning and it was very important. When she didn't answer her phone or open the shop yet…and I was worried."

The woman's eyebrows rose. "Well, Jenna might not know where she is either. I don't think they're on good terms," she said conspiratorially. "They've had words if you know what I mean. It was all about that husband of hers. I never thought he was right for Rina, and…"

Dora held up her hand. "I do not want to know about her personal life, madam. I want to find her."

The woman's lips thinned. "Rina has a condo near the bridge in the fancy district. The Hampton Downs Estates. I don't know the address, but I think there's a business office on the premises."

When Dora swung out of the shop, the book owner's mouth twitched. Sliding another book onto the shelf, she watched Dora drive away.

Ten minutes after leaving the bookshop, Dora guided Magda's car into the circular driveway of Hampton Downs Estates. She marveled at the glass windows that filled one entire side of the building along brick-lined walls and archways. The building appeared to have been beautifully constructed in the late 1900s, and then, with an eccentric twist of the wrist, the architecture was thrust, screaming, into the 21st century. She wasn't sure if she could live in a place so wildly different from her lovely flat in Paris.

The office manager was unwilling to provide any information. "Yes, Rina Silvan has a condo here, but I certainly cannot divulge her unit number." The woman's red hair was so bright that it hurt Dora's eyes. The vivid green tunic she wore over gold-colored leggings made Dora wonder if the woman was living in a perpetual St. Patrick's Day mode.

"Well, can I wait here while you check her condo? It's important. She's sort of missing." Dora had no intention of leaving.

The woman's eyes narrowed slightly. "Sort of missing?" She moved around her desk to perch on the front, one leg supporting her on the floor while the other was bent at the knee, hanging lazily off the desk. She tapped her manicured fingers on her knee and stared at Dora.

"Yes, we had an important appointment, and I know Rina wouldn't miss it unless she had a very good reason. She could have fallen in the shower or slipped on the stairs or…" Dora's face reflected her worry, and she couldn't stop pacing.

The woman raised her hands in the air like a football referee calling a timeout. "Ok! I'll go. But you stay here." She grabbed the keys from her desk drawer, confirmed that Dora wasn't following her, and then jogged out the door.

Dora laughed at her clothing, which was so over the top, even though she was worried about Rina. Her flair for fashion had provided her with an excellent career, and even now, her creative mind scoffed at the woman's attire. The phone began to ring before the woman returned, adding another layer of stress to Dora's already overactive mind.

Dora fidgeted, straining her head around the column to watch for the woman. Within a few minutes, the redhead surfaced, and the green bombshell returned with a smile. "No, she's not there. She wasn't knocked out, in the bathroom with her head bashed in, or sound asleep. She isn't home." She plopped the keys back into her desk and turned toward Dora again. "Sorry."

Dora was certain the woman wasn't sorry, but she was forced to leave empty-handed, left to wonder what happened to Rina all over again. She had no choice but to return and ask the people in the restaurant next to the antique shop. Why hadn't she gone there first before coming here? Her mind was in shambles. "Merde. Now I have to face this damn traffic again."

She shifted the car and slowly drove away, hoping Rina wasn't lying in a ditch somewhere. She suppressed the thought and retraced her way to the antique shop.

Meanwhile, back at the hospital, Jacob and Magda sat side by side next to Ash, willing him to wake up. They took turns standing by his bed and then sitting down again, each silent in their vigil. Lunchtime came and went, but they were oblivious to their growling stomachs.

Jacob and Magda smelled the food before Dora entered the room. "Anyone hungry?" Ash's sister glanced toward the bed. Her hair was disheveled, and her face was blotchy from stress. "I found food for us, and thank God, I didn't have to drive anywhere to get it. There's a little restaurant a block away." She set three paper bags on the small table beside her brother's bed and then looked at her father and Magda.

Magda turned to look at her without replying.

"No. I couldn't find her. I went to the bookshop by her shop and the café next door. I also visited her condo building, and the manager looked into her apartment. It was a fight for me to get her to look for me. But Rina isn't there either." Dora's eyes welled with tears, and she wiped her hand across her cheek.

Jacob walked toward her, but stopped abruptly as Ash's croaking voice peeled into the room, "You can't find her either?"

Everyone turned toward him at once. His mother reached his side first and began to cry. Jacob put his arm around her shoulders, and the men exchanged glances.

"Rina?" Ash felt agitated as he attempted to lift the light blanket that covered him.

"You aren't going anywhere. We don't know where Rina is because she's not answering her phone," his mother whispered.

When Dora arrived at the bedside, she slapped her hand on the sheet and said, "Well, it's about time you woke up, you lazy bum. We had a date this morning, remember?" Her voice cracked as she fought back tears that threatened to choke her.

He stared at all of them for a heartbeat before allowing a brief smile to slide across his face, but it vanished as quickly as it appeared. He looked out the door and down at the bed. "Somebody crashed into me while I was looking for Rina. And if she's still missing. I need to get out of here."

"Wait! …Still missing? What do you mean, Ash?" Dora's voice cut through the commotion. Everyone spoke at once. Her fingers twisted the sheet that covered his large body, and her knuckles turned white.

Nurse Rice heard the timbre of Ash's voice from the hallway as she was passing the room. "Well, Mr. Mahone. It's nice to hear you're awake. I'll get the doctor." She quickly walked away, and then she was gone.

"Rina was missing last night? You two left together. I don't understand…" Dora's voice faltered, and her questions blended with the others. Their confused inquiries merged as one while they waited for Ash to address some of them.

"She disappeared when we were at Lola's Bar. We ordered wine, and she went to the bathroom. That's the last time I saw her. I drove around for hours trying to find her. It was probably stupid. Where did I think I was going to find her, running through the streets? I went to the police, but…" His chest rose and fell with the telling, and he ran a finger along the top of his neck brace.

The doctor arrived just as Ash finished explaining that Rina was missing from Lola's bar the night before. The doctor pulled a stethoscope from his white jacket pocket and gently moved the others aside. When he shone the light into Ash's eyes, he stepped back and smiled.

"Welcome back, Mr. Mahone. The police want to take your statement so they can find the driver of the car who put you in here. Do you know what day this is?" The doctor held a light up to shine into Ash's eyes.

"Tuesday? Please call the police. I need their help. I think my car accident might have been connected to my missing girlfriend." He dropped his head down onto the pillow again, feeling weak and slightly disoriented.

"Your girlfriend?" Magda whispered, her lips curling into a smile.

She and Jacob exchanged a smile before they patted Ash's leg, both relieved that he wasn't injured more seriously. Sharing their son, even in this situation, deepened their love for each other. Magda reached for his hand, while Dora patted both of them with her own.

Thirty-Three

Earlier that morning, far from the hospital, thunderbolts of pain shot through Rina's skull. She groaned and squeezed her eyes shut in self-defense. The room was dark and smelled wrong. Where was she? This was not home; she was certain of it.

Rina's hair fell across her cheek, but when she attempted to push it aside, she felt a burning sensation from the tape on both wrists. She whimpered and turned her head away from the foul-smelling pillow beneath her aching head. Her throat hurt so much that she struggled to swallow. It had to be a nightmare; I'm dreaming.

Then she remembered. She jerked upward, lifting her head just enough to focus on the room. "Ahhhh," she groaned, immediately regretting the movement. Her mind cleared. She had been with Ash at Lola's. She had gone to the bathroom while he ordered wine and then... Her thoughts turned hazy. Someone had grabbed her from behind, and she didn't remember anything else.

Suddenly, a bright flash of light blinded her as a large man yanked the door open. "So, you're awake. I knew you'd only be out an hour or so. You and I are going to have a little heart-to-heart, Miss Nosy Boobs."

Gabe switched on the overhead light, and the brightness flooded into Rina's head like lightning. She instinctively shut her eyes tight. The harsh lights made it impossible to pry open her eyelids, and she flinched away from the man. Pulling her knees up into a sitting position, she pressed her elbows against her sides. Trying to appear fierce, she struggled to recall one of the defensive moves she had learned in her police self-defense classes.

She heard a crunching sound as a heavy body settled down across from her. Rina held her taped wrists up to shield her eyes, trying to squint them together for a better look. She knew it was a man. When she saw his face, her heart jolted. "You!"

"Yep. Me again."

"What have you done? Why am I here? Where's Ash?" She turned her head slowly, attempting to see every corner of the mismatched room.

"He isn't here. That's why **you're** here. To get **him** here." Gabe laughed at the look on her face.

"What? Why?" She twisted her wrists, trying to dislodge the silver duct tape, but it wouldn't budge.

"Because he has something that I want. And I'm sure you know exactly what that is. You two are too cozy for him not to have shown you that cloisonné box, Missy. And he owes me big time." He grunted and swiped a hand over his chin.

She sucked in a breath. "Why does he owe you anything? Where's your buddy...the one who was on the cruise ship with you? I heard that thieves stick together...or did you dump him because you wanted it all for yourself?"

Gabe nearly fell off his chair when his foot slipped on the loose rung below. His eyes glared toward her, and she shook her head animatedly. "I knew it."

"You don't know **anything!**" He shot up from the chair and laughed when he saw her wince. He started pacing in front of his dirty apartment window and placed his hands inside his pockets. "Mahone ruined my military career, and now I'm going to ruin him."

He snatched her purse to search through it. When she lunged at him, he yanked it out of her grasp and swatted at her hands. He pushed his fingers inside again until he grasped her iPhone in his hands.

"What's your PIN?"

She didn't answer.

"I asked you for your PIN?" His eyes turned flat.

"1090 dammit!"

He tapped in the numbers. Scrolling through the recent calls, he chuckled. "It looks like you're very popular. Ash called you, let's see...fourteen times since you and I left Lola's. Must be missing you...Let's give him a call, shall we?" His face lit up like a kid's as he punched the screen. The call went to voicemail. "Guess he's not taking your calls. But don't worry; we'll keep calling until he gets my message."

She growled at him. "How could one man ruin your military career? Ash wasn't in the military." Her head felt like a sledgehammer; she lifted her manacled hands to her temples.

"He wrote a story that tossed me out of the army on my ass."

"You must have deserved it."

"Oh, yeah? You don't know shit."

"I have to go to the toilet."

He grimaced. "Don't try anything fancy in there." He helped her up and pointed her down the hall. "And leave the door open."

"Like hell, I will," she said as she slammed it shut with her foot.

He laughed.

Rina surveyed the grimy bathroom and pursed her lips in dismay. Black hairs were scattered across the sink, and a few lay behind the toilet seat. A rust line encircled the toilet bowl at the water line, and the dust was so thick that she could write her name in it. Towels were strewn across the floor beside the tub, and one was draped over the shower rod. Bile rose in her stomach. She picked up the cleanest towel she could find from the floor to wipe off the toilet seat.

"Oh. My. God." She shivered and struggled to pull down her slacks before she peed her pants. Rina was sure she'd never seen a room so filthy or sat on a toilet so deplorable. But she had to pee.

"Hurry up in there, Missy."

"Shut up."

He laughed harshly again and pounded on the bathroom door.

"Okay! My God!" She noticed a small window above the tub but realized she probably couldn't fit through it even if she climbed up there. She examined the tiled soap niche built into the wall and the small rod across the top. Could she use it for a foothold? How high was this building? Where did the window lead? As quietly as she could manage, she stepped onto the side of the tub and leaned her throbbing face into the window. First floor. It would be a fall, but she might be able to...

"I said, Hurry up. If I have to come in there, I will." His voice was turning nasty as he tapped the door with his knuckles again.

"Sometimes it takes a while. My stomach hurts, and I can't go on demand." She listened as his footsteps retreated down the hallway.

Back up on the tub, she snapped open the lock and grimaced at the squeaky sound that filled the room. Her head throbbed. The soles of her canvas shoes were slick, and she knew she was running out of time. She slipped the lock back and slid the window open. Turning her head slightly to listen for the man, she decided it was safe and took off her shoes. Her toes curled around the soap bar as she pulled herself up with her elbows, wishing for the hundredth time that her hands were free.

A slight scuffling sound distracted her, causing her elbow to slip. When the man burst through the door, he caught her before she could hit the side of the tub. Everything felt upside down. He grabbed her by the tape around her wrists and shoved her toward the toilet, spinning her away from the window.

"Hey, Nosy Boobs, you aren't going anywhere until I say so." His gruff voice was close to Rina's ear, and she could smell his onion-scented breath. He was breathing heavily.

She jerked her face away from him. When he pushed her toward the toilet, she lunged for the seat to avoid falling to the floor. She was trying to think quickly, but got derailed when one hip slipped off the toilet. She realized she had no easy escape now. Would Ash ever find her?

He righted her onto the toilet seat with a snarl. "Next time, you leave the damn door open or pee your pants. Your choice," Gabe bellowed. He glared at her as she tried to balance herself on the closed toilet seat.

In contrast to his statement, Rina's voice was faint. "Ahhhh, right. I'll pee my pants all over your dirty couch then. I'm not leaving the bathroom door open to give you a peep show."

Gabe shot her a withering stare, and his scowl deepened. "Come, now!" As he reached for her, Rina forced herself to break the panic that had paralyzed her and moved toward the brute. He pulled her back into the living room and tossed her onto the smelly couch. He glared at her with a 'don't you dare move' look.

She shot him a glare. Her hip throbbed, but it couldn't compare to the onslaught of angry insults she carried in her head. Uncertain about what he might do next, she didn't want to risk getting knocked out again.

"Not so feisty now, Nosy Boobs?" He moved around the room, picking up scattered clothing and dirty food containers. His mobile phone rang, but he ignored it. As he pushed the debris into a small garbage bin, he kept glancing at her, as if his mind were in a million pieces.

"What are you going to do with me? No matter what Ash did to you, it has nothing to do with me. And I don't have what you're looking for. Is it worth going to jail for, Mr....? What's your name anyway?"

"You don't need to know my name, Missy. Just leave me the hell alone! I need to think." He tossed the containers into a large garbage bag and walked out the door, slamming it behind him.

His mobile phone rang again. Rina slid off the couch as fast as she could and grabbed it. "Hello? Hello? Help me, please! Call the police. This man is holding me..." She heard Gabe coming back. She dropped the phone and hurried back to the awful couch, scuttling into the corner before he opened the door.

Gabe took a deep, labored breath. As he inched his boots off, he sat back and stared at Rina. "This is beginning to be a hell of a mess. You are probably right. I don't want to see the inside of a jail. It might be too late to walk away, but maybe that's exactly what I need to do." He rubbed his hands over his scruffy black chin, feeling the prickly beginnings of a beard against his fingers. He ran his hands over his face and shook his head as if a conversation were happening inside his mind.

"Let me go then." Rina felt cold again. The stench of used food containers and empty wrapping paper made her gag. It was nearly as bad as the filthy bathroom. She wondered how someone could live in this messy apartment. The smell, the dirt, the cold—did he even have a heater? If he did, it wasn't turned up enough to feel its warmth.

"I'll think about it." Then he left her alone once more.

Much later, he still hadn't returned. Rina continued suffering from a pounding headache. She opened her eyes cautiously to regain her bearings. A chill ran down her spine when she heard sounds coming from beyond the doorway. When he entered the room again, he sat across from her.

She began to shiver and reached for the tattered blanket he'd thrown at her during the night. She could tell it was nearing noon by the sunlight streaming through his grimy windows. She refused to cry or show him that she was afraid. Watching him through her half-closed eyes, she leaned back and rested her head on the armrest.

Gabe Pizelli steepled his fingers and stared at Rina. His expression betrayed his inner conflict. After releasing a deep sigh, he hunched over and sank his head into his hands, resting his elbows on his knees. He whispered, "Oh, God. What to do?"

She heard him mumble, but she didn't respond. When he fell silent, she lifted her head and watched him. The smell of onions wafted over her again, causing her to wrinkle her nose.

They stared at each other warily. The sounds of the city invaded the room. Neither moved. When she noticed his eyes drop to the silver tape wrapped around her wrists, hope bloomed in her belly. What in the hell was he going to do? His jaw tightened as if he were overthinking the whole situation. She counted one, two, three, four. Rina couldn't let him see that she was scared spitless. Where was Ash? Why did this guy want to hurt her? She tried to remember what he had said about Ash and the military. Her wrists throbbed. She wanted the tape gone.

Suddenly, they heard police sirens cutting through the haze of their jumbled thoughts. In that part of town, it wasn't unusual to hear the blare of sirens from time to time, so Gabe paid it no mind. He glanced at the ceiling, as if he could uncover answers there.

He walked around the room. He turned to stare at Rina again, and then Gabe moved toward her. When he bent down to her, she kicked both of her feet into his groin. As he doubled over in agony, he fell on top of her. When she tried to push him off, he struggled to regain his balance. In their effort to right themselves, his oniony breath filled the air between them.

"You ditzy broad! I was going to cut off the damned tape!" He cradled his aching privates for a few seconds before carefully sitting down beside her. He groaned loudly near her ear and glared at her. After readjusting himself to ease the throbbing, he turned toward her again. And then his fingers began to slash at the silver tape with his pocket knife. "Sit still and let me get this off without stabbing you accidentally." His breathing sounded labored.

Rina jerked away from him as her raw skin tore when the tape released. "You shouldn't have put it on me!"

He exhaled loudly. "That's what I've been thinking. All this drama isn't worth it, and I've made a real mess of things. So, shut up and let me think my way out of it."

Thirty-Four

Detective Rom Brady walked into Ash's room. He noticed several people finishing their lunch and a nurse checking the patient's vitals. He pulled out his small notebook and retrieved a pencil.

Everyone stared at him.

"Ashton Mahone?"

"Yes, that's me. I asked for help last night, but the precinct on Valencia wouldn't give me the time of day. I was told I had to wait until twenty-four hours had elapsed." Ash ground out the words.

The detective scrunched his face. "Say, what? You had problems before your car accident?" He glanced at Jacob, Magda, and Dora, who were edging toward the door. "Yes, please give me some time with Mr. Mahone. I'd appreciate that."

When the family left, he turned toward Ash again. In just five minutes, the detective had heard his story and scratched his head. "So, you think there's a connection, and you have three suspects. Interesting." He sat down in the chair, pulling it closer to Ash's bed.

~

Across the bridge in Richmond, two uniformed officers received a 911 call from a man who reported that a woman needed help. Unsure whether she was in danger or if it was indeed a tactical situation, they followed protocol and proceeded with caution. The address indicated an apartment on the ground floor.

Officer Marley Austin nodded to his partner, Officer Kristin Bloom, who understood his intentions. She watched him jog across the grass toward the apartment, where large windows overlooked a grassy area and walking path. When he reached the edge and peered into the window, he gave her a thumbs up, prompting them to quickly rush toward the building.

Gabe jumped back from Rina when he heard boots pounding down the hallway toward his apartment. He looked around in a panic, but before he could move an inch, the door swung open violently. Two cops stood in the doorway, guns drawn, and he froze in place.

Rina nearly fainted from relief. Sobs bubbled up from her throat as she pressed her hands to her eyes. Had her call worked? The caller had contacted the police. Who was it? As she saw the officers rush toward Gabe, the tears flowed; her cheeks were wet before she could choke back the next sob.

The officers kept Gabe within range with their pistols. He stared at them, bewildered. Officer Austin had seen the man hovering over Rina through the window, so he acted based on her imminent danger. He pushed Gabe down onto the shabby chair near the couch, wrinkling his nose at the smell of onions. With one hand holding Gabe down, he reached behind him to grab his handcuffs and nodded toward his partner and the victim.

The female officer exchanged a glance with her partner and rushed over to Rina. She whispered urgently, "Ma'am. Are you alright? Have you been sexually assaulted?"

"No, he didn't touch me that way. I'm okay." Rina nodded blankly at Officer Bloom while the policewoman cut the duct tape from her wrists.

Kristin Bloom shot Gabe an angry glare as her partner cuffed him and called for a transport to take the man into the station. She understood that the victim was traumatized and wanted to separate her from the abuser as quickly as possible.

Rina trembled so violently that she struggled to walk down the stairwell with the officer supporting her. The muscles in her legs felt like jelly. As she rubbed her sore wrists, she glanced at the angry red welts left behind after the tape was removed. All this for that beautiful cloisonné box? And something Ash did to ruin a military career? Ridiculous was the word echoing in her mind.

"Ms. Silvan, your cry for help was turned in by a man named Harry Dalton. He's Gabriel Pizelli's employer, and he'd been calling him for a few hours. When he heard your frightened message, he called 911." The female officer led Rina to a flashing patrol car with its blue and red lights. Several apartment dwellers watched the scene with growing excitement.

Rina took a deep breath. "I need to find Ash. He'll be worried about me. This Gabriel guy took me from Lola's last night when we were there and..."

The policewoman pulled out her notebook and flipped through several pages. "Would this friend be Ashton Mahone?"

Rina's head jerked up. "Yes, it is."

"Stay here, ma'am, and I'll be right back." The woman had short dark hair, like a cap around her head. With her eyes blazing, she shot Rina a look that promised the haven Rina needed.

She watched the policewoman jog toward the porch where her jailer now stood in handcuffs. His head hung low, and his face was turned toward the ground. She saw the woman speak to her partner, and then she jogged back to the car. "Good news, ma'am. Mr. Mahone is in the hospital and..."

"What? In the hospital? Why?" Rina's mouth formed an O.

"We're on our way to San Francisco General, ma'am. I don't know any more than that." Kristin Bloom buckled her seat belt and shook her head at Rina.

"*Please* stop calling me ma'am. I'm Rina Silvan. When you call me ma'am, I feel a hundred years old." She looked at her from the back seat and they shared a grin.

"Yes, Rina. By the looks of your face and the way you're limping, you probably should be checked out at the hospital too." She stared hard and whispered in a voice only a woman understands, "You are **sure** he didn't touch you, hurt you…"

Rina sank into the back seat. "No, thank God." Her fingers drummed against the armrest as the police car turned south and then sped west across the bridge toward San Francisco. Her watch showed one-thirty. Rain pelted against the windows, giving her a blurry view of her beloved bay. She was afraid to ask any more questions. She just wanted to get to the hospital and find out what had happened to Ash. If he were in the hospital, maybe she was the lucky one with a few scrapes and bruises. Her heart thudded against spindly ribs, and she felt the tears rush up again.

Thirty-five minutes later, she exited the elevator with the policewoman and was directed to a hospital room. Just before reaching the door, she heard a slight squeal as Dora flew toward her.

"Oh. My. God. Where have you been? We have been so worried." Dora's voice shook. When she saw Rina limping toward her and the bright red welts on her wrists, Dora started crying.

Jacob and Magda followed and hugged Rina so tightly that she was sure her ribs cracked. "I'm okay. Where's Ash? Why is he here?"

Three sets of eyes stared at her as they shook their heads. Magda spoke first. "Ash is finally awake. He was in a deep sleep or a coma, I don't know which. Someone rammed into his car last night. He has a concussion and whiplash. It was a hit-and-run driver."

Rina's hand flew to her chest, and concern washed over her face once again. "Where is he?"

Dora led the group into the room and interrupted Detective Brady. He greeted the policewoman, and they stepped into the hallway for a private discussion.

Rina walked toward Ash. When she lifted her hands to him, the lump in her throat tightened, and she couldn't speak at all. She didn't care that they weren't alone; she leaned down and kissed him, being careful not to hurt him. When she pulled away, he held her close and whispered, "I promised I'd protect you, and I didn't. Please forgive me, darlin."

Rina's tears soaked his hospital gown as she lifted her head to gaze deeply into his eyes. "Ash, why do we keep meeting like this? You know how much I hate hospitals." She smiled through blurry eyes.

Everyone in the room gathered around, and then the police detective returned. He gestured for Rina to join him in the hallway. She didn't want to leave Ash's side, but she recognized that she had no choice.

"Ms. Silvan, we need to take your statement. Are you feeling up to going to the station with Officer Bloom? The doctor will examine you first. Okay? We mustn't miss anything. Mr. Mahone thinks there may be a link between Gabe Pizelli abducting you and the car crash that put him in that hospital bed. He mentioned your ex-husband and Gabe Pizelli and... well, he mentioned your sister too."

Rina's pulse raced. Before she could respond to the man, she was taken to a small examining room. A nurse applied warm salve to her wrists, and her neck was examined, where bruises appeared purple. "I need to see Ash again before I'm taken to the police station. Thank you, but I'm sure I'm fine now." She thanked the nurse and hurried down the hallway.

His body was wracked with pain. At first, it was just pain in his head, and then moving his head became a struggle. Trying to lift it off the pillow, he leaned slightly toward Rina and whispered, "Did he hurt you...you know, what I mean?"

She gently stroked Ash's brow and leaned in close to his ear so that he was the only one who could hear her, "No, he didn't do that. But he told me you'd ruined his military career. I didn't ask him anything about it. I'll be back after I give my statement."

Her head felt as if marbles were rumbling around inside it. Could Jeff or Jenna possibly be responsible for Ash's accident? She pushed her reddened wrists up to run her trembling fingers through her hair. Officer Bloom led Callie down the hall, into the elevator, and outside to the police cruiser. A rock lodged in her throat as she drove away from the hospital and toward the police station.

Two hours later, her statement was typed and signed. Her head still throbbed. Rina called Dora. Although she longed to be with Ash again, she wasn't ready to face the hospital just yet. Officer Bloom offered to take her back to the hospital.

"Fish tacos always make me feel better… oh, and a salad." The little restaurant near the hospital was just a short walk away, and Dora responded to her text immediately.

"How's Ash? I wanted to tell you what happened last night without Jacob and Magda listening. Ash will be livid no matter what, but I needed to talk to someone, and you're the one."

Dora grinned. "And my job was trying to find **you**. I thought the traffic couldn't match the craziness of Paris, but San Francisco and San Rafael traffic have it beat, my friend. Oh, and your condo manager? The one with the crazy red hair. Oh, my goodness. Do you think she's Irish?"

It was the first time Rina had laughed in many hours. As Rina finished the last bites of her fish taco, Dora swallowed the final drop of her Malbec wine, just as her phone dinged. Dora glanced at the text message and scowled.

"It's Laura. She's angry that I took Papa away without telling her. She said her friend wanted to meet him and asked why nobody told her he was gone." Dora was thoughtful for a moment.

Rina watched as confusion spread across Dora's face. "A new friend?" Her voice sounded confused and suspicious.

"I will ask her." Dora's fingers flew across the miniature keyboard on her phone, which pinged back almost immediately. "My friend wants to see Ash. Where is he? The man has now returned to America." When Dora read the words aloud, both women scowled.

"How does he know Ash? He hasn't been in Paris since he wrote for the newspaper. This is strange. How does he know Laura?" Rina stuffed the last piece of fish taco into her mouth and moved the coleslaw around with her tongue. Their eyes met again.

"Tell Laura that Ash is at my antique shop in San Rafael." Dora appeared dumbfounded before she typed the message. After setting down her phone, she gently tapped the wine glass with her fingernail. She avoided meeting Rina's gaze for a moment, and when she finally did, her lips quivered.

"Is it possible that Laura…?" Rina felt her head spin. She didn't want to believe that this beautiful woman's twin sister could have anything to do with the events that she and Ash were facing.

"No, it can't be. It would kill Papa. No…" Dora's eyes flashed. "I won't believe it until..." She tossed the small square napkin onto the table and lifted her glass to the waiter in a mock salute. When he arrived at her table, he promised to return with two more glasses of wine.

~

Laura Safra sat in her office at Sorbonne University in Paris and read her sister's message. She then sent a message of her own to Gabe Pizelli. However, it was a police officer who intercepted and read her text, and who immediately called Detective Brady.

When Ash saw the detective frown while listening to someone on his phone, he assumed it was bad news. As the detective turned toward Jacob, Ash felt sure of it. His head throbbed and felt like it would explode. He couldn't tell if it was from the knock on his head, hearing he'd been connected to Gabe while still writing about the war, or his aching neck. He wanted the brace removed, but the doctor was adamant with a firm no.

Detective Rom Brady nodded toward Ash before turning to his father. "Mr. Safra, would you please join me out in the hallway for a moment?" He looked drained, as if the weight of his job had nailed him to the ground. He stared at the floor for a few moments, wishing he were a hundred miles away.

Jacob was surprised and curious, but followed the police officer into the hallway. Nurses hurried around, so they made their way to the waiting room ahead.

"Mr. Safra. I'm not sure how to tell you this." The detective shook his head, seeming as if he wanted to be anywhere but there.

Jacob narrowed his eyes, raising one white eyebrow. "I do not think anything you say will surprise me. We've been so worried about Ash, and now with Rina missing, just tell me." He sat down on the couch, and the detective joined him, a sad look in his eyes.

~

Magda felt perplexed when the men left the room, sharing a bewildered glance with Ash. "What do you think that was all about?"

Ash lifted his hand, and she walked toward the bed. When she laced her fingers with his, she whispered, "It must be important or he would have discussed it with all of us, don't you think?"

He squeezed her fingers and lay his head back on the pillow to ease the headache that had become his constant companion since waking up. His mother's hand felt warm, and he wondered if he could curl up and be a little boy again, free from all the drama of the past few days.

They remained like that until Jacob returned to the room ten minutes later, pale and shaken. He struggled to swallow and reached for Magda's other hand. After three attempts to speak, he could barely get the words out and said, "It was Laura."

"What do you mean it was Laura?" Ash's voice remained stony.

Magda turned toward him with a furrowed brow, glancing between both men. Jacob closed his eyes but couldn't stop the tears that streamed down his face. "The police just intercepted a text message between Laura and Gabe Pizelli telling him where you could be located." The room vibrated with its silence.

Thirty-Five

Gabriel Pizelli's fingertips tapped against the interrogation room table. His face was drenched in tears, but nobody cared. His mind was in a quandary. Should he tell them everything about Laura Safra's request that he kill a man? Should he keep her out of it? He hardly knew the woman. But since he had refused the hit on Ash Mahone, maybe they'd go easy on him. He hadn't hurt the woman; he had just taped her up and tossed her around a bit. He lifted his hands to his aching head. When he rubbed the stubble on his jaw, his mind went blank.

"Mr. Pizelli, why did you pinch Rina Silvan at Lola's last night? Did she make you angry? Like you wanted something, she refused to give it to you?" the policeman barked, a sneer on his face.

"No. It wasn't like that. I never touched her, not sexually…" Gabe's eyes shifted from one man to the other. "She never said I did, did she? If she did, she's lying. I only wanted to…"

"You only wanted to what? Scare her? And when did you slam into Ash Mahone's car? You wanted to finish him off after you tried to kill him twice already? Once in that alley in San Francisco and Mazatlán?"

Gabe looked stony. "What? I didn't try to kill him or hurt the woman. I don't rape women. I don't kill people either."

The police officer stared at Gabe for a heartbeat before continuing, "Oh? You mean, not since you got thrown out of the Army after doing just that? You just beat them senseless and hope they don't die. Is that it?"

Gabe didn't answer. He pressed his lips tightly together. This wasn't going at all as he had hoped. Maybe he should just tell them everything. He slumped in his chair and closed his eyes. His breathing became shallow, and the hairs on his arms stood up like pins on a pincushion. With his eyelids shut over his panicked eyes, he took another deep breath.

"And who's your Paris friend who wonders if you've found Ash yet? They just sent a text telling you where to find him. Quite a coincidence, don't you think?" The officer placed his foot on the rung of the chair where Gabe sat, tapping his knee as he waited for Gabe to respond.

This time, Gabe's mouth went slack; he felt sucker-punched. "I want to see a lawyer." He wasn't going to reveal anything until he spoke with someone smarter than him.

The policemen stared at him and left the room. He'd said the six words that told them their questioning was over.

~

Several miles away, Jeff Sebring slammed his phone down onto his desk. Several bank clerks stared at him. He rose and paced around his office, mumbling and cursing. Then he called Jenna Silvan.

"Hey. What did your attorney say?"

"You don't want to know, Jenna. And I need my car back."

He heard her snort loudly. Jenna paused before answering. "That's not right, Jeff. You're still married. You should get some of that money. It's not fair."

Jeff caught his breath and adjusted the knot in his tie, recalling Rina's words when she told him Jenna didn't want him at all. Taking his time, he carefully chose his response. "Jenna, we don't need her money. Let's start fresh. I earn a good salary, and so do you. When the divorce is final, let's go away for a week and celebrate." His lips tightened, and his eyes narrowed.

He heard the breathy sound she always made with her lips when she thought she'd heard something ludicrous. "You're joking. I'm not going anywhere with you unless you …"

Jeff slammed the phone down for the second time that morning, ripped the tie from his neck, pulled open the first two buttons of his shirt, and reached for his bottom drawer. He got up, shut his office door, and took out the Jack Daniels and a glass. Then he vowed to get drunk.

~

Back at the hospital, Ash had finally convinced his parents and Dora to go home. His head was no longer in danger of exploding, and he wanted Rina all to himself. His family had left about thirty minutes earlier.

Rina sat beside him, holding his right hand and gently stroking it up to his wrist. She looked at him from beneath her long, dark lashes, her moist lips parting to release a sigh.

Ash forced himself to concentrate on the conversation. As they spoke softly, Harry Dalton walked into the room. He appeared shaken, his shirt hanging outside his normally creased slacks. His jacket was drenched from the pouring rain, and Ash sensed that the man had something weighing on his mind.

"Ash. I am so sorry." He looked at Rina.

Ash's face creased in confusion. "What are you talking about?"

"Gabe. I've just been to the police station."

Ash stared at his friend. "Why?"

Harry took a breath. "Because it's probably my fault that Gabe has been chasing around the world trying to rob you, that's why. I finally put the pieces together. He's been absent or late from work for the past week, inquisitive about your friend who came looking for you, and overly interested in that cloisonné box. We already figured that part out. And then when I called him today and…" he turned to look at Rina again.

"…And you called 911 after you heard me beg for help."

"Yes," he said simply.

The puzzle pieces fell into place. She stood up and wrapped her arms around this stranger, saying, "Thank you for saving me. I was afraid I wasn't going to get out of that mess. I'd nearly given up. It was a fluke that he left the room when you called, and he'd forgotten to tie me to something and…" Rina broke down.

Ash stared, open-mouthed. "Harry, you may have started this ass's ball rolling in the wrong direction when he saw the box, but you didn't do it. And you saved my girl." The headache was returning with a vengeance, so he lay back on the pillow and closed his eyes.

When he felt Rina's hands on him again and her kiss on his lips, he knew his friend had left the room. "Ash. When are you going to get out of here and replace that glass of wine? Did you drink mine last night, plus yours? Or did you tell Sam to save it for me because we were coming back?" Her voice was soothing, and even though his eyes remained closed, he smiled. When she kissed him again, he almost forgot he had a headache. Almost.

~

Near Mission Dolores, Jacob sat on the couch, dumbfounded. His daughter held his hand, and her chest ached with tears. She still couldn't believe that her twin sister could be involved in this terrible plot to harm Ash and steal his beautiful blue box. She had heard the story, knew it was valuable, and never doubted that he might be in danger because of it. But Laura?

Magda brought a decanter of whiskey and three glasses balanced on a glazed tray. "You drink wine in France, but here…when our lives turn upside down, we drink whiskey." She set it down on the round table between the ecru-colored couch and two wingback chairs facing west. She poured whiskey into each glass, and without a word, they reached for them and gulped them down. After Jacob swallowed the last drop, he held his glass aloft, and Magda filled it again.

"Do you think she knows the police read her message instead of that horrible man?" Magda's voice was low.

Dora noticed that Magda was horrified by the idea of Ash's sister being involved in this insidious scheme against her son. Dora felt the whiskey rising again, but she swallowed hard several times. No more for her. Red wine, please, her mind pleaded.

Magda must have seen the look on her face. She reached for the heavy glass from Dora's fingers and set it on the tray. Dora closed her eyes, trying to make the horror of the day fade away. When she opened them, she saw a glass of red wine on the tray where the whiskey glass had been. "Magda, you are everything and more than Papa said you were." She gave a wan smile and sipped, unconcerned whether she would get sick from using the wine as a chaser for the nasty brew.

Jacob seemed to have shrunk from his usual self. His breathing was shallow, and his lips curled around the glass, drawing in more whiskey. When he turned to Magda, he said wearily, "You know, of course, that everything must be set on pause. I must talk with Laura because I know the police will interrogate her." He turned to Dora.

Dora said, "No," louder than she intended. She looked at her father and Magda as one. Shaking her head, she said, "Papa. You stay. I'll go. It is something I must do. And then I will return. We came for an adventure, and we will have one. But first, I will finally stand up to Laura and do what I can after we have a long talk. I hope I can beat the police. If not, we will talk at the police station, but we will talk."

His face softened. When Dora saw her father perk up, she hoped she had made the right decision. Her mind was racing and her bitch mode was set to go. Laura would not get away with this, and she couldn't wait to tell her so.

Jacob lifted Magda's hand, and they shared a sad smile.

Dora looked at their entwined hands and began to make plans. The airfare to Paris was astronomical, but she was so furious and disappointed in her twin that she paid it without a second thought. The flight on Air France was scheduled to depart in six hours, and she'd be ready.

She had always been intimidated by her twin, but that was over. Never again would she allow Laura to shame her into making decisions that weren't her own. They had always laughed because Laura was born first; as the older twin, they had a tug-of-war all their lives. Laura had pressured her into selling her apartment after Jacques' death, but she liked it. And Laura chose her friends. She would kick their brother out of their lives. This time, Laura was not in control.

Now it was Dora's turn. Ash's entrance into their lives had opened a door that gave her strength she hadn't known she had. It had knocked Laura back a step, and maybe that's what this was all about. Laura had always been the other part of Dora; now there was Ash. Why couldn't Laura see it as a benefit rather than a setback? And now she was in such a mess that Dora wasn't sure she could ever forgive her. She'd crushed their father and nearly devastated their brother and Rina. Dora sank to her knees in Magda's guest room and laid her head on the bed. When the tears came, they arrived in great, wrenching sobs.

Downstairs in the living room, Jacob and Magda sat together on the couch, turning to face each other as the sounds from upstairs broke their hearts. When Magda began to go to the girl, Jacob pulled her back.

She hesitated, sighed in despair, and sat down again.

"I think she needs time to get past this shock, just like we do. She's had a rough few years in her personal life, and I think she depended on her sister as her stabilizer. I never thought so, but if the girls worked on their relationship, believing that was what they needed, I didn't step between them. This twin thing is strong and delicate, and sometimes there are no words to explain it. They aren't one person, but they aren't two people either. It has always mystified me. Now, Dora is feeling the complexity that cracks her mind as well as her heart. I don't know how she will come out on the other side yet. Maybe she needs these tears to wash away the old life and reflect on what lies ahead?" His eyes misted.

"Oh, my dear Jacob. I don't have words to tell you how sorry I am to hear about poor Dora and to think that…" She stopped and lifted her handkerchief to her trembling mouth. When she blew her nose, she felt Jacob shaking beside her. He rubbed his hands on his thighs and walked his fingers toward his knees. Then he repeated the motion until Magda placed her fingers over his to stop the next movement.

He glanced at their hands, one resting atop the other, and noticed the wrinkles and raised blood vessels. It reminded him of his father. How could those hands belong to him when he was young just yesterday?

"Perhaps," he said, pulling her into an embrace. "First, let me tell you that the more I am with Ash, the more I see my father in him. He was a wonderful, caring man, and I am better for knowing him; just like our boy."

She didn't respond except to squeeze his fingers.

"Maybe I am getting too old for this... Time has gotten away from us, and the children are making me feel even older."

She lifted her face to his and kissed his lips. Magda moaned with pleasure at kissing him after all the years behind them. "And maybe you're not that old after all?"

He laughed and kissed her neck. "As much as I hate to admit it, I have always worried about Laura and how she views life. She is a taker and a user, just like her mother was. This DNA thing is real. And now I worry for Dora. She has always allowed Laura to take advantage of her. Since Ash came into the family, I have noticed a positive change in her."

"She is a beautiful girl and seems very independent."

He smiled sadly. "I hope she can remain strong and go to Paris more boldly than ever before." He reached for Magda's handkerchief and wiped his nose with it."

"Well, I guess if we can share a son, we can share hankies?" Magda chuckled softly. "I am sorry for it and hope you are right. Dora is a truly special girl, and she is beautiful, intelligent, and caring. I want to get to know her and be part of her life." Her salt-and-pepper hair curled near her cheek. Jacob reached to push it behind her ear.

When she smiled at the gesture, she angled toward him again. They kissed each other, softly at first, and then the kiss turned much deeper. Her arms went around him.

"I feel young again."

He squeezed her tightly. "You feel young to me."

"I guess turning seventy years old is just a number and doesn't mean a toot when it comes to kissing, right, Jacob?" She lifted her fingers to caress his cheek and ruffled his white hair.

He answered her with another kiss, and they held each other like that for a long time. Neither of them wanted to move, and they both marveled at how their kisses had ignited a fire within them.

"Just a number," Jacob whispered.

"That's an understatement," she answered.

They exchanged meaningful grins, still holding onto that spark. Both were stunned to realize the ember had never been fully extinguished. Each wondered if they could recall everything that came with it. They shared a lingering gaze, and their next kiss escalated into something much more.

~

Meanwhile, upstairs, the sounds of crying had ceased. Dora lay on her bed, gazing up at the ceiling. She kicked off her shoes and tucked her feet onto the quilt, pressing her toes into the folds. When she drew the box of Kleenex closer and blew her nose, her eyes stopped leaking.

Although she ached from a loss as deep as death, she knew she'd taken a step toward oneness and would no longer rely on her connection with Laura. The break had been developing for years, but she had refused to admit that she could live without her sister controlling the strings of her life. The room was growing dark, and the sounds from below the stairs became muted. With one last loud sigh, she threw the box of Kleenex across the room, where it bounced off the wall.

Thirty-Six

Jenna stamped her foot and let out a howl. "Rina won't get away with this. She took the shop and Uncle James' money, and now she wants Jeff's too." Her eyelids tightened, and her mind began racing from one scenario to another. Borrowing Jeff's car had been a bad idea. Now she wasn't sure how to tell him it was probably totaled. She had been lucky to make it three blocks before leaving it by the curb and walking away on foot. She thought Rina had been in the car with her boyfriend. She stamped her foot again and poured herself a brandy.

By the time she finished the second glass, she knew what she was going to do. Since Rina hadn't answered her phone for hours, she would use her key again to give her a little surprise. First, she had to ensure she wasn't home and then call her two young thugs again.

Mona picked up her phone on the first ring. Her bright red hair clung to her skin after her shower, but she never missed a call. That's why her phone rested on her bathroom countertop.

"Yes? Again? Okay, I'll check and call you back. Give me a few minutes; I just got out of the shower. Uh-huh. Okay."

When Mona ran the errand, she sent a quick text and then got ready for her date. She pulled out a green dress with sparkles on the hem and looked for matching earrings. By the time she left a little while later, she truly looked like a leprechaun.

Jenna swung her car into the parking lot and lifted the black device buried in the ground. It looked like an ordinary water sprinkler head, but the top could be unscrewed, revealing a key dangling from its lid.

"Yes." She pumped her hand in the air. A few minutes later, she was inside Rina's condo, waiting for her young hoodlums to arrive.

~

Before Dora climbed into the cab that would take her to San Francisco Airport that evening, she focused on her confrontation with Laura. Could she stand up to her? Would she feel guilty, as she usually did when she disagreed with her twin sister? Anger surged in her mind as words twisted through her head. How could twins be so different? When had she first admitted to herself that her sensitivity didn't reach her sister's heart? Maybe at the same time, she longed to feel it from their mother. She replayed her conversation with Ash at the hospital a few hours earlier.

She had asked Magda to drive the car to the hospital. No more San Francisco traffic for her, at least not for a while. She was so filled with angst and worry that she didn't even notice the miles speeding by. She didn't see the tall buildings, hilly streets, cobblestones, or the streetlights illuminating their path. Dora only remembered walking into her brother's room.

I'll discuss it with Detective Brady. He was surprised to learn that Laura is a professor at the Sorbonne and was shocked when he found out that Laura is our sister. Her position will assure them she's not going to run away. He mentioned he'd wait until your plane landed before contacting the French police. Will that give you enough time?" Ash appeared worried.

Dora took a deep breath and gazed into her brother's face. Rina had been in the waiting room talking to Jacob and Magda, giving Dora and Ash some time alone. They knew she had made a decision, but she hadn't shared it yet. She was eager for a confrontation but also frightened.

Ash pulled her hand to his lips. "Be safe, little sister. We have a lot of adventures to catch up on. And Rina is getting antsy to get you connected with these clothiers here in town." He grinned.

"Antsy? What is this word?" Her forehead creased.

"*Anxieux*. Anxious to get started." Dora smiled, but her heart felt so tightly wound inside her chest that it was difficult. She bent down to hug her brother before walking out the door.

~

After ten hours of mental aggravation and six thousand miles in the air, Dora landed at Charles de Gaulle Airport in Paris. It was three in the afternoon in France, precisely the right time for her sister to be leaving the Sorbonne. She timed both phone calls within minutes of deplaning, and her plan was set into motion.

At five o'clock, she heard her sister turn the key in their father's front door. She had poured two glasses of Cabernet and arranged slices of hard cheese and chilled green grapes on the front table in front of a roaring fire. Despite her exhaustion, she felt prepared.

Within minutes, Laura, though cautious, lifted her glass in a silent salute and then waited for Dora to begin. She hadn't been in the house since spending hours cleaning up the mess that Gabe had left behind.

When Dora placed her wine carefully on the glass table beside her, she put her hands in her lap and clasped her fingers together. "Now, tell me what you have done, Laura."

Laura's eyes widened, and she lifted her chin in defiance. Hesitantly, she asked, "What exactly do you mean, what have I done? You're the one who's done something. You took Papa to America chasing after that son of his, and then you left him there." She reached for a slice of cheese and grabbed some grapes with her fingers before slipping them into her mouth.

Dora's lips twitched. "Yes, there is that. It seems like you've gone to a lot of trouble to get rid of him, haven't you?" She lifted her glass to her lips again. Her stomach churned against the food, but she managed to hold it down.

Laura's head came up. "What are you talking about?"

"Laura. Laura. Laura. Don't pretend with me. We both know about Gabriel Pizelli, don't we?" Dora narrowed her eyes as she watched Laura choke on the grape and attempt to wash it down with her wine.

"Who?"

Dora shook her head in disgust and stared into the fire. The room had always been a haven in bad times and a pleasure in good times. This evening, she wasn't sure what it held for her. She tapped her finger on the arm of the chair and turned her gaze toward her twin sister. Before she could say another word from her arsenal of thoughts, Laura's voice caught her off guard.

"I was there for you when Jacques died, Dora. Now you need to be there for me. That man found me. I didn't look for him..." Laura's voice hammered out the words, daring her sister to refute her statements.

"Oh, you admit to knowing this man now? A man who has tried to hurt Ash over and over again? A man you hoped would hurt him again and bring Papa home without his son in our lives?" The sigh Dora directed toward her sister was not lost on her.

Laura knew she was losing ground, and Dora could see frantic emotions flashing across her face. As twins, they often shared those same feelings and sometimes spoke words simultaneously. This time, Dora frowned and felt elated that Laura was off balance.

"Why do you bring up Jacques now, Laura? I am finally moving past the grief of losing him. Yes, you helped me when it happened. You were so close to the accident then, and I couldn't see beyond the pain. You know I needed your shoulder, and I loved you for it. But that was then, and this is now."

Laura gulped the dregs of her red wine. "Nobody forced Jacques to take those pills, Dora. When he fell out of my office window, he wanted..."

"What pills?" Dora's shocked voice was no longer in control. Her eyebrows shot up, and her eyes blazed. "You told me he came to you raving about a science report, and then he stumbled by your window and fell…" Her voice cracked.

Laura's head spun around to stare at her sister.

"I said, **what** pills, Laura?"

"They were…it was…it wasn't my fault."

"What wasn't your fault?" Dora's fingers dug into the armchair. She leaned forward, glaring into Laura's face. When she reached across the space to grip Laura's arm like a claw, Laura jumped.

"The pills," Laura whispered. "He kept wanting more and more of them. That day, I said no. And he didn't like it. His eyes were wild. He pushed me, and I… pushed back." Laura's usual stoic manner crumbled. Trembling, she pulled Dora's hand from her arm and held her sister's fingers tightly, imploring her to listen.

Dora stared at her twin and stood up.

Laura leaped up from her chair and positioned herself in front of Dora. She placed a hand on each of Dora's shoulders to look into her face. All it earned her was a deafening, teeth-rattling slap across the face.

Dora's shocked eyes stared at her hand as if she couldn't believe what she had done. She turned to look at Laura and noticed the red mark blooming on her face.

Laura recoiled and swung her head back, testing her jaw to determine if it was broken. Then she slumped back into her chair. Before she could speak, the doorbell rang.

"There is one other thing I wanted to mention…" Dora whispered.

Laura was puzzled by her sister's words. Before she could reply, Dora walked stiffly toward the front door. When Dora invited two officers in blue uniforms from the Police Nationale into the house, Laura's head dropped to her chest.

Fifteen minutes later, Dora watched as they guided her twin sister down the front steps. Her heart no longer thundered in her chest, and her eyes were dry. Something had shifted within her. She had always wondered when she would think of herself as an adult. Today was that day.

"Dora, please…" Laura's cheeks were wet, her eyes still glistening with tears. She shrugged away from the policeman with disgust, remaining haughty and unable to fully comprehend what was happening. "I can walk. I'm a professor at the Sorbonne, for God's sake, not a peasant! Please, Dora…?"

"Not this time, Laura." Dora's eyes blazed with fury as she wrapped her brightly colored scarf around her neck and slipped her hands into the pockets of her silk slacks. She took a step toward the house but turned back to look at Laura again before going inside.

When Laura stumbled because her hands were shackled and she needed help getting into the car, Dora didn't blink. When her sister's frightened eyes met hers through the window as the police drove her away, Dora shook her head and walked into the house. Then she ran to the bathroom and vomited all the cheese, grapes, and red wine into the toilet.

Thirty-Seven

When Detective Brady walked into Ash's room the next day, he found him fully dressed in a blue blazer, gray slacks, and a striped shirt open at the neck. Ash was arguing with the doctor. The rain had stopped, and the fog was lifting, bathing the room in sunlight from the oversized windows and reflecting the beauty of the day.

Dr. Muñoz turned to the visitor, shook his head, and left the room. Rina sat in the easy chair, eager to take Ash away from there. "I have news." Both Ash's and Rina's ears perked up.

The detective shook Ash's hand and nodded at Rina. "It appears we have another puzzle solved. And again, it's sort of in the family."

"What?" Ash and Rina both voiced the word in unison.

He opened his small notebook after flipping the cover off and traced his fingers down the notes. "Jeffrey Sebring's car was just found three blocks from the accident site. The front was caved in; the radiator is dry, and paint chips from your car are embedded in the grill."

Rina covered her mouth with both hands, and she looked at Ash.

He, in turn, stared at Rom Brady, his lips thinning. "Good God. Now what? First my sister, then my friend's employee, and now Rina's ex-husband?" He sat down on the bed with a thud.

"It's good to see you're leaving behind your tubes and monitors today. Glad I caught you. There's a tow truck on its way to pick up the Sebring." He nodded toward Rina. "For now, go someplace safe and stay off the streets. We have no idea what this guy is capable of, and picking him up for a hit-and-run is just the beginning."

After he left the room, Rina sat on the bed next to Ash. When he lifted her hand to his lips, he whispered, "Let's blow this joint."

They left the hospital after he refused the standard wheelchair exit, and the nurses weren't happy. The sun finally emerged from the clouds. The bright winter day was unusual for San Francisco. The breeze was cold, the sky was blue, and they hoped to escape. But, of course, they were mistaken.

"I ordered Chinese food, and it'll be delivered in--" Rina looked at her watch. "-One hour. That will give us time to get to my place across the bay. I called your mother to tell her not to expect you. She laughed at me and said, "Okay, today he's yours, but tomorrow...""

Ash chuckled. When Rina drove into her condo's parking garage, Ash tapped his lips with a finger, signaling her to move toward him. The kiss shifted from a gentle touch to something more passionate as her arms tightened around his neck. Ash moved a hand to cup her cheek, and they both groaned with pleasure.

"One would think I'd get tired of this, but...nope. Not yet."

Rina laughed shakily as they walked hand in hand to her front door. "I could get used to it easily, Mister Mahone."

When she slipped her key into the lock and opened the door, the words died on her lips and echoed off the walls. The front room was empty. Her couch, two chairs, artwork, and tables were all gone. The kitchen counter was missing the toaster, blender, and her Bose CD player.

"Oh. My. God." Rina leaned against the doorjamb. "Jeff again?" He got into the condo last time, and I haven't changed the locks yet. I don't understand..." She slumped against Ash and looked around her.

Ash pulled out Rom Brady's card and his phone. His heart was ready to burst as he pulled Rina close to his chest. She was shaking so much that he wanted to sit her down, but where could he put her? The furniture was gone. "Go check your bedrooms while I call Rom."

She returned with a dazed look on her face. "All gone. Every damn stick of furniture in my house is gone." Her words spilled out like wind against a loose picket fence.

He hung up the phone and pulled her in for another hug. Just as he kissed the top of her head, the doorbell rang. Dinner had arrived.

After he paid the driver, they'd lined up all the small white boxes of Chinese food on her kitchen counter like little soldiers. When Rina opened a drawer, she nearly cried with relief when she found them still filled with utensils, knives, and scissors.

As they munched on their Kung Pao Chicken and Chinese noodles, the doorbell rang again. When Rom Brady entered her condo, they pushed the white boxes toward him, and he took a fork from Rina.

You won't believe the phone call I received on the way over here.

Ash's mouth was stuffed with Chinese pork and white rice as he waited for the detective to finish swallowing his noodles. He couldn't remember the last time his life felt normal—before the blue cloisonné box, his mother's revelations, and the cruise ship. When would he return to that life? Now, he had another father, two sisters, a girlfriend, and an ex-husband pursuing him.

Rom Brady swallowed his dinner and began again. "We've picked up Jeffrey Sebring, and he's in the interrogation room now. He says he loaned his car to someone and he's thrown her under the bus." He pressed his tongue into his cheek and looked at Rina. "Maybe you should sit down, Ms. Silvan."

"Call me Rina, please."

Ash lifted her and set her on the counter after he remembered there wasn't anything in the place to sit down on. Her eyes never left the detective's face. She kept her arm around Ash's shoulder.

"Who did he lend his car to?"

"Your sister, Jenna Silvan." He lifted his fork, stabbed it into a piece of Chinese pork, and tossed it into his mouth.

Rina dropped her fork and lowered her chin to her chest. Both men chewed their food, uncertain of how to lighten the atmosphere around them. The sun streamed through Rina's windows, casting millions of dust motes dancing across her empty carpet.

"Okay, I will have to digest that one," she said when she lifted her face and her mind went back to work again. "Someone must have seen all my furniture removed. If my sister had anything to do with it, I want to take care of this once and for all. If it was Jeff, you can throw his butt in jail. But, if it was Jenna who moved me out of here, her ass is mine."

When she grabbed a new fork, she stabbed it so forcefully into the small food box next to Ash's hand that he jerked away from her. She laughed and jumped down from the counter. It was the first time she had laughed since entering her house.

Ash watched Rom Brady wipe his mouth, nod at them, and walk out the door. He turned to Rina and saw her tossing the empty containers into the trash. He followed suit and grabbed a paper towel. At least the thief had left the towels.

"I just can't believe my sister would do this. She's done some ratty things in the past, and when I thought I couldn't put anything else past her, she tried to hurt you. She told Jeff about you, so she must be following me. How did she know where you were that night? And this? Emptying my condo? Why would she do that? I know she's angry because Uncle James left me the shop, but she never cared about it. She didn't even care about the old guy when he was alive, and he knew it. She never cared about Jeff, and he must know that by now, too." She bit her lip.

Ash let her ramble as she brainstormed out loud. He wasn't sure what he could add and scratched his head in confusion.

"My sister."

He jerked his head up. "Really? You think your sister has the corner on betrayal and stupidity?" He blew out a breath of air beside her. The day couldn't get any worse, could it?

Rina turned to him. "Touché, my dear."

When she drove her Beemer out of the parking garage, she noticed Mona staring at her through the condo office window. She stopped the car, put it in reverse, and parked quickly. "I'll be right back, Ash."

She burst into the manager's office and saw Mona recoil away from her. "Mona, my condo's been emptied. The police are going to talk to all my neighbors. If you saw anyone moving me out of here, you need to get your ducks in a row. The police are on their way."

"I didn't see anything. When did this happen, Rina?" Her red head bobbed up and down. Her fingers clutched at her open-necked collar as she sat down in her office chair with a thud. Her bangle bracelets clicked against her desk, and she pushed her glasses up on her nose.

"I don't know. I've been at the hospital with my friend. I have no idea when it happened. Everything was there when I left. It's too ridiculous. Surely someone saw something. And if they did, I'll have the thief by the short hairs." Rina sputtered and left Mona open-mouthed and reaching for the phone.

She drove straight to Magda's. The bridge was packed with cars; traffic was a nightmare. When they arrived, Magda's face was confused when she opened the door. "Rina? You said…"

"Yes, Ma. But we need a chair to sit …"

"What?" They entered the living room where Jacob waited.

"It's a long story, and I need a drink." Ash headed toward the kitchen. They heard the clinking of glasses and the slamming of cupboard doors.

When Jacob and Magda turned toward Rina, her phone rang. As Jenna's face lit up her screen, Rina stood and walked out of earshot.

She sat on Magda's stairs and nodded to Ash as he entered the large room carrying glasses, wine, and a bottle of whiskey.

"Jenna?" Her voice answered slowly.

"Well, well. Big sister is now taking my calls. I understand you had a nasty surprise when you got home."

Rina thought she heard a faint cackle on the line. Then, Jenna's voice shifted to a meanness that Rina couldn't explain.

"Where are you, Jenna? I think we need to have a talk, clear the air, and get some closure." Rina's words intensified.

"Ah, **now** you want to talk. Well, we should probably meet at a public place. You're probably in the city. Let's meet at that little piano bar in Ghirardelli's Square…say, an hour?"

"Get there now! I'm on my way." Rina stabbed the end button on her phone and joined the group in the large room. Mind chatter shot in every direction. Jenna was going to stop making her life hell. It had been a long time coming. She'd tried a hundred times to give her sister the benefit of the doubt, even though her heart had given up on her years earlier. But she was the only sister she had, and dammit, weren't sisters supposed to look out for each other? Rina frowned. Jenna must have missed the memo. She re-entered the large room with forced nonchalance.

When Ash looked up, she noticed the concern etched on his face. She took the glass of wine he offered her. As he patted the cushion next to him, she sat down and felt his warm thigh through her leggings.

She understood he was curious about the phone call, but she also realized he would try to prevent her from meeting Jenna. She sipped her wine and listened to Jacob recount what happened in Paris.

"The police are holding Laura. Dora said it is much more complex than this Gabe fellow trying to hurt Ash over the cloisonné box. She mentioned it also involves her husband, Jacques, who died a few years ago. Although Dora wouldn't explain further, I have a terrible feeling. Her voice sounded different, as though she had something heavy to deal with." Jacob's voice went soft.

"It sounds as if neither of our sisters is acting like sisters, Ash. Why are relationships so difficult?" She stared up at Ash for a moment. "How did Dora's husband die, Jacob?"

Ash squirmed next to her, and she knew he was aching to ask her about the phone call. She changed the subject.

"He fell from a window in Paris and died instantly. It was a tragic end to a life that held such promise. He was working on a secret science project at the Sorbonne at the time, just a temporary position with a clear path to something much bigger. Laura said he stumbled and fell against the window."

"Laura was with him? There must have been some piece of information Dora learned about his death." She mulled over the thought.

"That is exactly what I think. You see, he had been in her office at the Sorbonne. Many questions went unanswered, but after the police investigated his death, they told Dora it was an accident. She loved him very much. After his death, she became very ill and threw herself even deeper into her work. She was able to buy the shop with Chloe using the life insurance money she received from Jacques' death. That's why finding connections here in San Francisco is so important to her, because Jacques helped her start the company. She wants it to grow and…" Jacob's eyes turned inward. "Now with Laura…" He sighed loudly.

Rina's stomach rebelled against the wine, but she sipped it anyway. Ash reached over to tap her knee for her attention, yet she simply placed her hand over his and took another sip. There was tension between them, but she needed to face this alone, just like Dora had to do it alone. It was a sister issue, no less.

"Who was on the phone?" He asked, straight to the point.

She put down her wine and smiled up at him. "I need to leave for a little while, Ash." The room felt too warm. She wasn't being fair to him, but she had no choice. His face mirrored her uneasiness, and her stomach flip-flopped when his eyes urged her to trust him.

"What? Where are you going?" His voice was troubled. A nervous muscle jumped in the curve of his throat.

The look on his face was priceless. Rina said, "Trust me." She turned toward Magda. Magda and Jacob stared at her, their faces mirroring Ash's concern. Their eyes conveyed that they knew something was wrong; she never avoided Ash.

"Please tell them what happened, won't you, Ash? I won't be gone very long, but there's something very important I must do." She stood up, put her purse on her shoulder, and leaned down to hug him. With a quick look of apology toward the old couple, she pulled away and looked at his face, urging him to understand.

Ash was so surprised that he stood up to pull her hands into his. Prepared to argue with him, she quickly shook her head to warn him it wasn't up for debate. He was angry and began to follow her as she inched her way out of the house.

"Please, Ash. I need to do this alone." Rina's expression showed him it was pointless to try to change her mind. Her small black purse swung in the air as she pivoted on her heel and waved a hand behind her.

When Rina closed the front door, Magda's face darkened. Jacob, on the other hand, turned to his son. "Tell us what happened tonight. She was shaking, and in the short time I've known her, she has never looked so focused. It was as if her eyes were somewhere else, and demons were after her." He gripped Magda's hand and looked at Ash for answers.

Ash shook his dark head. "Ma, I need your car keys."

Thirty-Eight

Several miles across town, Rina passed through Fisherman's Wharf and found a parking spot close to the square. She walked toward the piano pub. It was dark outside, but the streetlights guided her, and she felt no fear. The street was crowded with people, and laughter echoed behind them. The bay was frothy, and the moon shone on the water like a Monet painting. Her shoes slapped against the pavement. She glanced at her watch and then pulled her coat tight. The breeze from the water, mingling with the usual San Francisco wind, wasn't ideal for walking around at night in the winter.

She heard the lilting sounds of piano music as she pulled open the door to The Pub on Beach Street. Looking around, she saw that Jenna hadn't arrived yet, so she chose a table in the corner where she could lean against the wall and keep an eye on the door. She wanted no more surprises.

Rows of empty liquor bottles hung suspended above the bar, and she was ready for a drink. By the time her sister inched her way into the pub, she had a Moscow Mule in hand, the copper cup raised in Jenna's direction. Her sister looked like a woman on a mission as she marched toward Rina, as if there were a marching band playing in her head.

"So, here we are," Rina said as she lifted the copper cup.

"Starting without me, I see." Jenna slid into the chair across from her sister with a smile that didn't reach her eyes. She removed her gloves and the white scarf around her neck, noting that Rina's neck was bare. "It's cold out there. Where's your winter garb, sis?"

Rina gripped the handle of the cup as she swallowed the strong drink, allowing the mixture of ginger beer and vodka to slide down her throat. "Stop the shit, Jenna. Jeff has already told the police you borrowed his car, and they've already proven it was the car that rammed into Ash's car."

"Ash? Oh, is that your new lover?"

"Don't change the subject. Jeff threw you under the bus."

Jenna ignored the barbs. "Come on, Rina. Tell me about your new friend. He's gorgeous, at least from what I could see of him." Jenna raised her hand to the waitress who was weaving her way between several tables. "Jeff's just trying to save his own skin. I didn't ram anyone's car."

The cold sides of the copper cup seemed to cling to Rina's hands as she cradled it and gazed at her sister. "You cannot lie your way out of this one, sweetie." Her voice dripped with sarcasm. "And since Jeff is at the police station right now, I guess the ruckus you caused at my house was all you." Rina clenched the edge of her seat with one hand while observing Jenna's face up close.

"You can't prove anything. I had nothing to do with it."

"With what, Jenna? You already mentioned the surprise I went home to when we spoke on the phone," she spat out. Rina's eyes bored into hers.

Jenna took the cold IPA from the waitress's hand and licked the froth off the beer before responding. She shrugged. "Mona called me."

Rina shook the table, and the beer sloshed across the front of Jenna's silk blouse, drenching it. Her breasts were now clearly outlined through her bra. When Rina laughed, Jenna upended the table. Everyone stopped to stare, and the barkeeper nodded to a big man near the door.

"What the hell...?" Jenna stood up, dumbfounded, and Rina laughed. "Let's take this outside, Rina. You stepped over the line."

"No, **you** stepped over the line, and tonight we are dissolving it."

Before Jenna could respond, the big man picked up the table and set it upright. "You ladies want to leave now or sit down and behave yourself?" Large muscles pulsed through his shirt, and his gold earring swayed in the air as he hissed each word.

When Rina started to stand, a familiar voice interrupted. "They're with me. I'm sure they'll be just fine. Sorry for the mess. Will you girls ever just wait for me like ladies?" Ash's face dared them to argue.

Jenna paused for a moment before turning her smiling face toward him. "So, I finally get to meet the new man. My, you are something," she said as she glanced towards Rina.

Rina's face reflected the surprise Ash had anticipated. He leaned toward her sister. "So, you must be Jenna." He extended a hand toward her, and she slipped hers into his. When he squeezed her hand tighter than Jenna expected, she tried to pull away.

"Not so fast." He let her pull away slowly, painfully.

"Who the hell do you think you are?" She wiped at her blouse.

"Me? You said I'm the new man in Rina's life. And I am." Ash turned his gaze toward Rina, expecting a rebuke but finding amusement instead. She was enjoying this.

Jenna lifted her hand again and ran it down the length of Ash's arm. "Mmmmm…I like you." Her dark hair swirled around her shoulders as she pulled her scarf tightly around her neck, in a coquettish manner. Seemingly oblivious to his disdain, she inched her chair closer to his.

He looked at her through hooded eyes. "Well, I don't like you."

Jenna's head snapped up. "You can't believe everything Rina says about me, Ash. I'm a very nice person, and I think we should get to know each other." She patted his arm again.

Rina had enough and grabbed her purse from the chair rail beside her. When she stood up, the look exchanged between Ash and Jenna was broken. "I'm out of here. You two can get to know one another on your own time."

Jenna reached for her gloves. "Hey, we aren't done here."

Ash grabbed her wrist and squeezed hard. When she flinched, he brought his face close to hers. "Yes, you are damned well done here. The police are on your tail, and if I were you, I'd think up a good alibi. Because your butt is cooked as far as I'm concerned. If you even think of touching a hair on your sister's head, you'll answer to me."

When he got up to follow Rina out of the pub, Jenna's phone pinged. It was Mona. "Police just left. Someone saw you in Rina's condo." Jenna grabbed her gloves, tossed down a ten-dollar bill, and then raced for the door.

The barkeeper wasn't sad to see them leave.

Thirty-Nine

The dark San Francisco night didn't slow Rina down as she double-timed it toward her car, leaving Ash behind. Huffing ahead of him, she glanced back toward him. "I told you I needed to do this alone!"

"Really? And you had it all under control? I've never seen a bouncer move so fast to stop two ladies ready for a catfight. When that table crashed to the floor, I thought she'd taken you with it." He struggled to keep up with her as she raced away from him.

"We weren't having a catfight," she said through bared teeth. "She didn't like getting her blouse all wet to outline her breasts for everyone to see her nipples...And she knew I wanted to kill her."

"Yeah, that's what I mean." He reached for her arm, but she pulled away from his grasp. When she beeped her car unlocked, he stepped in front of her and backed her up to the Beemer. Her eyes were blazing with anger.

"Rina. She tried to kill me. Did you think I'd sit there drinking wine with Ma and Jacob while you played Wonder Woman on your own?" He looked into her eyes, seeing the reflection from the street light above them.

She dropped her head on his chest. "No, but..."

"No buts. We're a team, aren't we?"

"Are we?" Her anger faded from her face, and she grinned at him.

"I'm one block to the south. I'll drive back here so you can follow me, okay?" When she nodded, he jogged away. When he drove around the corner a few minutes later, he wasn't surprised to see her Beemer gone. Slapping his hand against his mother's steering wheel, he swore so loudly that it was probably heard across the rippling water to Alcatraz.

The brisk, cold wind whipped at Jenna's scarf as she left the pub and wound her way around several blocks to find her car. Mona's text had her hurrying to unlock it and jump inside. As she drove away toward her house, she didn't notice Rina's Beemer creeping along behind her.

The moon was bright, but she wasn't looking at it, the bay, or the water beyond. She wanted to get home, pack a bag, and drive south. "That stupid Jeff," she mumbled as her Volvo drove toward her townhouse on Lombard Street. When she turned onto the historic street, she cursed the hairpin turns that slowed her down. Turning into her house, the garage door lifted, and she sped inside.

Five minutes later, a noise made her pause a hand in midair. She craned her head to listen and thought she'd imagined it. Jenna tossed panties, bras, blouses, and two pairs of jeans into her polka-dot bag. When she reached for her purse and car keys, she heard the noise again. This time, she flipped off the light and inched her way toward the small elevator door. She took off her shoes and walked barefoot toward the kitchen to punch the button that would take her to her garage one floor down. She stubbed her toe in the dark and leaned against the wall, holding her breath against the pain.

And then the kitchen light switched on. Rina lounged against her counter. "Going somewhere? I told you the police were on their way. Did you think I'd let you get away with all the chaos you've left behind?" Rina pointed a flashlight at Jenna, who laughed at her.

"Really." Jenna laughed. "You plan to clobber me with a flashlight? You're a piece of work, Rina. All the times you could have fought back, and you just weren't smart enough. You never did get it, did you? Mom loved you best, and I hated you then, and I hate you now. I thought you were inside Ash's car when I rammed him. Too bad. Put your stupid flashlight away. I'm leaving." Jenna laughed and lunged for the elevator button again.

Rina's face glinted with stunned anger as she moved the switch to its second position. Zap...

Jenna stopped laughing and screamed as she crashed to the floor. She continued writhing on the brightly colored European-tiled floor when the doorbell rang.

Rina strolled toward the front door, allowing Jenna to savor the aftereffects of the blast. *She should have taken me seriously.* As she turned her head back to look at her sister, she vaguely wondered if she should have zapped her twice.

Detective Rom Brady stood beside Ash. When Rina pulled open the door to let them in, her sister was still groaning loudly from inside. She looked at them as if she had expected them and opened the door wider. Her hair was a mess, and her eyes blazed with energy.

Ash's eyes gleamed as he mouthed the word "taser?" He nodded sharply toward her pocket, prompting her to push her flashlight out of sight.

The detective stared at Rina and jerked his head toward the sounds coming from the lit room behind her. "Your sister?"

She nodded and stepped back to let him in. Following Detective Brady, Rina pressed her lips together. When she felt Ash's hand on her arm, she shook her head. Her eyes communicated that she was okay.

When the detective saw Jenna writhing on the ceramic floor tiles with her luggage beside her, he turned to Rina again. Unspoken words hung between them as he bent down to help her off the floor.

By now, Jenna was pointing a finger at Rina, and the words pouring from her mouth would have made a sailor blush. He backed her up against the counter, and she took a breath. "You won't get away with this, Rina Silvan. You wait until the cops hear about this..."

Once more, the detective stared at the woman. "Jenna Silvan? You have the right to remain silent. Anything you say can and will be used against you in a court of law. You have the right to an attorney. If you cannot afford an attorney, one will be provided for you. Do you understand the rights I have just read to you? With these rights in mind, do you wish to speak to me?"

Jenna was sputtering. "Of course, I want a lawyer. I'm going to scream until someone listens to me. I haven't done anything wrong. It was her. She shot me with a flashlight!"

Once more, Detective Brady turned to Rina, raising an eyebrow. He gave her a knowing look. "A flashlight, eh?" He tried to suppress a chuckle as his lips twitched.

Ash let out a soft groan. As he pulled Rina closer to his side, he glanced at the detective and made an effort not to roll his eyes.

Rina stared at Jenna and then smiled at her. It was the same smile Jenna had given her all those years ago after chopping off her baby doll's hair and pushing Rina down the front steps of their house.

Now, she was the sister watching from the top step.

Forty

Magda pulled Rina into the house when they got home again. The young woman seemed dazed, her face lit up with emotion. Ash had called her from his car and briefly explained what had happened. Neither she nor Jacob could fully grasp it. They were stunned to learn that the police detective had taken Jenna Silvan into custody.

Her old heart fluttered so wildly that she was sure everyone could hear it. Now that Rina had settled her sister issue, Magda was eager to share her news. Life was suddenly galloping forward, and she didn't want to slow it down.

Lights blazed in every room downstairs. An electric tension filled the air. Ash's face showed that something was wrong the moment he stepped through the door.

"What's going on, Ma? I can't handle another crazy event." He and Rina followed his mother into the brightly lit room.

"Sit down, Ash." His mother's face urged him to relax, but her own was so animated that it made her feel giddy.

"Enough already. I want my stable life back." Ash stood beside her, holding her shoulders firmly. After dipping his face down to look into her eyes without getting an answer, he turned toward his father.

Jacob sat on the couch with a toothy smile. His leg bounced up and down while his foot nearly danced on the carpet beside Ash. His white hair was fluffy, as if he'd been running his fingers through it.

"Ok, Ma. What's going on?" Ash looked from one to the other.

"Well," she said primly before sitting down next to Jacob. "I think we have a wedding to plan..." She held up her fingers one at a time, tapping each one as she said, "There's cake, flowers, chamber music."

Rina looked sharply at Ash as thoughts tumbled and rolled. "Did you tell her we...that you and I...?" She swallowed hard and abruptly sat down on the wide loveseat.

"No, dear. Jacob and I," Magda replied simply. "We decided it isn't fifty years too late after all. I'm in remission, and he thinks we should grab whatever time we have left and spend it together. We're just trying to figure out whether we want to live in San Francisco or Paris." She clapped her hands together like a child and stood up again.

Time reset itself.

Jacob flashed his son another toothy smile while gently patting Magda on the rear. Without hesitation, she reached back to caress his fingers.

When Ash saw his mother lovingly caressing his father's hand, his face revealed the thoughts racing through his mind. It was never about the jewels. In fact, it wasn't even about the cloisonné box. He visualized a keyhole in a heart-shaped lock. His mother had opened the box with her story. And he had unlocked her past and walked right in.

Ash dropped like a stone into the seat beside Rina, who stared at the older couple with a toothy smile of her own.

The End

Patricia says I'm a West Coast girl who moved to the East Coast and back again. Twice. My imagination has always been etched in music, color, and rose-colored glasses. I've had crazy characters and stories banging and fluttering around in my head, dying to get out, since I was old enough to hold a pen. I'm a fan of historical fiction filled with adventure and romance. And I'm addicted to genealogy! My sense of humor runs a little rampant at times, I'm no stranger to laughter, and I love a good anticipation scene.

She is one of the administrators for the Hawaiian Spaniards Facebook page and a volunteer for Find a Grave. Patricia was born in Woodland, California, but grew up in Oregon, where she raised her children. She now resides in the Pacific Northwest, accompanied by her laptop and a glass of red wine.

Patricia

www.patriciabbsteele.com

www.facebook.com/patriciabbsteele

PLEASE LEAVE A REVIEW on your purchasing site and/or Goodreads.

Thank you!